Taught by the Students

Taught by the Students

Culturally Relevant Pedagogy and Deep Engagement in Music Education

Ruth Gurgel

Published in partnership with
National Association for Music Education

ROWMAN & LITTLEFIELD
Lanham • Boulder • New York • London

Published in partnership with National Association for Music Education

Published by Rowman & Littlefield
A wholly owned subsidiary of The Rowman & Littlefield Publishing Group, Inc.
4501 Forbes Boulevard, Suite 200, Lanham, Maryland 20706
www.rowman.com

Unit A, Whitacre Mews, 26-34 Stannary Street, London SE11 4AB

British Library Cataloguing-in-Publication Information Available

Library of Congress Cataloging-in-Publication Data

Gurgel, Ruth, 1974–
Taught by the students : culturally relevant pedagogy and deep engagement in music education/ Ruth Gurgel.
  pages cm
Includes bibliographical references.
ISBN 978-1-4758-1338-8 (cloth : alk. paper) — ISBN 978-1-4758-1339-5 (pbk. : alk. paper) — ISBN 978-1-4758-1340-1 (electronic) 1. Music—Instruction and study—United States. 2. African Americans—Education. I. Title.
MT3.U5G84 2016
780.71'073—dc23   2015024850

∞™ The paper used in this publication meets the minimum requirements of American National Standard for Information Sciences—Permanence of Paper for Printed Library Materials, ANSI/NISO Z39.48-1992.

Printed in the United States of America

To Doug,
who reminds me that *Jehovah-jireh*
["God will provide"]

Contents

Figures and Tables

Foreword

Alicia Beckman

Most people don't know just how difficult it is to be a good music teacher. They remember their choir classes in school as relaxed and low on pressure. "What a fun job!" they say. "It must be nice not to have to worry about all of that academic stuff and teach one of the easy classes." Therefore, it must be fun being the person responsible for facilitating the blow-off class? These are the same people who think that if you can push "play" on an iPod, you can teach music. What they fail to remember is that choirs can often contain some of the largest class sizes with a wide range of student skills and interests. Add the challenges of puberty to this equation and you've got yourself one tough job. My 10 years teaching middle school choir were the most difficult, and, as it turns out, the most rewarding, of my career.

For the 8th-grade class of 2001 (my first year at Clark Middle School), I was their third or maybe fourth choir director. They had low expectations for me and for themselves. The school staff, having had 14 choir teachers in 10 years, expected very little from me too. They all wished me well and were kind, but it was clear that no one expected me to last long. Proving them wrong, I stayed 10 years before moving on to teach reading, which is what I've done for the past five years. When I look back on my time as a middle school choir director, I credit my success to three things: my teaching team, using a student-centered approach, and having an expectation of excellence.

In a profession where isolation is commonplace, it's important to find your people. I was lucky that the band and orchestra teachers in my school were not only great teachers but also wonderful people. I didn't realize it at the time, but my relationships with these two people were going to be the best of my teaching career. Had it not been for David and Terri, I would have quit more times than I can count.

David and I shared a classroom—his orchestra classes meeting oppo-site my choir classes. After one particularly discouraging 8th-grade choir rehearsal, he found me crying at my desk. He said, "Get in your car and drive down to the lake. Sit there until you feel better and then come back." When I said I was fine, he practically pushed me out the door. Of course, he was right and I came back ready to give it another try. Do the best you can, but give yourself a break if it doesn't go perfectly. Come back and try again tomorrow.

Happy-go-lucky David was a great balance to serious Terri—my go-to per-son for meltdowns and troubleshooting. She was an endless source of solu-tions and an expert on all things middle school. Perhaps the smartest thing I did was to take Terri's advice regarding absolutely everything. She knew the kids, the staff, and the history of the school. She knew what worked and what didn't work, what to do, and what not to do. I listened and we became fast friends.

Terri and I supported each other any way we could think of. We team-taught our toughest classes and built relationships with each other's students in attempts to help them find their way in our classes. We told each other about our challenges and took turns bringing the morning coffee.

The relationship with my team kept me coming back to work day after day, but it was the students who made my job worthwhile. Rehearsals always went best when I kept my cool and remembered that each student was someone's beloved child who wanted desperately to be liked and to fit in. This perspec-tive helped me care about them and, believe it or not, it made a difference because each and every student knew he or she belonged in my classroom.

In case you don't remember from your own school experience, kids have a sixth sense that allows them access to a teacher's private feelings about them. They can tell if you don't like them, and pretending won't do you any good. You *must* truly care for and enjoy that child. While this connection comes easily with some students, others require more work. But when you do this, you will be happier and so will your students. Better yet, your students will start seeing each other differently.

Have you ever been in church when no one around you is singing? Unless you're different from the majority of the population, you won't want to be the one belting it out alone. Musical expression, especially when your voice is your instrument, is intensely personal. Kids who are midpuberty aren't exactly keen on calling attention to the most private aspects of themselves, unless they are supremely confident, which—let's face it—is an oxymoron.

In most cases, middle schoolers are reluctant to sing in front of their peers. The only way I got kids—all kids—to do so was to create an environment in which they trusted me as well as each other. They used to say that being in my classroom felt safe and like home. They weren't just talking about me but about how they felt around their peers as well. Kindness is contagious and when it is demanded, the culture changes, if only for that one period per day. They were friends with people in my class that they wouldn't talk to outside of the room because it was what I expected and what I modeled.

In all my studies in education, I was told to set the expectation bar high because kids will work hard to meet it. If expectations are set too low, the kids will go just far enough and never reach their full potential. Expecting excellence from my students brought both great pride and great disappointment. While some classes were more successful than others, I found that students worked hard to meet the expectations that were set for them. We never would have gotten there without the relationships we built with each other and my unrelenting demands for hard work. Most of the time. Unfortunately, no matter how hard I tried, there were some classes that saw only limited amounts of success. As much as I blamed myself at the time (and hence was greatly disappointed), I can now see that the important thing is to not give up. Keep coming back fresh each day with something new to try and make sure they know that you care about them. What else can you do?

The 7th-grade class that became the case study for this book is one of those groups that stretched and challenged me. This was my last year of teaching music. They were one of the most difficult classes that I had in my 10 years of teaching middle school choir. I don't feel like I gave up on them that year, but I just didn't have it in me to go another entire school year. Had it been earlier in my career, I would have made a different choice. I was just ready to move on.

Looking back, there are so many things I would do differently if I got a second chance to be a new teacher. I hope that Ruth's research will save others from making the same mistakes I did and that their first years of teaching will be somehow less painful as a result. Being a music teacher is not an easy job. It is definitely more than pushing "play" on an iPod or a YouTube video. Having been a reading teacher for the past five years now, I can honestly say that I believe that the music teachers have the toughest jobs in the entire building. But I can also say that those jobs have the potential to be the most tremendous and gratifying jobs as well. Leading students to be a part of something bigger than themselves—something that feeds their souls and lasts a lifetime—is a privilege experienced by very few teachers. A lot of teachers think they know what this feels like because, yes, teaching a child to read is very important and fulfilling. But having taught both music and reading, I know that those who teach music get to glimpse a part of humanity that is truly special and unique. Don't forget this when you feel jealous of the academic teachers who get credit for doing the "important" work. Trust me when I say that if they knew what you get to do, they'd be the jealous ones.

Best wishes to all of you music teachers out there. Enjoy the journey.

Preface

Since the Tanglewood Symposium in 1967, the field of music education has acknowledged its need to better serve students of color.[1] However, in school districts in the United States, the data still show that students of color elect to truncate their music education experiences in schools sooner than their white counterparts do. Ideally, the demographics of students enrolled in music classes would mirror the demographics of the school district. However, no such picture exists in most racially diverse schools in the United States.[2] Instead, the percentage of students of color enrolled in elective music programs is often markedly lower than the percentage of students of color in the total school population. Regrettably, these percentages become more disproportionate as students advance through the grades.

Issues of racial inequity in classrooms often overlap with other areas of inequity, including gender, class, (dis)ability, and language. In fact, students from families of lower socioeconomic status, students whose parents have attained a lower level of education, and students whose native language is Spanish are also less likely to enroll in school music programs.[3] However, race provides a particular area of analysis, with its own complexities. Race is often difficult for teachers to discuss and examine, and focusing on race can encourage the continuation of this necessary discussion in music education. By exposing and discussing racial inequity in music education, we can continue to move forward in understanding and dismantling the systems that currently support racism in our field.

The terms used in the United States today to talk about race are often coded. When they are used, they signify a system of labeling or categorizing people based on physical characteristics. For example, when a person enters a room filled with people they have never met, he or she may (perhaps subconsciously) label the people present based on how they look. If a person has mahogany skin, kinky hair, and full lips, he or she might be perceived as "black" or "African American." If a person has brown skin, deep brown hair, and brown eyes, the individual might be perceived as "Latino" or "Hispanic." These labels are not initially applied based on the language that a person speaks, where he or she lives or used to live, or where that person's family is from—labels generally associated with ethnicity or nationality.[4] However, these labels sometimes overlap with the concepts of ethnicity and nationality, making them more confusing, and making "colorblindness" seem an attractive alternative. (I will further discuss the concept of colorblindness and some of its associated problems in chapter 1.)

As an example of how these terms overlap and yet are distinct, consider how you might refer to yourself in terms of race versus ethnicity. For example, if your grandparents came from Germany, would you introduce yourself as "German American"? Most white people would not refer to themselves in this way. They might say, "My grandparents came from Germany, and I am an American." If they describe themselves in terms of race, they might say, "I am white," or "I am Caucasian." If they describe something as ethnic or diverse, they generally refer to something or someone outside of the construct of whiteness. For example, the terms "ethnic music" and "world music" presently carry a connotation of music from outside the Western European tradition, even though Western European music also originates from a particular time and place.

Throughout the history of the United States, the construct of who is white and who is not has shifted. For example, people from Ireland arriving in the United States in the 1840s were also seen as outside the construct of whiteness. The shifting construct of race makes it difficult to pin down, analyze, and talk about. Each person develops ideas about his or her identity and the identity of others based on exposure to race labels and categories. In the United States, a system known as institutional or systemic racism confers a set of advantages and privileges on white people, based solely on their whiteness.[5] These advantages often remain hidden to white people, and this hidden nature of racism unfortunately serves to perpetuate it. A resulting idea, known as "meritocracy," is that the United States provides a level playing field whereby opportunities are open to anyone regardless of race (or gender, etc.), and that one's life is completely determined by what one makes of it.[6]

In this book, the idea that institutional racism supports inequality in the field of music education provides an underlying assumption in line with Culturally Relevant Pedagogy (CRP).[7] Throughout the book, I will explain the facets of CRP as they become salient, beginning in chapter 1. Culture, as a construct embedded in CRP, not only includes racial identity, but also incorporates all facets of human identity, and is rooted in one's discursive communities, shifting over time and influencing how one thinks, values, believes, and acts. All classrooms, by this description, are cross-cultural, with each student participating in unique discursive communities, even if all students appear to be racially similar.

The analysis I present compares the students' and their teacher's interpretations of classroom pedagogy. I also provide a link between engagement in music classrooms and CRP, an important and underexplored area of research in music education. I compare the six prongs of CRP with the themes identified by the students and their teacher regarding engagement in their 7th-grade choir classroom. I use this comparison as a way to organize themes and analyze students' experiences with (dis)engagement.[8] The lens of CRP in this book allows for a deep analysis of music students' perceptions as they relate to the body of literature on effective teaching of students of color.

So, how did this come to be a book focusing on the (dis)engagement of students in music classrooms? I began with an interest in the phenomenon of disproportionate membership of students of color in music classrooms. If the data demonstrate that music education in the United States is not serving these students well,[9] then these questions remain: *How are these programs not serving students well? And why?*

As the research for this book took shape, I realized that the students' voices were often found in the music education research base as responses to surveys in quantitative work, but not found in the extended analyses of qualitative studies. The valuable survey-based studies have identified *teacher effectiveness, instruction*, and *classroom climate* as factors that influence students' continued participation in school music classes.[10] I wanted to build on these studies by finding a music classroom to study that *did* have racial demographics mirroring those of the school district in which it was situated. I needed a music class where the students had not elected to drop out. These were the students I wanted to interview. I wanted to know why they continued to enroll and to ask them to share their perspectives on their experiences in a long-term study.

Ms. Alicia Beckman's 7th-grade choir classroom at Clark Middle School in the Lake City School district was an ideal site.[11] Her class contained racial diversity that approximated the district's.[12] The choir class from which the research participants were drawn consisted of 54 percent African-American students, 30 percent white students, 11 percent Latino/a students, and 5 percent Asian students. The choir class contained 34 students in the 7th grade, 15 male and 19 female. This class met twice a week for 50 minutes and once each week for a 50-minute rehearsal with the other 7th-grade section of choir at Clark.

As I began preliminary observations in Ms. Beckman's choir classroom, I found that her students demonstrated a desire to not only study music, but also to study music with *her*. They had each chosen to take her class again after singing in her 6th-grade choir (they could have chosen a study hall), and told me in their initial interviews that Ms. Beckman was one of their favorite teachers.

During my early observations, I noticed that sometimes, the class as a whole would sing as Ms. Beckman instructed, attend to her suggestions and ideas, and offer on-topic comments during class discussions. However, there were other class periods during which the students as a whole would choose not to sing when asked, but would talk or laugh with each other, and generally goof off (as the students put it). All eight students in the study told me in initial interviews that they enjoyed music and especially singing; singing was an engaging activity for them, both in and out of school. Because the students would at times disengage from an activity that they were initially drawn to and enjoyed, their perceptions on the contexts surrounding their varying levels of engagement in class are especially worth examining.

The shifts in student engagement were a source of frustration to Ms. Beckman. For her, very similar lessons could produce very different levels of student engagement. The students could not describe for her (to her satisfaction) what made this shift occur, although they were willing to answer her questions. Most often, they said that they chose not to sing because they were tired or they "just didn't feel like it." When I began to design the research study, I hoped that perhaps I could learn to understand the conditions that caused the students to (dis)engage, how they signaled their (dis)engagement, the effects of (dis)engagement in the classroom, and how the students' perspectives aligned with CRP.

Engagement in the music classroom is not equivalent to entertaining students sufficiently so they will comply with teacher instructions. The students in this study offer a rebuff to the idea that they can be tricked into participation based on superficial "engagement." They engaged in the classroom work when it was interesting and challenging, and when their teacher made the learning relevant. This form of deep engagement is a foundation for high achievement, autonomous learning, and learning that transfers beyond the classroom. By examining the students' perspectives on (dis) engagement, we learn what types of relationships, music, and instruction lead to high levels of musical achievement and continued music learning beyond the classroom.

I chose eight students who represented five different racialized categories to interview extensively. They self-identified as Native American and white (Estephanie), African American/black (Gregory, Mila, Jacobi), Caucasian/ white (John), Latino/a (Ángel and Alice), and Asian American (Blossom). These eight students discussed their experiences and perspectives in choir class—in this case, a racially diverse choir class. I observed the music class in which they were enrolled and then interviewed one of them following each class period. I also held focus group sessions with the students, during which I asked them to discuss their experiences with me and with each other.

What I found during initial interviews clued me in to just how interesting this study would become. The students were *just as* willing to discuss their (dis)engagement with me as they were with Ms. Beckman, and my question "Why did you choose not to sing today?" yielded very similar (and nonilluminating) answers in my eyes. Yet, their descriptions of their experiences were rich and detailed. I felt that perhaps the students were doing an excellent job of giving me answers and I needed to abandon my own perspectives and work to see it from their point of view.

A qualitative approach allowed me to make detailed analyses of the interactions between the teacher and the students as well as their unique contexts both inside and outside of the music classroom. I explored how the students' experiences at home, in school, and with music intersected with their membership in 7th-grade choir. As I interviewed the eight students in this study and Ms. Beckman, I also looked across their perspectives to find commonalities that suggest important focal points for those of us who work in music education as we strive to become effective cross-cultural teachers. My analysis does not provide a way to generalize "best practices" for instruction of students in a racial group. However, as the students describe their perspectives, they highlight links between engaging musical pedagogy and CRP that suggest best practices for every classroom.

AUTHOR/TEACHER AS RESEARCHER

What a researcher views as the "realities" of the research participants is already filtered through a set of values that influence what that researcher "sees" and describes.[13] As the researcher in this study, my beliefs and systems of reasoning (especially as a music teacher) play a role in constructing the analysis of the data in this study. My interest in students' perspectives on music instruction began during my initial years of teaching in the public schools of Denver, Colorado. My first teaching experience was in a neighborhood elementary school with a student population consisting of 60 percent African-American students and 40 percent Latino/a students.

My second teaching experience was in an elementary school with students from all over the world, including many from multiethnic families. Many of my students at this school were multilingual. These experiences led me to examine my own culture and situated-ness as a white woman (and teacher) from a mixed-European background. I began to examine my teaching practice through the lens of the influence of institutional racism on our country and found that this lens presented opportunities to work for social change.

My interest in these matters grew, especially as I learned from my colleagues, students, and the parents in Denver, who demonstrated characteristics of what I now call an intercultural personality.[14]

These experiences, combined with my doctoral work, allowed me a chance to examine whiteness and institutional racism and their connections to pedagogical practices in schools, especially in music classrooms. I became interested in the connections between students' perspectives in music classrooms and the literature on CRP, which led to the formation of this book.

WHO WILL FIND THIS BOOK VALUABLE?

Even though this study produces findings that are based on one music classroom, the themes that emerge provide a framework that can assist both preservice and in-service music teachers in examining their practice, their cultural assumptions about students, and the multiple manifestations of high achievement in music education. There is no prescription for music curriculum in this book, but the students in this study do clearly describe their views on effective music teaching and learning. Their perspectives provide a starting point for music teachers to understand their own students' ideas on engaging and Culturally Relevant musical pedagogy, enabling them to analyze and refine their pedagogy in the areas of relationships, instruction, and repertoire choice.

Music teacher educators will find this book to be a useful resource for their graduate and undergraduate courses. I have included moments (titled "Reflect") in chapters 1–8 for readers to consider and discuss their students and their classroom practices. I also include a "Take Action" section at the end of chapters 2–9, providing ideas for further exploring the issues discussed within the chapter. Music departments within districts will also find a useful resource in this book for encouraging discussion among teachers and students. Using the book in this way will also lead to a deeper understanding of CRP and how this theory can be applied in music classrooms all over the world.

OVERVIEW OF THE CHAPTERS

Chapter 1 contains descriptions of engagement theory and CRP, thus forming the theoretical framework of the research in this book. In particular, this chapter reviews the literature within the discourses of CRP and music education surrounding the concepts of sociopolitical consciousness and cultural competence.

Chapter 2 introduces the students and the teacher who participated in the research for this book. It begins by presenting the students' perspectives on relationships with their classmates and their teacher, Ms. Beckman. The students' strong relationship with Ms. Beckman is based on her *conceptions of social relations* and *conceptions of self and others*, two prongs of CRP. The students discussed how these relationships developed and how conditions in the classroom influenced their mood toward their peers and teacher. This chapter also analyzes the intricacies of mood contagion in the classroom and how mood contagion is linked to the students' choices to engage (or not) in classroom instruction.

Chapter 3 counters the following myth found in some corners of music education: teachers in racially diverse settings must use popular music if they expect the students to pay attention. The students in this study confirmed that it is important to them to enjoy the songs they sing. At times, however, they disliked singing a song in music class that was a favorite outside of school. Students also discussed how they grew to enjoy a song through the influences of a song's lyrics, groove, familiarity, context, and instructional presentation.

Chapter 4 provides students' perspectives on two additional myths found in music education: some students enter the music classroom without much motivation for learning music and some students do not want to learn traditional musical techniques.

The students in the study described their desire for a challenging environment in which they can sense their own achievement. They discussed a desire for a teacher to hold them to a high level of musical accomplishment; to craft an organized, well-planned curricular trajectory; and to include their ideas, experiences, and knowledge in student-centered lessons. This chapter also discusses the pitfalls of deficit thinking, teacher-centered pedagogy, and low expectations.

Chapter 5 demonstrates the need for teachers to become culturally competent in their classrooms. The students discussed how they signaled their positive engagement in music class through culturally situated vocal and physical behaviors. This chapter also focuses on students' expressive movements and their verbal interactional styles during class.

Chapter 6 describes how students' behaviors can signal their disengagement in music class. In the music classroom, the teacher's interpretations of and responses to these behaviors are filtered through cultural lenses, and this chapter discusses how misinterpretations can result in confusion, frustration, and low engagement for students.

Chapter 7 describes the effects of (dis)engagement in the music classroom. It describes how both engagement and disengagement function as cycles in the music classroom and how teachers and students respond to these cycles.

Chapter 8 complements the other chapters in the book by discussing key moments in the disengagement cycle that are important triggers for further disengagement. This chapter also discusses interventions designed to reverse the disengagement cycle in Ms. Beckman's classroom. In doing so, it counters the following myth: because of student behavior, students in racially diverse settings require a firmer classroom management style that includes maintaining a higher level of control than is needed in white classrooms.

Chapter 9 summarizes the lessons from the students in light of CRP. It peers into the future of music education, discussing how music education (and music teacher education) can become stronger in meeting students' needs.

Appendix A provides the research questions that prompted this study. Appendix B describes the data-gathering methods and the analysis procedures.

NOTES

1. I use the term "students of color" to refer to students who are "raced and outside the construction of whiteness" (Gloria Ladson-Billings and Jamel Donner, "The Moral Activist Role of Critical Race Theory Scholarship," in *The Sage Handbook of Qualitative Research*, 3rd ed., ed. Norman K. Denzin and Yvonna S. Lincoln [Thousand Oaks, CA: SAGE Publications, 2005], 298.)

2. Barbara R. Lundquist, "Music, Culture, Curriculum, and Instruction," in *New Handbook of Research on Music Teaching and Learning*, ed. Richard Colwell and Carol Richardson (New York: Oxford University Press, 2002).

3. Kenneth Elpus and Carlos R. Abril, "High School Music Ensemble Students in the United States: A Demographic Profile," *Journal of Research in Music Education* 59, no. 2 (2011): 128–45.

4. Ethnicity most often refers to a person's country of heritage (also distinct from a person's nationality, or country of residence).

5. Derrick A. Bell, "White Superiority in America: Its Legal Legacy, Its Economic Costs," *Villanova Law Review* 33 (1988): 767–79; Richard Delgado, ed., *Critical Race Theory: The Cutting Edge* (Philadelphia: Temple University Press, 1995); and Gloria Ladson-Billings and William Tate, "Toward a Critical Race Theory of Education," *Teachers College Record* 97 (1995): 47–68.

6. Peggy McIntosh, "White Privilege: Unpacking the Invisible Knapsack," *Independent School*, Winter (1990): 31–36.

7. Although Ladson-Billings does not capitalize her theory, in this book, I will capitalize references to Culturally Relevant Pedagogy, or CRP. I do this to distinguish her theory from theories of others who use the term with different meanings, or slightly different titles, such as "culturally responsive pedagogy," "culturally appropriate pedagogy," or "multicultural education." I also refer to teachers who practice CRP as Culturally Relevant teachers. This makes a reference to qualities of these teachers and their practice that line up with Ladson-Billings' theory.

8. In this book, I use the term "(dis)engagement" to signal a discussion of "engagement and disengagement."

9. Vicki R. Lind, "Classroom Environment and Hispanic Enrollment in Secondary Choral Music Programs," *Contributions to Music Education* 26, no. 2 (1999): 64–77; Vicki R. Lind and Abby Butler, "The Relationship Between African American Enrollment and the Classroom Environment in Secondary Choral Music Programs," in *The Phenomenon of Singing* (St. John's, Newfoundland, Canada: Memorial University, 2005), 105–10.

10. See Abby Butler, Vicki R. Lind, and Constance L. McKoy, "Equity and Access in Music Education: Conceptualizing Culture as Barriers to and Supports for Music Learning," *Music Education Research* 9, no. 2 (2007): 241–53; Lind, "Classroom Environment"; Lind and Butler, "Relationship"; Carolee Stewart, "Who Takes Music? Investigating Access to High School Music as a Function of Social and School Factors" (PhD diss., University of Michigan, Ann Arbor, 1991); Linda M. Walker and Donald L. Hamann, "Minority Recruitment: The Relationship Between High School Students' Perceptions About Music Participation and Recruitment Strategies," *Bulletin of the Council for Research in Music Education* 124 (1995): 24–38; and Michelle Watts and Christopher Doane, "Minority Students in Music Performance Programs," *Research Perspectives in Music Education* 5 (1995): 25–36.

11. All names of schools, districts, principals, teachers, students, or family members of students in this study are pseudonyms.

12. Lake City School District, located in a large Midwestern university town with a population of approximately 233,000, served 25,000 students in grades K–12 during the 2011–2012 school year. From 1991 to 2011, Lake City School District had seen a decrease in the percentage of white students. In 1991, the district served 79 percent white students, 21 percent students of color; in 2011, the students self-identified as 46 percent white, 20 percent African American, 18 percent Hispanic, 9 percent Asian, 7 percent more than one race, and 1 percent Native American (Lake City School District, *District enrollment*, 2011, retrieved June 4, 2012, from the World Wide Web). During the 2010–2011 school year, Clark Middle School itself served over 500 students whose racial identities closely matched the district statistics. Clark served a slightly lower percentage (36) of white students and a higher percentage (27) of African-American and Latino/a (22) students. Lake City School District, as a whole, reflected the phenomenon of disproportionate membership described by Lundquist in elective music classes. In 2008, Lake City's district demographics for 11th grade included 58 percent white students and 42 percent students of color (Lake City School District, *District demographics*, 2008, retrieved May 27, 2009, from the World Wide Web). Percentages of 11th-grade students of color in elective music classes did not reflect the district demographics. The elective music class enrollments showed that 77 percent of the students were white, while 23 percent of the students were of color.

13. Joe Kincheloe and Peter McLaren, "Rethinking Critical Theory and Qualitative Research," in *The Sage Handbook of Qualitative Research*, 3rd ed., ed. Norman K. Denzin and Yvonna S. Lincoln (Thousand Oaks, CA: SAGE Publications, 2005), 327.

14. See William B. Gudykunst and Young Yun Kim, *Communicating with Strangers*, 2nd ed. (New York: McGraw-Hill, 1992).

Acknowledgments

This book was only possible because eight students and their choir teacher believed that music in the schools is important. Alicia Beckman worked unswervingly each day to teach, sing, craft, and collaborate. Her students Mila, Gregory, Jacobi, Alice, John, Blossom, Estephanie, and Ángel explained their thoughts and ideas with grace. I hope that this book does what they envisioned, namely, provide perspectives that can influence music classrooms.

This book began as my doctoral thesis. Julia Eklund Koza and Deborah Bradley, my advisors, provided valuable insight into the work of a music teacher–researcher. They spent many hours discussing the thesis with me, helping me revise and reorder the material. I am forever changed by my time spent learning from Carl Grant and Gloria Ladson-Billings, who served on my dissertation committee along with Susan Cook and encouraged me to pursue the publication of this book.

Finally, I don't have the words to thank Mira, Levi, and Doug for their encouragement and love. Thank you also to my parents, Susan, Robert, Barb, and Karl, and to all of my siblings for their love and support. Joanna, thank you so much for all of your support and encouragement and for believing that this work was important. Of course, I give all credit and praise to God for his help and strength. I hope that I have done the students of Clark Middle School and Alicia Beckman proud.

Part I

THE PATH TO ENGAGEMENT: WHAT ENGAGES STUDENTS IN MUSIC CLASS?

Chapter 1

Introduction

Culturally Relevant Pedagogy, Engagement Theory, and Music Education

You know, it's funny that these six prongs [of Culturally Relevant Pedagogy] . . . to me, it's just being a human, being a good person.

—*Alicia Beckman*

Students' perspectives on (dis)engagement in their racially diverse music classrooms provide insights that assist teachers in designing more Culturally Relevant and therefore more engaging pedagogy. As teachers continue reading what the students say in this book, they may think: this is pedagogy that is *just good teaching.* Yes. However, as Ladson-Billings notes, it seems that "good teaching" does not happen with great regularity in classrooms populated with students of color.[1] This chapter asks why such "good teaching" might not reach students of color in music education. The two theoretical constructs of student engagement and CRP suggest hidden areas of pedagogy that currently serve to disengage students, especially students of color, in music classrooms.

ENGAGEMENT THEORY: WHAT IS IT?

Student engagement is causally linked to academic achievement and school completion.[2] Students who are engaged in the classroom are constructive, enthusiastic, willing, emotionally positive, and participate with a cognitive focus on learning activities.[3] A deep level of engagement facilitates academic achievement and is the "direct (and only) pathway to cumulative learning, long-term achievement, and eventual academic success."[4]

3

Deep engagement moves beyond compliance with school rules for attendance, compliance with teacher-requested behaviors, even beyond compliance with educational expectations, such as completing assignments or acing tests. Deep engagement is more concerned with intellectual engagement and emotional investment. It incorporates a person's identity. In the words of Ruth Deakin Crick, deep engagement

> is when a learner becomes personally absorbed in and committed to participation in the processes of learning and the mastery of a (chosen) topic, or task, to the highest level of which they are capable. This means that he or she will be aware of, and attend to, the processes of learning, rather than just the outcome, and will utilize his or her own power to learn and serve his or her chosen purpose—developing his or her learning identity and mindfully using the scaffolding provided to pursue the journey towards his or her chosen outcome.[5]

Deep engagement involves a teacher who is able to provide scaffolding that can facilitate an ethical process of identity formation combined with support for "processes of knowledge creation in a world where relevant outcomes can no longer be predetermined."[6] Contemporary theories of student engagement must take into account the "person who is learning, his or her development as a person in the community and the ways in which proximal and distal social environments influence that learning."[7] From the teacher's perspective, engaging the students is not only critical to achievement outcomes, but also critical from the ethical standpoint of acknowledging and allowing all that the student is and brings into the classroom knowledge production.

Student engagement is preceded by motivation or "willingness to exert effort to achieve a learning goal."[8] Without the motivation to engage, another form of coercion must take place to force compliance with the learning tasks, and this forced compliance is likely to lead to less challenging, lower-level learning tasks as the teacher focuses more on behavioral compliance than on increasing the challenge and excitement of classroom learning experiences.[9]

Engagement as a general phenomenon takes place in various social settings. In these settings, the person who is deeply engaged is "an intentional participant in a social process which is taking place over time."[10] Students may choose to participate in church-related, community-related, family-related, or school-related activities. In the school arena, students may participate in a variety of curricular and extracurricular pursuits. Within the classroom, students engage with the teacher, their peers, and the curriculum.[11] The system or context of the classroom influences students' levels of engagement. The context for engagement includes the learner (with his or her identity and values), the social setting, the learning facilitator (teacher), and the school setting.[12]

Student engagement in the classroom is a multidimensional construct, but the dimensions have not been consistently defined in the scholarship. Most often, the dimensions that researchers have examined are behavioral, cognitive, and affective. Behavioral engagement refers to how the students act as a measure of how engrossed they are in the learning task.[13] Engagement behaviors are physical ways of participating in the learning tasks and can vary from student to student.

Cognitive engagement refers to the mental strategies the student employs to purposefully and willingly accomplish difficult skills and cognitively complex tasks.[14] Cognitive engagement includes a high level of concentration and interest in the learning task. Affective engagement refers to students' emotions regarding their school, classroom, and learning tasks, including their feelings of belonging.[15] The affective component of engagement can be described as enjoyment, or "flow," and is heightened during an activity in which learners participate in a challenge that they meet with a high level of skill.[16]

Reflect 1.1

- What does "student engagement" look like in your classroom?
- How does it feel to you when students engage?
- What behaviors do *you* tend toward when your students engage?
- Conversely, what does "student disengagement" look like in your classroom? How can you tell when students are disengaging or misbehaving?
- What do you do when you sense students are disengaging?
- Define "student disengagement" and "student misbehavior." Compare and contrast these two terms.

CULTURALLY RELEVANT PEDAGOGY: WHAT IS IT?

In 1994, Gloria Ladson-Billings wrote a book titled *The Dreamkeepers* that described her research with eight successful teachers of African-American students and documented the qualities these teachers had in common. She found that the teachers did not exhibit similarities in background, training, or even teaching methods, but they all exhibited similar ideologies. She categorized their ideologies as *conceptions of social relations*, *conceptions of self and others*, and *conceptions of knowledge*. These ideologies guided how the teachers encouraged their students to be *academically successful*, to be *culturally competent*, and to have *sociopolitical consciousness*.[17] She referred to this type of teaching as Culturally Relevant Pedagogy (CRP) and declared that this type of teaching need not be used exclusively with African-American students (her focus in the study) but is sound practice for students from all backgrounds.[18]

Ladson-Billings described the three common ideologies of Culturally Relevant teachers in this way:

> Teachers who practice culturally relevant methods can be identified by the way they see themselves and others. They see their teaching as an art rather than as a technical skill. They believe that all of their students can succeed rather than that failure is inevitable for some. They see themselves as a part of the community and they see teaching as giving back to the community. They help students make connections between their local, national, racial, cultural, and global identities. Such teachers can also be identified by the ways in which they structure their social interactions: Their relationships with students are fluid and equitable and extend beyond the classroom. They demonstrate a connectedness with all of their students and encourage that same connectedness between the students. They encourage a community of learners; they encourage their students to learn collaboratively. Finally, such teachers are identified by their notions of knowledge: they believe that knowledge is continuously re-created, recycled, and shared by teachers and students alike. They view the content of the curriculum critically and are passionate about it. Rather than expecting students to demonstrate prior knowledge and skills they help students develop that knowledge by building bridges and scaffolding for learning.[19]

Part I of this book expands on five of the prongs of CRP in the context of Clark Middle School choir. Part II of the book focuses on applications of the sixth prong, *cultural competence*, to music education.

Reflect 1.2

Dig deeper into the six prongs of Culturally Relevant Pedagogy. Begin by reading "Toward a Theory of Culturally Relevant Pedagogy" by Gloria-Ladson Billings (*American Educational Research Journal*, 1995, vol. 32, no. 3, pp. 465–91). Discuss the following questions with your group:

- What does *academic achievement* encompass in music education?
- What does a *culturally competent* teacher do in the music classroom?
- How can a music teacher encourage students to engage in *cultural critique* (develop *sociopolitical consciousness*)?

SOCIOPOLITICAL CONSCIOUSNESS

To promote sociopolitical consciousness in their classrooms, music teachers need to understand that culture is linked to power in society in multiple ways, and that these relationships are often "rendered invisible, underemphasized, or ignored."[20] Joyce E. King provided guidelines for teaching with a sociopolitical perspective. She felt that the content of schooling for African-American children should

1. give students an enhanced sense of mutual responsibility for their own learning and the learning of their peers; enhance their commitment to use their cultural knowledge and school learning for the benefit of their community, the society, and for humanity.
2. enable children to analyze and understand the strengths and weaknesses of their community's cultural patterns and the inequities and opportunities in the society and the global community in which we live. Instruction should also enable students to think critically about, and act positively to support, community and social transformation.[21]

According to the descriptions of sociopolitical consciousness by scholars such as Ladson-Billings, Banks, King, Sleeter, and Grant, simply including "world music" in the curriculum (even if it is presented with its context) does not mean that music teachers are using this approach. While music educators may go into depth on a particular culture's music, studying various aspects of the culture, learning to experience the music, even learning from a culture-bearer, these lessons fall short of examining the "infusion of various perspectives, frames of references, and content from various groups that will extend students' understandings of the nature, development, and complexity of U.S. society."[22]

Teaching from a sociopolitical perspective involves analyzing both the diversities between people and the commonalities that "unite all humans."[23] Sociopolitical consciousness can be furthered when students and teachers learn not to categorize or stereotype according to cultural, ethnic, gender, or religious groups, but understand that individuals within these groups also vary in their beliefs, values, and behavioral patterns.[24] Using these principles can assist a teacher in examining the sociopolitical elements of music with his or her students.

Developing sociopolitical consciousness involves examining how societal structures in the United States create unequal power hierarchies among groups of people. To open up discussion about reforms in the field of music education regarding race, teachers can look for manifestations of institutional racism that may work to provide inequitable experiences for students of color. The primary facets of institutional racism include meritocracy, color-blindness, and deficit thinking. Within these facets, themes emerge that are fleshed out and applied to education in CRP and overlap with the themes in student engagement theory.

The problem with colorblindness. White teachers may propose that they see children, not color. They may say, "It doesn't matter what color my students are, I treat them all the same." This notion of colorblindness, or that color does not matter, enables teachers to deny their own racial identity as well as their students' racial and cultural contexts and how their students experience institutional racism.[25] Colorblindness can be described in this way:

> If we accept the notion of whiteness as normal, then any person who is *not white* is abnormal. Thus, within polite, middle-class mores, it is impolite to *see* when someone is *different*, abnormal, and thus, *not white*. Hence, it is better to ignore, or become colour-blind, than to notice that people of colour have the physical malady of skin colour, or *not whiteness*.[26]

The dominant discourse positions colorblindness as a means of promoting social justice in classrooms. But to ignore how the historical and social realities of a person are connected to his or her race can only serve to "place severe limitations on the possible remedies for injustice and thereby maintain a system of white privilege."[27]

The prevalence of deficit thinking. The literature on deficit thinking suggests that when teachers assume that the academic or social behavior of a student of color is linked to a negative aspect of his or her culture, they view that child as having cultural deficits that need to be remedied.[28] In this way, a teacher can view the culture of students of color as static, and argue that the students have inappropriate values, show lack of effort, or come from family structures that are the cause of their behaviors or academic failure in schools. Teachers often resort to "cultural explanations" when a student does not conform to their (cultural) expectations for how students are to interact in the classroom.[29] This means that white teachers who see themselves as not having a culture, or being "just normal," infuse the word "culture" with anything nonwhite.[30]

Bonilla-Silva and Dietrich labeled this phenomenon "cultural racism" and described how this can result in a "blame the victim" mentality.[31] In this way, the term "culture" becomes linked to the terms "race" and "ethnicity." If a classroom is "culturally diverse," the embedded/coded idea is that the classroom contains students who are nonwhite. Even describing a classroom as "diverse" holds assumptions about the race of the students in that classroom, and that many are nonwhite. While, in the United States, racial identities are complex and multifaceted, they do comprise an element of one's "culture." Culture itself is multifaceted and links to one's discursive communities: family, hometown, religion, travels, experiences, race, and much more.

Like colorblindness, deficit thinking allows educators to place blame on the students or their families for unequal achievement patterns along racial lines. Educators and administrators are then absolved from examining the link between their own practices, schooling structures, and student outcomes.

As García and Guerra stated, "Because these educators do not view themselves as part of the problem, there is little willingness to look for solutions within the educational system itself."[32] It then follows that teachers may see no need to examine their own cultural expectations and thus how their pedagogical practices, choices of curriculum, and the structure of schooling itself place value and emphasis on their Western European cultural values.

Reflect 1.3

Institutional racism manifests in many ways, and an important step in recognizing these manifestations is examining whiteness as a culture: something that shapes what people value; how they behave and interact; and how they believe other people should behave and interact. Read "White Privilege: Unpacking the Invisible Knapsack" by Peggy McIntosh (*Independent School* [Winter/1990], pp. 31–36). With your group, consider and discuss the culture of "whiteness." Use the following quote from McIntosh (p. 34) as a start:

> I can swear, or dress in second hand clothes, or not answer letters without having people attribute these choices to the bad morals, the poverty, or the illiteracy of my race. I can speak in public to a powerful male group without putting my race on trial. I can do well in a challenging situation without being called a credit to my race. I am never asked to speak for all the people of my racial group. I can remain oblivious of the language and customs of persons of color, who constitute the world's majority, without feeling in my culture any penalty for such oblivion.

CULTURAL COMPETENCE: HOW DO CULTURALLY RELEVANT PEDAGOGY AND MUSIC EDUCATION DISCOURSES ALIGN?

The issue of student disengagement from music education in schools is not equivalent to disengagement from music altogether. For most youth, participation in music (whether listening, singing, creating, or playing an instrument) outside of school is engaging. Their musical environments provide them with a sense of identity that links them to other people who share in those environments. Students who engage in music outside of school do so willingly and enthusiastically.

In music classrooms, one of the challenges for teachers is to foster the sort of environment that continues to encourage deep engagement within a group of students who may differ in musical tastes, learning styles, prior experience, and cultural background. Applying CRP to school music classes means, in part, that participating does not require students to abandon their preferred ways of engaging with music outside of school.

Within a Culturally Relevant music classroom, the teacher establishes a climate where students' home musical practices are celebrated and incorporated into the fabric of the classroom. In this environment, students achieve success in many musical genres while still maintaining links with musical learning patterns that are valued in their homes and communities. To do this, music teachers must be (or become) culturally competent: valuing different paths to excellence in music, defining musical excellence in multiple ways, and functioning in multiple music-making cultures.

If a teacher believes that her students' valued ways of interacting and making music are not valid and does not structure the class so that these patterns are also used, she conveys to the students that her way is the better, more valued way, and the students' ways are to be suppressed in the classroom. Teachers can avoid this pitfall by analyzing how the cultural knowledge of students allows them to participate meaningfully in their own cultures.[33] They can then work to use students' culturally preferred interactional styles in the classroom and therefore align the process of music teaching and learning "more closely with students' cultural knowledge and their indigenous ways of knowing, learning and being."[34] This alignment is called "cultural congruence" or "synchronicity."

Cultural congruence in a classroom does not mean that teachers have mastered all of the details of all of the cultures of students represented in their classrooms, perhaps assuming, for example, that all African-American students learn/interact in a particular, homogenized way.[35] Individual students, who are all members of a cultural group (or multiple groups), maintain individuality within that group. Irvine stated,

> Teachers can acquire the necessary pedagogical and anthropological skills to make reasonable instructional decisions. These classroom decisions are based not on stereotyped cultural profiles of ethnic groups but rather on how culture may or may not contribute to an understanding of an individual student's behavior. . . . Because the concept of culturally responsive pedagogy is so logically and emotionally appealing, teachers must be particularly cautious in their interpretation and application of this type of teaching. In the process of creating authentic discourse and culturally relevant examples, inexperienced teachers might resort to a style of teaching that further isolates diverse students from mainstream society.[36]

If a teacher attempts to promote cultural congruence in her classroom but has not examined her own cultural contexts or become competent in multiple cultures herself, she will continue to engage in "premature attempt[s] to package, label, and simplify this culturally specific teaching style [that] will result in yet another failed attempt to convince teachers that, indeed, 'all children can learn.'"[37] Teachers who do not understand and employ cultural congruence in their classrooms are at risk for lowering expectations of their students, engaging in deficit thinking, and hindering the achievement of their students by wasting instructional time on behavioral matters.[38]

In order for a teacher to encourage cultural competence in his classroom, he must be aware of how and when he provides cultural congruence or synchronicity in the classroom. Theories on cultural congruence suggest that students will do poorly in schools where there is a constant mismatch between students' home culture and the culture of the classroom.[39] When a student does not experience cultural synchronicity within the classroom, the results for the student may include discomfort, disengagement, and a deteriorating relationship with the teacher. Within a music classroom, cultural expectations for body comportment and singing styles also can influence the degree to which a student experiences cultural congruence.

CLASSROOM INTERACTIONAL PATTERNS

Even among persons of similar cultures who know each other well, interactions (either verbal or nonverbal) can produce misinterpretations and misunderstandings. In classrooms, misinterpretations on either the students' or teacher's part can be more easily identified and minimized if the teacher understands his preference for particular cultural interactional patterns and how those patterns align with those of his students. In this way, teachers can then reduce the risk of alienating and humiliating their students by being aware of when they are asking their students to participate in an interactional structure that might be unfamiliar to the students.[40] Wills et al. found that

> if the social participation structure is familiar to students, then performing with new academic content is not very alienating. On the other hand, if the academic content is familiar and engaging, then students may be willing to try out new ways of interacting and using language. The issue underlying both cases is safety: not having to risk looking clumsy or stupid in front of others. Lesson content and form, taken together or separately, can reduce the risk of embarrassment, which in turn triggers resistance—the withholding of assent to learn and to participate in learning activities.[41]

Patterns of verbal communication; assumptions about when to speak, when to defer to others, when to raise a hand; chances of one interrupting the other; and differences in the rhythm, tempo, and pitch of speech all play a role in how classroom interactions are approached and interpreted by both teacher and students.[42] Nonverbal communication patterns, including issues of personal space, gaze, and frequency of touch also play a role in communication.

A study by Byers and Byers described the interaction of two white girls and two African-American girls with their white teacher in a nursery school. The more initiating white girl looked at the teacher 14 times, and the teacher responded eight times. The more initiating African-American girl looked at the teacher 35 times, but the teacher responded only four times. The researchers concluded that the African-American girl, unlike the white girl, "did not share with the teacher implicit understanding of cultural nuances, gestures, timing, verbal and nonverbal cues."[43] This resulted in a frustrating experience for the African-American girl, demonstrating an example of how contrasting interactional patterns can function.

A teacher who instructs using solely white-normed classroom interactional patterns may assume that her teaching is understandable and comfortable for all students. However, the cultural context of schooling is most congruent with those students who expect to passively learn information transmitted by the authoritative teacher, exert individual effort toward completing a task, perform for recognition, and avoid confrontation.[44] For students who do not expect to interact this way, their interactional behaviors may appear disruptive to the teacher.

For example, Shade described one particular area of cultural mismatch that stood out in classrooms. A standard African-American practice is that of "breaking in and talking over people" during the course of a discussion. For some teachers, this practice can appear disruptive and disorderly, while for students, this practice might signal that the "individual is listening, comprehending and has anticipated the point being made. In conversations and discussions within their cultural settings, there is little need to finish explaining an idea if the listener has already assessed the intent, meaning, and outcome."[45]

Mismatches such as this can begin a deficit thought pattern for teachers when they approach their African-American students. A teacher with a deficit perspective might expect African-American students to have short attention spans, be easily distracted, speak without raising hands or being called on, be impulsive rather than reflective in their responses, interrupt the class by talking to their classmates, experience difficulty with learning tasks, and fail to complete those tasks on time.[46] For the students, however, these behaviors seem natural and appropriate as they seek relief from being bored, attempt to understand a teacher who is not clear, support each other in the learning task as they do when they learn outside of school, interject their ideas at relevant points, seek to be creative and spontaneous, and work at their own speed to be thorough.[47] If these behaviors result in a cycle of punishment and misunderstanding, frustration can build for both teacher and students. However, if teachers can recognize a particular communication style as demonstrating engagement instead of being disruptive, they can better assess and value student participation.

BODY COMPORTMENT

Teachers in music classrooms often require their students to portray certain types of body comportment as they listen and respond to music.[48] Gustafson found that music education in the 1900s laid a foundation that has worked to ensure that Western European classical music is listened to with an introspective, reverent contemplation. She stated,

> The contemplative listener was at the pinnacle of civilization; the primitive listener and music maker were frozen in a childish attitude toward music. . . . The unreasonable listener indulged in "indecorous" movements such as foot tapping, lacking the reverence that would qualify him as the individual with an aura of cultural nobility. The overarching idea, supported by the burgeoning influence of child study in the academy, was that movement to music and extroverted emotion was for younger children and, as such, was a more primitive form of musical appreciation.[49]

In music classrooms today, body comportment plays a role in how students are taught not only to listen, but also to produce and respond to music. In fact, teaching from a Western European perspective produces a way of separating music making, listening, and movement.[50] In many cultures outside of this tradition, these separations are not made. Ben Aning, professor of music at the University of Ghana, described how listening to music is viewed in some African cultures:

> However, the audiences or onlookers, unlike Western audiences—especially concert audiences—are not passive receivers but, instead, most often active participants, either as singers, hand clappers or voluntary dancers. In short, African musical behavior is an extension of the African's natural life activity. His attention, during aesthetic endeavors, is never diverted from life; he does not "stop living in his acts of daily life, or stop being directed toward their objects." Moreover, the act of listening (apparently a passive exercise for some cultures) occurs in a dimension that requires the involvement of the African's sense of being and behaving musically—*moving "with" existence.* (italics in original)[51]

In the societal structures of the United States, African-American children are afforded advantages if they possess a form of white cultural capital that includes the ability to be reserved, to subordinate emotions and affections to reason, to constrain physical activity, and to present a disciplined exterior. Cultural capital in the context of this country, particularly when applied to African Americans, necessarily includes these characteristics. Conversely, African Americans are disadvantaged if in their expressive culture they project those African-American cultural formations that are viewed as oppositional to what it means to be white.[52]

Gustafson reported examples of this cultural mismatch in school music resulting in students' disengagement from musical activities at the elementary level when they are asked to stop singing along with a teacher (since singing along would mean they are not listening) and to stop clapping on counter beats as opposed to main beats.[53]

When we view issues of body comportment in music education today through the lens of the theory of CRP, especially the tenet of cultural competence, it becomes possible to view this issue as a hidden curriculum that works to reinforce a Western European standard while negating other cultural styles. For students who display a cultural orientation to body comportment that incorporates expressive movement with music making and listening, congruence in this area is lost in music classrooms if the teacher expects and instructs a more white-normed style.

SINGING STYLES

In most traditional school music programs, one of the vocal goals is to produce a light, "pure," bel canto sound. This sound is a "single-voiced musical timbre [that] allows listeners to concentrate on the pitch dimensions of the performance—the melody and harmony—rather than to be captured by the complex sonic quality of the combined individual timbres of the singers' voices."[54] However, a variety of musical singing styles, such as gospel singing, value a complex timbre where individual voices blend in unique ways. In a music classroom, if the norm is seen as the bel canto style, while styles such as gospel, which may be a very strong part of students' identities, are seen as an add-on or ignored altogether, students may not experience cultural congruence in this area.

Ben Sidran described the meaning of particular singing styles for African Americans during the time of slavery in the United States (modern readers should understand the word "man" given below as the more inclusive "person"):

> The slaves were only able to express themselves fully as individuals through the act of music. Thus each man developed his own "cry" and his own "personal sound." The development of "cries" was thus more than a stylization; it became the basis on which a group of individuals could join together, commit a social

act, and remain individuals throughout, and this in the face of overt suppression. It has been suggested that the social act of music was at all times more than it seemed within the black culture. Further, to the extent the black man was involved with black music, he was involved with the black revolution. Black music was in itself revolutionary, if only because it maintained a non-Western orientation in the realms of perception and communication.[55]

A teacher who does not recognize the bel canto style in which she instructs as one possible cultural vocal style therefore views her students' alternate styles as needing correction, a deficit. If she can, however, recognize her students' singing styles as individual expressions, as unique as their personalities, yet also as a tool for uniting socially and communicating with others, she may be able to create more culturally congruent environments for students.

MOVING FORWARD

Does Culturally Relevant music teaching mean that teachers must abandon Western European music and music-making practices? No. In fact, the students in this study suggest that they desire more and better musical instruction in this tradition. But music teachers can develop cultural competence and teach with sociopolitical consciousness, placing music within its historical and social contexts and fostering a climate of social critique in the classroom. In the following chapters, Ms. Beckman and her students paint a picture of how this can happen.

NOTES

1. See Gloria Ladson-Billings, "But That's Just Good Teaching! The Case for Culturally Relevant Pedagogy," *Theory into Practice* 34, no. 3 (1995): 159–65.

2. Sandra L. Christenson, Amy L. Reschly, and Cathy Wylie, "Preface" in *Handbook of Research on Student Engagement*, ed. Sandra L. Christenson, Amy L. Reschly, and Cathy Wylie (New York: Springer, 2012), v–ix.

3. Ellen A. Skinner and Jennifer R. Pitzer, "Developmental Dynamics of Student Engagement, Coping, and Everyday Resilience," in *Handbook of Research on Student Engagement*, ed. Sandra L. Christenson, Amy L. Reschly, and Cathy Wylie (New York: Springer, 2012), 21–44.

4. Ibid., 23.

5. Ruth Deakin Crick, "Deep Engagement as a Complex System: Identity, Learning Power and Authentic Enquiry," in *Handbook of Research on Student Engagement*, ed. Sandra L. Christenson, Amy L. Reschly, and Cathy Wylie (New York: Springer, 2012), 679.

6. Ibid., 678.

7. Ibid.

8. Ibid., 680.

9. Catherine D. Ennis, "Teachers' Responses to Noncompliant Students: The Realities and Consequences of a Negotiated Curriculum," *Teaching and Teacher Education* 11 (1995): 445–60.

10. Deakin Crick, "Deep Engagement," 678.

11. Ibid.

12. Deakin Crick, "Deep Engagement."

13. Susan Yonezawa, Makeba Jones, and Francine Joselowsky, "Youth Engagement in High Schools: Developing a Multidimensional, Critical Approach to Improving Engagement for All Students," *Journal of Educational Change* 10, nos. 2–3 (2009): 195.

14. Jennifer A. Fredricks, "Engagement in School and Out-of-School Contexts: A Multidimensional View of Engagement," *Theory into Practice* 50, no. 4 (2011): 328.

15. Ibid., 328.

16. See Mihaly Csikszentmihalyi, *Flow: The Psychology of Optimal Experience* (New York: Harper & Row, 1990); Mihaly Csikszentmihalyi and Isabella Csikszentmihalyi, eds., *Optimal Experience: Psychologic Studies of Flow in Consciousness* (Cambridge, MA: Cambridge University Press, 1988); David Elliott, *Music Matters: A New Philosophy of Music Education* (New York: Oxford University Press, 1995); David J. Shernoff and Mihaly Csikszentmihalyi, "Flow in Schools: Cultivating Engaged Learners and Optimal Learning Environments," in *Handbook of Positive Psychology in Schools*, ed. Rich Gilman, E. Scott Huebner, and Michael J. Furlong (New York: Routledge, 2009), 131–45.

17. Sociopolitical consciousness (Gloria Ladson-Billings, *The Dreamkeepers: Successful Teachers of African American Children* [San Francisco, CA: Jossey-Bass, 1994]) means that students learn to understand that social inequities exist in society and also that students are taught to think critically about actions they could take to advocate against unequal power structures. Sociopolitical consciousness includes components that allow students to analyze materials and events from a political perspective, encouraging them to engage in social criticism and make decisions regarding social change. Furthermore, sociopolitical consciousness allows students to challenge mainstream structures and mainstream "official knowledge" (Michael W. Apple, *Offical Knowledge*, 2nd ed. New York: Routledge, 2000) in order to advocate for the exposure and reduction of unequal power structures in society.

18. Ladson-Billings, "But That's Just Good Teaching!"

19. Ladson-Billings, *Dreamkeepers*, 25.

20. Theresa Perry, "Up from the Parched Earth: Toward a Theory of African-American Achievement," in *Young, Gifted, and Black*, ed. Theresa Perry, Claude Steele, and Asa G. Hilliard (Boston, MA: Beacon Press Books, 2003), 64.

21. Joyce E. King, "The Purpose of Schooling for African American Children: Including Cultural Knowledge," in *Teaching Diverse Populations: Formulating a Knowledge Base*, ed. Etta R. Hollins, Joyce E. King, and Warren C. Hayman (Albany: State University of New York Press, 1994), 42–43.

22. James A. Banks, "Approaches to Multicultural Curriculum Reform," in *Multicultural Education: Issues and Perspectives*, 3rd ed., ed. James A. Banks and Cherry A. McGee Banks (Boston, MA: Allyn & Bacon, 1997), 237.

23. Beverly J. Armento, "Principles of a Culturally Responsive Curriculum," in *Culturally Responsive Teaching: Lesson Planning for Elementary and Middle Grades*, ed. Jacqueline J. Irvine and Beverly J. Armento (Boston, MA: McGraw-Hill, 2001), 27.

24. Ibid., 19–33.

25. Louise Derman-Sparks and Patricia Ramsey, *What if All the Kids Are White? Anti-Bias Multicultural Education with Young Children and Families* (New York: Teachers College Press, 2011).

26. Adrienne D. Dixson and Celia K. Rousseau, "And We Are Still Not Saved: Critical Race Theory in Education Ten Years Later," *Race Ethnicity and Education* 8, no. 1 (2005): 16.

27. Ibid., 15.

28. Daniel T. Solorzano and Tara J. Yosso, "From Racial Stereotyping and Deficit Discourse," *Multicultural Education* 9, no. 1 (2001): 2–8.

29. Gloria Ladson-Billings, "It's Not the Culture of Poverty, It's the Poverty of Culture: The Problem with Teacher Education," *Anthropology and Education Quarterly* 37, no. 2 (2006): 106.

30. Ibid., 107.

31. Eduardo Bonilla-Silva and David Dietrich, "The Sweet Enchantment of Color-Blind Racism in Obamerica," *The ANNALS of the American Academy of Political and Social Science* 634 (2011): 193.

32. Shernaz B. García and Patricia L. Guerra, "Deconstructing Deficit Thinking: Working with Educators to Create More Equitable Learning Environments," *Education and Urban Society* 36, no. 2 (2004): 151.

33. King, "Purpose of Schooling," 26.

34. Ibid., 27.

35. Jacqueline J. Irvine, "The Critical Elements of Culturally Responsive Pedagogy: A Synthesis of the Research," in *Culturally Responsive Teaching: Lesson Planning for Elementary and Middle Grades*, ed. Jacqueline J. Irvine and Beverly J. Armento (Boston, MA: McGraw-Hill, 2001), 2–17.

36. Ibid., 14.

37. Ibid., 15.

38. Tyrone C. Howard, "Telling Their Side of the Story: African-American Students' Perceptions of Culturally Relevant Teaching," *The Urban Review* 33, no. 2 (2001): 135; Jacqueline J. Irvine, *Black Students and School Failure: Policies, Practices, and Prescriptions* (New York: Praeger, 1990); Ladson-Billings, *Dreamkeepers*.

39. Kathryn H. Au and Alice J. Kawakami, "Cultural Congruence in Instruction," in *Teaching Diverse Populations: Formulating a Knowledge Base*, ed. Etta R. Hollins, Joyce E. King, and Warren C. Hayman (Albany: State University of New York Press, 1994), 5–24.

40. John S. Wills, Angela Lintz, and Hugh Mehan, "Ethnographic Studies of Multicultural Education in U.S. Classrooms and Schools," in *Handbook of Research on*

Multicultural Education, ed. James A. Banks and Cherry A. McGee Banks (San Francisco, CA: Jossey-Bass, 2004). For research done regarding classroom instructional patterns prevalent among white, middle-class teachers, see Courtney L. Marlaire and Douglas W. Maynard, "Standardized Testing as an Interactional Phenomenon," *Sociology of Education* 63, no. 2 (1990): 83–101; see also Hugh Mehan, "The Structure of Classroom Discourse," in *Handbook of Discourse Analysis*, vol. 3, ed. Teun A. van Dijk (London: Academic Press, 1985), 119–31.

41. Ibid., 167.

42. Irvine, "Critical Elements," 17.

43. Ibid., 8.

44. Barbara J. Shade, "Understanding the African American Learner," in *Teaching Diverse Populations: Formulating a Knowledge Base*, ed. Etta R. Hollins, Joyce E. King, and Warren C. Hayman (Albany: State University of New York Press, 1994), 177.

45. Ibid., 182. See also A. Wade Boykin, "Afrocultural Expression and Its Implications for Schooling," in *Teaching Diverse Populations: Formulating a Knowledge Base*, ed. Etta R. Hollins, Joyce E. King, and Warren C. Hayman (Albany: State University of New York Press, 1994), 243–73; see also King, "Purpose of Schooling," 25–56. These researchers did not seek to create a stereotype or declare that all African Americans prefer this style, but they did highlight how the inclusion of this style (and other) styles in the classroom can create a more culturally congruent classroom climate for all students.

46. Shade, "Understanding African American Learner."

47. Ibid., 176.

48. Ruth Gustafson, "Drifters and the Dancing Mad: The Public School Music Curriculum and the Fabrication of Boundaries for Participation," *Curriculum Inquiry* 38, no. 3 (2008): 267–97.

49. Ibid., 280.

50. Mary Arnold Twining, "I'm Going to Sing and 'Shout' While I Have the Chance: Music, Movement, and Dance on the Sea Islands," *Black Music Research Journal* 15, no. 1 (1995): 1.

51. James A. Standifer, "Musical Behaviors of Black People in American Society," *Black Music Research Journal* 1 (1980): 53–54.

52. Perry, "Parched Earth," 75.

53. Gustafson, "Drifters and Dancing Mad."

54. Barbara Reeder Lundquist and Winston T. Sims, "African-American Music Education: Reflections on an Experience," *Black Music Research Journal* 16, no. 2 (1996): 324.

55. Ben Sidran, *Black Talk* (Boston, MA: Da Capo Press, 1971), 13–14.

Chapter 2

"Why Should I Sing for You?" Student Perspectives on Relationships

Who are my students? They're kids! They're young, confused. I like them so much, I really do. They're normal kids out there looking for guidance. . . . They just want to be happy.

—Alicia Beckman

The students in this study reported that the critical underlying element that fostered their deep engagement in music class was their strong positive relationship with Ms. Beckman. They felt connected to her and appreciated the fact that she shared details with them about her life, sought to make them comfortable in class, and learned about them as people. They often responded to her open invitation to come to her classroom on their lunch hour to practice a piece of music or talk about something on their minds. Ladson-Billings described these actions as resulting from teachers' *conceptions of social relations*.[1] Based on these conceptions, Culturally Relevant teachers maintain an equitable teacher-student relationship, viewing students' expertise and experiences as equally valid and important to the class.

In addition to her *conceptions of social relations*, Ms. Beckman's teaching identity also reflects her strong *conceptions of self and others*, another tenet of Culturally Relevant Pedagogy. Within this tenet, teachers see themselves as part of the community in which they teach, believe that teaching is an important profession, and hold a high opinion of themselves within the profession.

These teachers see the act of teaching as an art and feel that they have a calling to the teaching profession. They see the act of teaching like "mining"—pulling knowledge out of their students. They also see themselves as a part of the community where they teach and feel that they and their students are involved in giving to the community. Culturally Relevant teachers believe that all of their students can succeed, and they help their students make connections between various facets of their identities—community, national, and global.[2] Ms. Beckman reflected her beliefs about herself, her students, and social relationships in the classroom by implementing strategies to develop and maintain relationships and to foster a warm and inviting classroom environment.

STUDENT RELATIONSHIPS WITH MS. BECKMAN

Alicia Beckman has been teaching at Clark Middle School in Lake City for nine years. She is a 37-year-old white woman who graduated in 1997 with a music education degree from a music conservatory located within a private liberal arts university. Before coming to Clark, she spent time teaching in large, urban districts on the West and East coasts; then she moved with her family back to Lake City, near where she grew up. In choir class, Ms. Beckman often shares aspects of her life with her students, including stories about her family and her interests outside of school.

Ms. Beckman works pointedly to build trusting relationships among the participants in her choir. To encourage the students to support and trust each other, she told them a story in class about one of her past students who had extreme stage fright. During a concert, he began shaking and crying, later explaining that this was because he was made fun of in elementary school for singing. The students immediately engaged in this conversation, injecting compassionate remarks.

Ms. Beckman described how hurtful remarks can injure a person. She continued, "Point being, you can't break people like that. You don't know if you're going to be the one that's going to ruin them forever." Ms. Beckman also described a scene from her daughter's gymnastics class. She described how a student who struggled in class did a cartwheel and fell, and it was so cute that everyone laughed.

Shayla, a student in class, called out a rhetorical question, "Now, how did that girl feel?" The class and Ms. Beckman all responded empathetically. Ms. Beckman replied, "I know how I would have felt if that had been my daughter. My daughter sitting on my lap laughed, and we talked about it on the way home. Once she put herself in that position, as the one who might have been laughed at, she understood. And if we all think like that, if we put ourselves in that position, I don't think any of us is that evil that we can't imagine what that would feel like." The students described their own similar experiences, which Ms. Beckman encouraged them to share. She also encouraged them to get beyond the fear of being laughed at. Instead, she asked them to focus on how much they enjoyed singing and to trust each other.

This type of class discussion, in which Ms. Beckman shares life with her students, is a usual occurrence in this choir classroom. The effects on the classroom climate are palpable. There is a sense of warmth and calm among the students as they enter the classroom. Students greet Ms. Beckman, wish her good morning, ask how she is doing, and often give her a hug before the bell rings.

In addition to sharing her life with her students, Ms. Beckman also includes the students in selecting repertoire for their class. Her personal playlist recently included Henryk Górecki's Symphony no. 3 and music by the Rolling Stones. "But in the car, I usually listen to hip-hop because [*she pulls out a note from a student*] I found this note. It has song suggestions from the kids. So I need to know, when they suggest something, if it might work for our group. So I try to keep current on what they're listening to." While Ms. Beckman does not teach music solely from the students' current listening libraries, she chooses all of the music with their tastes in mind.

JACOBI

Jacobi, a 12-year-old African-American male, has attended Lake City Public Schools since moving to Lake City three years ago. He listens to R&B and hip-hop, and he played violin in the district's orchestra program in 5th grade. He enjoys singing and rapping. During the course of this study, he performed several raps for his choir classmates.

He described listening to gospel music with his family as one of his favorite musical experiences outside of school. "After my grandma passed away, we started singing her favorite songs to remember her. My mom thought we could do it every Sunday. We have our big dinner and then, around 8, we'll say a prayer and then listen to music. I like those songs." Jacobi also expressed positive feelings about the music Ms. Beckman selects for his choir class. "I like the music she be picking. And sometimes she be giving us a choice. That's one thing I like about her too. Yeah, I like the songs she be picking."

ESTEPHANIE

Estephanie, another student in the study, stated that she joined choir because she was attracted to the fact that Ms. Beckman encourages the students to participate in choosing the repertoire, which includes popular music. Estephanie is 12 years old. Her grandmother is Native American and she describes herself as white and Native American.

She moved to Lake City to live with her dad less than a year before the study began when she was in the middle of 6th grade; she had previously lived with her mom in Indiana. She feels comfortable at Clark Middle School and in the choir class. She listens to hip-hop music, counts choir as one of her favorite classes, and likes Ms. Beckman as a teacher. She participates on a cheerleading team outside of school and studied clarinet in 5th-grade band.

Estephanie reported an example of how Ms. Beckman forms deeper relationships with her students by connecting with them outside of class. "Ms. Beckman is the teacher I have who can do that [make connections]. One time I saw her in the hallway, and she said, 'Good job today.' And me and my friend Jason were like, 'That's because we were sitting with the people that we could sing around.' She makes sure that you feel comfortable."

Estephanie and the other seven students in the study described Ms. Beckman as one of their favorite teachers at Clark: in fact, at the end of this study, all of the students in her 7th-grade choir classes once again elected to take her class in 8th grade. As she teaches, Ms. Beckman incorporates her students' ideas and interests, and her students enjoy how she fosters connections between their lives and the music they sing.

Ms. Beckman compared her work at Clark with her previous job working with younger students: "Middle school? Yes, I prefer middle school. I understand them." Her students also sensed that she *liked* being with them. When asked what he felt Ms. Beckman would do for her work if she could choose all over again, Jacobi said, "I think she might want to be a singer or a music writer . . . or do *this* job."

Ms. Beckman also purposefully finds ways for students to share their lives with her, deepening her relationships with them. Following the choir's concert in January 2011, Ms. Beckman asked the students to fill out a self-evaluation sheet about the concert and their performance. One student asked, "Will you give us that question, 'Tell us something you want me to know about yourself'? That's my favorite question."

Ms. Beckman smiled. "That's my favorite question, too. I look forward to reading the answers to that question, because they are the most interesting. Tell me anything on that question that you want. I leave the back side of your self-eval blank in case you need more room or you want to suggest a song to sing in the future." The students' relationships with Ms. Beckman and their knowledge of her positive feelings toward them set the stage for their deep engagement and musical achievement.

Reflect 2.1

Take stock of your relationships with the students in your classroom. You could start with conducting an anonymous poll asking your students how they think you feel about them. This might be a difficult task, but can help you identify positive relationships in the classroom as well as relationships you might need to improve. Then consider the following questions:

- How do I let my students know that I like being in class with them?
- How do I share my life with my students and invite them to share with me?
- How do I form connections with my students outside of class?
- How do I show my students that I value their input into the content and trajectory of the class?

Use this activity to reflect on the alignment of your beliefs with the Culturally Relevant *conceptions of social relations* and *conceptions of self and others.*

STUDENTS' RELATIONSHIPS WITH PEERS

For the students in this study, their ideal regarding student relationships within the classroom included knowing each other's "stories." To them, sharing and knowing stories included sharing knowledge about backgrounds, life experiences, personalities, strengths, and weaknesses. The students felt that knowing and sharing stories would give them a strong connection with their peers and result in a classroom where they could all feel comfortable singing together.

JOHN

The students in this study described varying levels of satisfaction with the relationships in the classroom. John demonstrated the lowest level of connection with the other students in the class. John was a 13-year-old white male who had moved to Lake City from Iowa at the start of 7th grade. He had attended a Catholic school in Iowa where he enjoyed singing cantor parts during the Mass. He liked a variety of subjects in school, including choir, and he took piano lessons at home. In 7th grade, he was the only student at Clark Middle School to participate in the Lake City Boy Choir festival.

John expressed discomfort in navigating a new school setting at Clark and at times wished he could move back to Iowa. Even in April, late in the school year, he felt that he did not really know or understand anyone in the class. When asked about relationships, he frequently used the word "them" to describe his peers in class, and rarely used the word "we" to include himself as a part of the student body in choir.

> *Ruth (researcher):* What do you think the relationships are like right now with the kids in the class? How do all the kids feel about each other?
>
> *John:* I have no idea. I know nobody, and I've got no idea what anybody else thinks.
>
> *Ruth:* What if you could go like this [*snaps fingers*] and have it be any way that you like about the relationships between the kids in the class—what would it be like?
>
> *John:* First, probably just make it that everybody actually wants to sing, because I'm willing to bet that there's a lot of kids in the class that are either doing this just to get out of study hall or don't really want to sing or thought maybe it might be fun, but then decided it isn't. . . .
>
> *Ruth:* Okay. What about their relationships with each other? Like, your relationship with them, their relationship with you. What would a good, perfect relationship be like?
>
> *John:* One where everybody would be friends, working together, happy . . . doing what they're supposed to do. It's a little illogical, though . . . it's sort of illogical to get everybody being friends.
>
> *Ruth:* What if everybody could respect each other and understand each other? How could *that* happen? Do you think you would need to know more about them?
>
> *John:* Probably. Once again, I don't know any of these kids. I don't even know how they sing; it's my first year here, I haven't had enough time to meet everybody. Then once you're working together, you have to get them to actually enjoy the class, and then it just depends on their talent. On how good they are at singing, and how much they want to sing. (April interview)

John stated that he wanted to be in a choir where the kids are all there to sing. He was not so sure that his classmates *did* want to sing. He was also not so sure that everyone in the class could be friends (it seemed "illogical"), but he thought if they could work together and sing well, then he might consider choir a better class. He also subtly suggested that a variation in talent among the students might influence relationships.

In contrast, Jacobi felt that relationships between the students could be enhanced if they all viewed each other as musically capable and celebrated each other's efforts. Jacobi often demonstrated his own musical affinity for memorizing raps during class. During one class period, he sang along with a karaoke Wii version of a 1980s rap song and wowed his classmates.

He smiled as Shayla, another student in class, exclaimed, "He a beast!" Jacobi rated the relationships in the class as a "6" on a scale of 1 to 10.

Ruth: [In your ideal class] how would all the kids feel about each other and singing together and working together?

Jacobi: They would feel like, "Aw, that person can sing!" Like, everybody can sing in the classroom. Everybody would become friends.

Ruth: How do you think it is right now on a scale of 1 to 10?

Jacobi: A five . . . well, six. Yeah, about a six. They like . . . friends with some people, and not with the other ones. They don't hate the other person, they just don't talk to them, because they probably don't know them like that. (March interview)

MILA

Mila, another student participant in this study, described how she would like to be better friends with the other students in choir and would like to talk with them outside of class. Mila is a 12-year-old African-American female who has lived in Lake City since birth and has attended Lake City Public Schools since kindergarten. She played saxophone in the band at Clark Middle School in 6th grade and switched to choir in 7th grade because she wanted to sing. She listens to pop and hip-hop music and makes up dances to songs at the after-school program she attends. She likes to swim and jump rope. She has five siblings and enjoys many subjects in school.

Mila sometimes feels that she cannot sit by certain students in choir class because they might tease her. While Mila has the same desire as Jacobi for improved relationships among the peers in the class, her experiences are different. She is not as musically outgoing as Jacobi and does not volunteer to sing alone, as he often does; however, she is still looking for acknowledgment from her peers that she is valuable and worthy as a contributor to the group. Mila stated, "I just want to be friends with every single kid in class. And we can get along together and talk with each other outside of class . . . and sing. Sit by each other, and sing."

BLOSSOM

Blossom, a 13-year-old Asian-American female, has lived in Lake City since birth and has attended school in Lake City School District since kindergarten. She participated in the district's orchestra program in 4th grade and has always enjoyed singing. In choir class in 6th grade, Blossom demonstrated that her musical capabilities included solo singing, and she sang a solo with her choir that year.

Blossom practices her choir music with YouTube videos while her older brother gives her tips for improvement. She listens to music almost every day, especially pop songs "that have attitude" and music "you can dance to." She also likes to practice singing with a good friend. Blossom described how students in the class know basic facts about each other but do not know each other's stories. To illustrate this, she described two students in class who irritate each other because they do not understand each other.

Ruth: Do you feel like everybody knows and understands each other right now?

Blossom: Like . . . you know how we always stand right there [*points to risers*]? And there was Carlos on one half and then Mariah on one half. They're both screaming at each other, so I told them to shut up. And then they just kept on going. Carlos, he sings. And Mariah sings, but then, like . . . Mariah doesn't talk, that's the thing. Sometimes she talks. It depends on what mood she's in. Carlos, he always talks. So then he talks a lot, and then he'll be like, "No, *you* shut up." And stuff like that. . . . I think sometimes he takes it as a joke, but then sometimes it's not. I mean, she's a happy person. So . . . she's always happy, so she talks in a voice . . . in a happy voice, even when she's being serious. So Carlos, I think, thinks it's a joke between them or something, when it's not. You have to get to know Mariah, from school and stuff.

Blossom described how one classmate, Mariah, felt when another classmate, Carlos, joked with her in a way that demonstrated that he does not take her seriously. She suggested that Carlos just does not know Mariah and what her tone of voice might signify. Blossom used this story to illustrate a point that Estephanie also discussed. Estephanie, too, felt that better relationships among the students would increase participation.

Estephanie: Um . . . maybe some people, like the quiet people, I think that a lot of us don't know as well. But most of us, I think we know each other pretty well. Just some people are really quiet, so a lot of us don't know them as well.

Ruth: Ok, so you think most of you just kind of know each other pretty well? What if you could get to know each other even more? Do you think that would help the singing and the relationships in the class?

Estephanie: Yeah, because then everybody would feel comfortable to sing who they're by. Sometimes some people don't feel comfortable by who they're singing by. Then everybody would feel comfortable and I think that would help some people to start singing.

Ruth: Can you think of somebody in the class that you . . . if you were to sit by them, you wouldn't really know a lot about them?

Estephanie: John. Um . . . Alice. Trying to think who's in our class, um . . . Louis.

ÁNGEL

Jacobi and Ángel also desired stronger peer relationships in choir. Jacobi and Ángel each named the other as a person they do not "know anything about." Ángel is a 12-year-old Latino male who has lived in Lake City for two years; before that, he lived in Mexico. Spanish is his first language. He has four siblings and he enjoys listening to mariachi music, among other styles.

Ángel enjoys art and science in school and likes being in choir because he enjoys singing, especially popular music; however, he had not experienced any school music before he had come to Clark Middle School. Neither Jacobi nor Ángel reported that the other is necessarily mean or disrespectful—they just do not know each other's stories, and this prevents them from developing a high level of community with each other in class.

Ms. Beckman used a number of team-building activities with the students during the beginning of the school year. During a class period early in the year, she encouraged the students to get to know each other as she taught them about Mary Lou Williams, a jazz composer. She played *Zodiac Suite* by Williams, a piece that includes a different movement for each zodiac sign.[3] She identified students by name as she went through the 12 movements and asked them if the descriptors matched their personalities. As she played the music, she asked the students to listen for qualities in the music that mirrored the traits of each sign. The students learned about each other's personalities and engaged in musical analysis as a class.

During another class period, the students sang along with songs from the television show *Glee* on the classroom Wii. The students used microphones and could choose to sing in small groups or alone. Ms. Beckman encouraged them to support each other with applause, positive feedback, and by singing along. The students took musical risks in an environment of support. Even though Ms. Beckman incorporated multiple approaches to team building, the students still stated that the relationships among peers in the class were not what they could be and that they wished those relationships would improve.

Ms. Beckman believed that each of her students was valuable to the group and capable musically. She sought to have them see each other in this way, but during the year of this study, her class did not achieve "solidarity in community."[4] For solidarity in community to occur, cohesion must exist among students, fostering relationships based on mutuality, reciprocity, commitment, connection, and responsibility.[5]

The choir did have magical moments of connection, however. During their January performance of "He Still Loves Me,"[6] they functioned as a whole: they celebrated the solos, and they were all excited and "feeling it."[7] The audience responded with cheers and applause, and the students felt very proud. John summarized the thoughts that many of the students expressed regarding this moment: "Everybody was in it together. Everybody was singing. It was just like, the perfect moment. The highest moment of the year for our choir, working as a team."

However, during other moments in choir when some students participated through singing and some did not, the students became frustrated. The varying

Reflect 2.2

- Now, take stock of the peer relationships in your classroom. Do your students "know each other's stories"?
- How can you create learning opportunities for students to get to know each other musically and personally?
- How can you help them identify and value each other's strengths?
- Can you identify a moment when all of your students achieved a musical goal together and celebrated that moment together? How often do you have those moments? How can you plan for moments in which students achieve musically together?

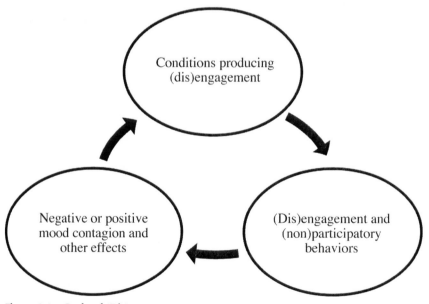

Figure 2.1   Cycle of (Dis)engagement

levels of participation among their classmates also influenced students' participatory behaviors based on proximity to certain peers. In this way, the students' perceptions of the (dis)engagement of the students near them contributed to a negative or positive mood contagion. As Figure 2.1 depicts, students' moods were affected by (dis)engagement in the classroom. Mood contagion, in turn, became a *condition* affecting students' (dis)engagement.

MOOD CONTAGION

Mood contagion is "conceived of as an automatic mechanism that induces a congruent mood state by means of the observation of another person's emotional expression."[8] Moods are an "affective reaction to general environmental stimuli, leading to relatively unstable short-term intra-individual changes, and can change readily."[9] The process of mood contagion occurs in two stages: first, people can begin to imitate the facial expressions and body language of the person they are observing; second, they begin to take on the moods portrayed by those particular actions. While Ms. Beckman's students' moods were sometimes affected by the physical or emotional conditions they brought with them into the classroom,[10] as Figure 2.2 depicts, their moods were also influenced by the instruction, the music in class, the teacher's mood, the other students' moods, and the students' work in singing with others as a group.

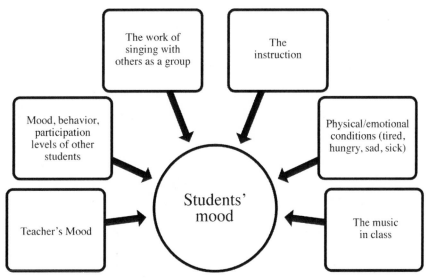

Figure 2.2   Conditions Affecting Students' Mood in Music Class

MS. BECKMAN'S MOOD

Ms. Beckman was aware of the multiple physical or emotional reasons why a student might not participate in singing on any given day or for extended periods of time. She let the students know that she would not hound them to participate if they were feeling sad, still in the process of growing comfortable singing in the presence of others, or just having a bad day. She described her approach in the following way:

> Hey, that's great [having all the students sing together]. But is that really the most important thing [getting them all to sing]? I don't know. At the expense of what? . . . Look at Allen. He didn't sing for weeks, months. And then, when he knew the songs, he started. Not always, but mostly. . . . But what if I was all over him, and being really strict with him, and deep down he knows that he can't, for some reason or another. And the other thing I try to tell kids, too, is that we don't know what is going on with other people. This may be an emotional issue. Because a lot of kids will . . . I've had kids just completely break down and start crying when they start singing. Or, they just can't. And . . . we don't know.

Ms. Beckman was also aware of how her mood could affect the students: "I'm a lot happier than I used to be. And that makes a difference in how they feel. Like, when I don't feel good, or I'm in a bad mood, or I have a headache or whatever. It's . . . not good. It can go bad very quickly."

While Ms. Beckman acknowledged that portraying a positive, enthusiastic mood is important in teaching, she was also concerned with staying true to herself. She wanted to be real with the students and felt that they would see through her attempts to be something she was not. During class, she told the students how their behavior could distract her from feeling the emotion in the song: "How many of you forgot to think about the words? How many of you forgot to put the heart into the song? I forgot. I'm sorry. It's not a crime! How many of you did? Because I was distracted by people talking. You're real people, I'm a real person." As Ms. Beckman observed and described, the reciprocal nature of mood contagion affects the mood of both teacher and students in music classrooms.

The students in Ms. Beckman's class described how their moods linked to hers. Jacobi described what an ideal choir class period looked like for him. "In this class? . . . I'd have everybody to sing loud enough, no interruptions. No wasting time. Have everybody in a mood to sing. And we sing loud. Teacher compliments us more. And . . . that's really all. Just be excited and compliment us." Jacobi described a desire for "everybody to be in a mood to sing," demonstrating how his classmates' enthusiasm for singing is reflected in his own enthusiasm. He also responded enthusiastically when Ms. Beckman demonstrated excitement and pleasure with their singing.

GREGORY

Gregory also described how mood contagion affected him. Gregory is a 12-year-old African-American male who has lived in Lake City since birth and has attended school in Lake City School District since kindergarten. He has three siblings and enjoys math and social studies classes, listening to R&B and hip-hop, and singing. Gregory describes himself as reserved, preferring not to express himself through movement or dancing. He shared that his sister once recorded him singing a choir song in the shower and then embarrassed him by playing it for his friends. When asked to describe if an enthusiastic teacher made a difference for him in class, he replied,

> I think so, because when the teacher is playing the piano really excited and everybody else is there with a boring face, it wouldn't be right, so I would probably have the same expression if somebody were . . . if she [Ms. Beckman] were the only one being excited. It wouldn't be right if we were all bored and she [Ms. Beckman] was excited.

Gregory gave an example of how the cycle of mood contagion can pass from the teacher to the students in a positive manner. Research confirms that the cycle of mood contagion in a classroom is reciprocal: when teachers' behaviors demonstrate their own interest in the subject matter and they have a lively presentation style, there is a positive effect on the learners' engagement and willingness to learn. This, in turn, affects the teacher positively.[11] When a teacher feels the students are motivated to learn and are engaged, these perceptions become the main source of a positive experience in the act of teaching.

The reciprocal nature of mood contagion bears implications for music teaching. Teacher perceptions regarding their students' engagement levels are linked to and influence teachers' own involvement/engagement in the classroom.[12] Teachers who conclude, based on students' perceived disengagement, that they are not liked or are not competent may experience affective disengagement themselves.[13]

If teachers view students' disengagement as an obstacle to lesson planning and teaching, they may experience motivational problems themselves, further leading to their own disengagement from the teaching and learning processes. Conversely, if teachers can interpret students' disengagement as a challenging and interesting puzzle that they can confidently solve together, they may be led to examine and implement more effective instructional methods, learning tasks, and classroom structures.[14] If teachers continue to display low enthusiasm or frustration, the classes can eventually be assumed to reflect those qualities back to the teachers in increasing measures.

ALICE

Ms. Beckman taught her students songs they enjoyed, even if she did not. In her interview in February, Alice, a student participant in the study, described her frustration with what she felt was too much class time spent understanding students' opinions regarding which songs they would like to sing. Alice is a 12-year-old Latina who was born in Mexico and moved to the United States when she was six years old. She and her four siblings have been living in Lake City for three years; Alice has attended school in the Lake City School District since then.

Alice enjoys music, especially hip-hop, and spends time singing and dancing with her cousins and friends. She participated in the district's orchestra program in 4th grade and joined choir at Clark Middle School in 6th grade. She had mixed feelings about joining choir in 7th grade and discussed possibly joining band; however, she remained in choir throughout 7th grade and elected to join again in 8th.

Alice brought up a practical point: the students had different songs that they liked, so she encouraged Ms. Beckman to spend more time in enthusiastic instruction of songs she herself liked. Alice stated, "Well, she [Ms. Beckman] should also choose songs that she likes, because, of course, a lot of people are going to like it and a lot of people are going to dislike it, so she should probably choose the ones that she likes." *Showing enthusiasm and vitality about what is being taught and learned* is also a Culturally Relevant practice.[15] Applying the research on mood contagion and CRP to music education, a teacher who clearly communicates enthusiasm for the songs the students are learning can make a difference in students' own enthusiasm and, thus, their engagement.

In class, Blossom sometimes chose not to sing for days at a time. In fact, from mid-March until April, Blossom rarely sang in class. She even declined to sing a solo assigned to her in rehearsal and ended up giving this solo to another student for the concert. In the following interview excerpt, and in a focus group session, she discussed aspects of choir class that she felt might encourage her engagement through singing, one of which was teacher enthusiasm.

Ruth: Ok. Do you have anything else that you've been thinking about . . . that you want to tell me about teaching in music class, and what could make a music class better?

Blossom: You know that chorus? That PS 22 Chorus you showed us?

Ruth: Yeah.

Blossom: Yeah, like . . . act like that teacher that's having fun all the time, no matter what. Like, Ms. Beckman, she told us that she really didn't like the song

"He Still Loves Me." But she sang it because we wanted to sing it, so she did it for us. So then we should always sing songs for them. For teachers, because they might care about something, and we didn't know their story.

Ruth: So maybe, if Ms. Beckman, like you said, acted more like that other teacher.

Blossom: Yeah. Because he looked like he was a fun teacher, always dancing around. And then when the kids sang "Just Dance," everybody started dancing, so then they had fun.

The last statement Blossom made was, "When the *kids* sang . . . *everybody* started dancing, so then *they* had fun." In this way, everyone in the class (students and teacher) can create the musical experience together. Blossom brought up Gregg Breinberg, director of the PS 22 Chorus. Mr. Breinberg identifies as a member of the choir himself, locating himself as a cocontributor to the overall performance. Mr. Breinberg has described his ideologies regarding the role of teacher enthusiasm in cocreating musical experiences:

Also important in achieving soulful performances I suppose is the fact that I don't park my behind on a piano bench and stare blankly at the keys while leading. I don't leave my students to do this on their own. We all, myself included, are responsible for putting the work together because that's what this process demands in order to be done successfully. As I basically said before, the teacher/director had better be prepared to give what he's asking for.[16]

As Breinberg leads class, he demonstrates the enthusiasm he requests of his students. His video blog[17] documents how he uses gestures, eye contact, and vocal excitement when the students achieve excellence to convey his enthusiasm and excitement for the music and the students. Ladson-Billings described this attitude as "we're all in this together" and states that this sense of community is important in establishing Culturally Relevant social relations in the classroom.[18] Similar to the way moods pass between teacher and students, mood contagion also occurs between students.

MOOD CONTAGION FROM PEERS

The students in the study discussed how mood contagion occurred between students within the choir. In a quotation earlier in this chapter, Jacobi described how "everybody being in a mood to sing" would positively affect him. Jacobi further described the effect this would have on his own participation.

Ruth: What if you came to choir and you felt like you had a good connection with the songs, and all the kids, even the kids who, like, right now don't sing.

Jacobi: Mm-hmm.

Ruth: They were all excited and singing, into it, feeling it.

Jacobi: That'd make me excited, and I'd sing too.

Alice described how the mood and behaviors of other students influenced her at times. She sometimes chose not to sing in choir because a person near her who was not singing influenced her. However, if she stood by someone who frequently sang in class, she was more likely to sing as well.

Ruth: [On the January concert] did you have a favorite song?

Alice: Mm-hmm . . . "He Still Loves Me."

Ruth: Why was it your favorite?

Alice: Because, almost the whole class likes it. And they . . . because if some kids, if they don't like [a song], they don't sing, and then it sounds kind of bad. And a lot of people like it ["He Still Loves Me"], and it makes it sound good.

Ruth: I noticed that on some of the songs, like especially in practice, some of the kids won't sing sometimes. How does that make you feel?

Alice: Not making me sing.

Alice connected excitement, participation through singing, and mood contagion. Barsade described the process of mood contagion among members of a group as "mood convergence."[19] Members of a group can "catch" the mood of others in the group if they attend to it to a certain degree, and may "compare their moods with those of others in their environment and then respond with what seems appropriate for the situation."[20] Barsade described not only how positive moods could converge, but also how negative cues from others in the group can begin a spiral into increasing negativity.

Alice and Jacobi discussed how both positive and negative mood convergence occurred among peers in the class. High levels of participation and engagement tended to motivate the students to remain engaged. The reverse also happened: when students disengaged by not participating, this "tuning out" was contagious and resulted in more students following suit.

In Ms. Beckman's classroom, Shayla, an African-American female, was a student who emerged as a leader who at times influenced who "felt it" or not. Like John, she sang when asked. She rarely, if ever, disengaged when she was asked to sing. She asked for clarification of a part if she did not feel confident in singing a melody and she encouraged the other students to sing and participate. In class, she added movement to songs, usually coordinating movements with two of her soprano friends, and answered Ms. Beckman's rhetorical questions. Shayla often caused her classmates to smile with her witty verbal contributions.

The students in the study labeled Shayla's behavior as ideal from the teacher's perspective and also as desirable from the other students' standpoints. Estephanie stated that she wanted to be in choir with Shayla next year and that she sings better when she sits next to Shayla. Gregory felt that an ideal student (from the teacher's perspective) cares about class and is willing to try anything the teacher requests. He felt that Shayla exhibited these characteristics most of the time. Blossom also described Shayla as having qualities of an ideal choir student:

Ruth: Think about the class right now. Is there a student who maybe has some ideal qualities, like those you just described?

Blossom: Shayla. Like, she sings. Sometimes she'll take things as a joke, but that's only because she wants everybody to still be happy. But take the thing seriously, that this is a class and not, just like, time off or anything. Because Ms. Beckman's really nice, so.

Ruth: So Shayla kind of takes it seriously? Like, "We need to do what she wants!"

Blossom: Yeah. Like, Shayla has her . . . she says her own opinions. She's not just going to stand there and just stand in line like everybody else. She'll yell it out if she needs to, for everybody to pay attention.

Ruth: Ok, so that's kind of a positive thing, like, she works to get everybody together and on the same page?

Blossom: Yeah.

Shayla definitely had an impact on the general mood of the group. Apart from Ms. Beckman, she spoke the most in class; it was impossible not to notice her. She had some leadership roles in the class, such as moving the lyrics to be visible when necessary on the computer screen, singing solos, passing out sheet music, and verbally encouraging other kids to participate in singing. Shayla demonstrated an example of positive mood contagion among peers, and perhaps, as Ms. Beckman did, music teachers could encourage students with strengths such as Shayla's to take on leadership roles in the classroom.

THE CHOIR'S WORK IN CREATING
PERFORMANCES TOGETHER

During a January focus group session, Blossom, Ángel, Alice, and Jacobi discussed their choir concert, which had just taken place the night before.

All of them agreed that the concert event was a positive musical experience, highlighted by the applause of their friends and family. During this focus group, they watched videos of the PS 22 Chorus in rehearsal and commented on this group singing "Just Dance" by Lady Gaga[21] and "Forever Young" by Alphaville.[22]

Ruth: Ok, what's going on?

Jacobi: They, like, feeling both of them. I think in both videos, they feeling both of the songs. In the first one, they had movements to the song, to show like. . . .

Ruth: Uh-huh . . . so, why?

Blossom: They like the songs?

Jacobi: Or maybe that's what they . . . like, the teacher asked them to do.

Ruth: How was the teacher . . . do you think *the teacher* was feeling the songs?

Jacobi: Yeah, he was the same. Mm-hmm.

Ruth: How was he . . . how could you tell he was feeling the songs?

Jacobi: Because he was, like, doing the movements and stuff. [*Demonstrates moves.*]

Blossom: He dances a lot . . . because he probably connected with the students.

Ruth: How do you think he did that?

Blossom: Like, asking them what kind of music they like. And then, maybe . . . the songs that they don't know.

As they viewed the videos of different choirs, the students discussed the choirs that they liked, mentioning that the choirs they liked most demonstrated cohesiveness in the group, which they thought manifested in students who were feeling the songs.

Ruth: Ok, so what I'm hearing is, you like singing if everybody is feeling it together?

Jacobi: Yeah.

Ruth: So, if your choir was feeling it together, would that make you want to sing more?

Blossom and Jacobi: Yeah. [*Ángel and Alice also nod agreement.*]

Blossom: I'd make a career with it. Like, a job with singing, like teaching or something.

Jacobi: It'd make it a way better class. [*Ángel nods agreement.*]

The students in this focus group discussed what group cohesion would look like for them and believed that the PS 22 Chorus provided a good example of students who were all "feeling it." They all considered this to be a desirable quality in a choir, one that would motivate them to engage and participate.

While community and group cohesion is an essential part of CRP, "the work that it takes to create community in the school and in the classroom should not be underestimated."[23] Gregg Breinberg described one way he builds a community of positive participation in a music classroom and thus also promotes mood convergence in a positive way:

> Creating the environment . . . is a slow process . . . encouragement is always needed, even with a seasoned group. I try to safely draw positive attention to a confident kid that is doing things correctly and can handle being made an example of. Of course it comes more naturally and easily to some than to others. But having a kid like Joey, who is very self-confident and popular among his peers, makes it okay for the kids that are perhaps a bit more inhibited. And sometimes the kids that perform the most genuinely are those that are the most reserved at the beginning of the year.[24]

Here, Breinberg referred to creating an environment where the students express themselves through the music physically and vocally. In Ms. Beckman's classroom, the students described a moment of community and connection when they experienced success as a class performing "He Still Loves Me." These examples of positive mood contagion can provide springboards to further meaningful musical experiences in which students engage together.

Reflect 2.3

Examine your mood during the course of a class period.

- Do you have "mood swings" during the class period?
- What causes your mood to change?
- How do your changes in mood affect your students?
- Can you sense how students' (dis)engagement might play a role in mood contagion in your classroom?

Monitor your mood for a day.

- How is your mood when you start the day? What mood do you project to your students?
- Are there times during the day when you are more enthusiastic/more tired/more content/more frustrated?

CRP, MOOD CONTAGION, AND RELATIONSHIPS

Relationships in a music classroom (any classroom!) are complex. Ms. Beckman provides a valuable window into how she developed strong relationships with her students. While her strategies can be studied and implemented in another music classroom, teachers should first examine their ideologies and beliefs. By developing strong Culturally Relevant conceptions of social relations and conceptions of self/others, teachers can identify additional creative strategies that match their personalities and the unique combination of students' personalities in their classrooms.

Ms. Beckman and her students also provide insight into how mood contagion functions in a classroom. Once again, teachers' and students' personalities will combine in different ways to form a unique alchemy. As teachers continue to work with students, they can learn to be more aware of the mood they project as they introduce new music, create collaborative experiences with the students, and design instruction.

Take Action 2.4

1. In your group, formulate a plan to strengthen relationships between you and your students. Choose a strategy to build strong relationships with students and make a point to implement this strategy throughout your day for three weeks. Document the relationships between you and two "focus" students throughout the three weeks. How do the relationships change/grow? Can you continue implementing this strategy and can you add other strategies?
2. Choose a class period during which you find it difficult to maintain an enthusiastic mood toward the musical content and/or your students. Make a determined effort to enthusiastically instruct and interact during this class period for three weeks. You may need to adjust your instruction so that you *do* become enthusiastic about the lesson plans you are implementing; perhaps, think of reasons that this class is a special class to you. Remind yourself of the goals of the class and the importance of the class to the students. Document these three weeks: How does the class respond each day? Do you notice a difference in the class's mood after the three weeks? How has this affected the students' (dis)engagement?

NOTES

1. Gloria Ladson-Billings, "Toward a Theory of Culturally Relevant Pedagogy," *American Educational Research Journal* 32, no. 3 (1995): 465–91.

2. Gloria Ladson-Billings, *The Dreamkeepers: Successful Teachers of African American Children* (San Francisco, CA: Jossey-Bass, 1994).

3. Mary Lou Williams, *Zodiac Suite* [Recorded by Geri Allen, Buster Williams, Billy Hart, and Andrew Cyrille on *Zodiac Suite: Revisited*], 2006 (first released in 1945 by Mary Records), Compact Disc.

4. Jeffrey L. Lewis and Eunhee Kim, "A Desire to Learn: African American Children's Positive Attitudes Toward Learning Within School Cultures of Low Expectations," *Teachers College Record* 110, no. 6 (2008): 1304–29.

5. Ibid., 1311. The events in the classroom during cycles of disengagement divided the students, and these events and their effects are discussed in the second section of this book.

6. This song was a gospel song from the movie *The Fighting Temptations.* In the movie, a gospel choir performs the song with several soloists, including Beyoncé Knowles.

7. The students describe a deep level of engagement in choir class as "feeling it." However, if the students are "blanked out," this indicates a low level of engagement, a time when their thoughts are not focused on the musical task at hand during class.

8. Roland Neumann and Fritz Strack, "'Mood Contagion': The Automatic Transfer of Mood Between Persons," *Journal of Personality and Social Psychology* 79, no. 2 (2000): 211–23.

9. Sigal G. Barsade (citing Tellegren, 1985), "The Ripple Effect: Emotional Contagion and Its Influence on Group Behavior," *Administrative Science Quarterly* 47, no. 4 (2002): 644–75.

10. The students describe how a negative physical or emotional state could affect their engagement levels, especially at the start of class. Influences from outside of the music classroom could affect students emotionally and influence their participation. Negative physical states included being tired, sick, hungry, or hurt.

11. Mareike Kunter, Anne Frenzel, Gabriel Nagy, Jurgen Baumert, and Reinhard Pekrun, "Teacher Enthusiasm: Dimensionality and Context Specificity," *Contemporary Educational Psychology* 36, no. 4 (2011): 299.

12. Jennifer A. Fredricks, Phyllis C. Blumenfeld, and Alison H. Paris, "School Engagement: Potential of the Concept, State of the Evidence," *Review of Educational Research* 74, no. 1 (2004): 59–109.

13. Ellen A. Skinner and Jennifer R. Pitzer, "Developmental Dynamics of Student Engagement, Coping, and Everyday Resilience," in *Handbook of Research on Student Engagement*, ed. Sandra L. Christenson, Amy L. Reschly, and Cathy Wylie (New York: Springer, 2012), 21–44.

14. Ibid., 36.

15. Ibid., 163.

16. Thomas J. Hanson, "Gregg Breinberg—The Teacher Behind the PS 22 Internet Sensation," *Open Education: Free Education for All Blog*, January 11, 2010, www.openeducation.net/2010/01/11/gregg-breinberg-the-teacher-behind-the-ps22-internet-sensation/.

17. *PS 22 Chorus Blog*, ps22chorus.blogspot.com.

18. Ladson-Billings, *Dreamkeepers*, 59.

19. Barsade, "The Ripple Effect."

20. Ibid., 648.

21. "PS 22 Chorus 'Just Dance' by Lady Gaga," YouTube Video, 3:12, posted by PS 22 Chorus, June 15, 2009, www.youtube.com/watch?v=h0FPZolbYns.

22. "PS 22 Chorus 'Forever Young' by Alphaville," YouTube Video, 3:01, posted by PS 22 Chorus, June 26, 2009, www.youtube.com/watch?v=KlfzbmPS3n4.

23. Kathy M. Robinson, "White Teacher, Students of Color: Culturally Responsive Pedagogy for Elementary General Music in Communities of Color," in *Teaching Music in the Urban Classroom*, ed. Carol Frierson-Campbell (Lanham, MD: Rowman & Littlefield Education, 2006), 46.

24. Hanson, "Gregg Breinberg."

Chapter 3

Hip-Hop in the Classroom

Student Perspectives on Musical Repertoire

I like hip-hop. It's movement . . . but romantic songs, I don't like the beat to romantic songs. They're kind of slow.

—Alice

I like to listen to pop songs that have attitude in it a little bit. They're not just slow.

—Blossom

All the eight students in this study stated that they liked singing. In choir class, however, if they did not like a song, they were probably not going to sing. For many choir teachers whose musical upbringing differs from that of their students, this becomes an issue of repertoire choice. The logic goes like this: I know my students will sing if they like the song. I know they like certain songs. If I choose a song they *already* like outside of school, then they will engage in choir and sing. If I choose a song they do not already know, they most likely will not enjoy it and therefore will not sing.

The students in this study confirmed part of this logic. They were interested in singing songs in choir that they enjoyed outside of school, and they *did* need to "like" a piece of music (a musical condition influencing their cognitive and emotional engagement) to sing it. However, this musical condition is influenced by many additional factors and is malleable over time.

The students in this study also confirmed the assumption that they will connect to school music if the music itself is relevant to their lived experience. However, the students could form connections to pieces of music that

41

were completely unfamiliar to them and develop these connections through multiple experiences. Figure 3.1 portrays the conditions that facilitated the students' affective and cognitive engagement with the music in their choir class.

Initial positive connections were formed through three musical conditions: when the students learned and could relate to the context of the song (story of the composer/performer, sociopolitical context), when the students understood the meaning of the lyrics, and when they perceived the groove of the musical arrangement. Students also engaged with a song initially if they enjoyed the song outside of class (an emotional condition) or were interested in the instruction regarding the song (see chapter 4).

FAMILIARITY AND ENJOYMENT
OF A SONG OUTSIDE OF SCHOOL
(EMOTIONAL CONDITION)

In the following excerpt from a January 2011 focus group session, Mila, John, Gregory, and Estephanie discussed the connection between students' enjoyment of a song outside of school and their willingness to engage with that song through singing in choir. The group viewed several videoclips of the PS 22 Chorus, including their rendition of "Viva la Vida" by Coldplay.[1]

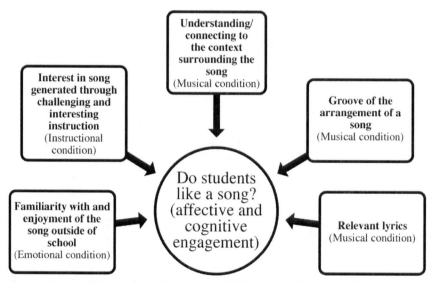

Figure 3.1   Conditions Influencing Students' Affinity for a Piece of Music in School

The students had multiple opinions about the clip, but all agreed that the students in the clip were "feeling it."

Ruth: Do you think that they were emotional about the song?

Estephanie: Yeah.

Gregory: Mm-hmm.

John: Yeah, they really liked the song. I have a feeling that this is a group . . . that they picked their song to sing. I think they picked this song, because they liked that song. So they're going to sing this song. It almost seems like that, because they enjoy it so much.

Ruth: But it seems like they picked it, it seems like they made it their own, because they enjoyed it so much?

John: Mm-hmm.

Ruth: Now tell me about your choir. Do you think all of the kids in your choir would say, "It seems like we picked all of the songs, because we enjoy them so much"?

Mila: No!

John: Noooooo! [*Shakes head.*]

Estephanie: [*Shakes head.*]

Ruth: What would be different?

Estephanie: Some of the kids act like they don't like it, because they're not singing at all. They're just sitting there.

Mila: Like, "Imagine." [*Referring to her own choir's version of "Imagine" by John Lennon.*]

John: I've heard a couple of kids call "Imagine" hippie songs and just . . . I've heard certain things about it that . . . I like "Imagine," personally. I've heard these people calling it certain things, which I don't really think . . . I actually like it, so . . . it don't sound right to me.

In this excerpt, John determined how "liking a song" can include a knowledge of the song before being introduced to it in class. John reasoned here that if the students were able to pick songs they already liked listening to and singing along with outside of class, they would participate. This is the logic described in the opening paragraphs of this chapter. Estephanie, in an individual interview, confirmed this idea, stating that singing popular songs in choir was a draw for her.

Well, I came for a tour of the school, and the social worker was showing us around. And she said, "Were you in band or chorus or anything?" And I said I was in chorus. And she was talking about the kind of music that they were playing [here]. Like, in my old chorus, they sang really old, old songs that you have no clue of, and they're really slow and old and stuff. Then she was talking about "Fireflies" [by Owl City, a song the Clark choir sang in a previous year], and that used to be one of the hit number one songs. So, I was kind of getting into it. . . . That would be kind of fun to do.

Other students agreed that enjoying a song outside of class positively influenced how they felt about it when it was introduced in class. However, for them, the mere act of selecting a familiar, loved repertoire did not sustain engagement, nor was it the only route to enjoying a song. For instance, in the Clark Middle School Choir, the students took a written class poll, indicating that they were excited to sing "Billionaire" by Travie McCoy.[2] But after two months of instruction, the students began to disengage when singing this song in class, sometimes talking or singing incorrect words during the rehearsal. In this case, the students initially enjoyed the song, but the instruction surrounding the song did not present them with either a vision for their own interpretation or a challenge they wanted to meet.

Students also expressed interest in learning new, unfamiliar music in choir. When Ms. Beckman introduced a new piece of music, the students' curiosity about how the music would sound facilitated their engagement with the piece. As time went on in the classroom, the students experienced and responded to instructional conditions in class, as well as musical characteristics of the piece itself. The musical conditions affecting students' engagement in both familiar and unfamiliar music are: connections with the *context*, relevant *lyrics*, and the *groove* of the song.

Reflect 3.1

Think back to when you were in 7th or 8th grade. What did you do when your favorite popular music group put out a new CD (or cassette tape, if you are like me)? For me, when I first bought Janet Jackson's album *Rhythm Nation*, I immediately put on my headphones and read the lyrics while I listened on my Walkman. This music spoke to me. I liked how it sounded, and I listened over and over again. In college, it was Sting's *Ten Summoner's Tales*. This album (CD by then) was the soundtrack to my undergraduate years; my friends and I had these songs playing during every gathering. Discuss with your group some of the "soundtracks of your life." What drew you to these albums/songs? How does this music speak to you still? What memories do you have of this music?

CONTEXT OF A SONG

The students at Clark Middle School recognized the role of knowing and understanding the context when forming connections to a song. As Ms. Beckman explored the context of John Lennon's "Imagine" with her students, this produced a deeper connection with the song, resulting in increased engagement and participatory behaviors in class. During class in January, Ms. Beckman and the students examined news footage and interviews with John Lennon, his critique of the Vietnam War, events surrounding his assassination, and other sociopolitical events of the time period.

Following her presentation of the context, Ms. Beckman asked, "Does this help you understand the song a little bit more?" Shayla replied, "Now that I know the story of the song, it ain't so bad." The effects of learning the context surrounding John Lennon and "Imagine" lingered in the students' minds. During a subsequent class period, two days before the concert, Allen, another student, spoke up in class. "My mom says we should really think about the lyrics [to "Imagine"]. This is her favorite song." Allen's engagement was sparked by the class's discussion of the context of the song "Imagine" and his knowledge of his mother's connection to the song.

Jacobi believed that the time Ms. Beckman spent teaching the context of "Imagine" helped him and his classmates to engage with the music. In a focus group discussion following this class period, he reasoned that perhaps the PS 22 Chorus members also engaged with their songs because Mr. Breinberg shared the context of the songs with them.

Jacobi: He probably brung that song to them like Ms. Beckman brought the "Imagine" song to us.

Ruth: When Ms. Beckman talked to you about "Imagine" and she gave you the backstory, do you think you *felt* the song after that?

Jacobi: Yeah, after that.

Blossom: [*Nods.*] A lot.

Gregory, in an individual interview, described how the musical condition of knowing the context of a song resulted in enjoyment of the song and engagement through singing.

Ruth: So your song "Imagine." Can you tell me some things that Ms. Beckman did with that song?

Gregory: She put on a video about John Lennon's death, and the video showed all of this . . . like, how much people cared about the song "Imagine" and that song will always be remembered. And that he was all about peace and stuff.

Ruth: Did that make a difference for you when she showed that stuff?

Gregory: Well, it did . . . it did make me sing louder. I kind of liked the song a lot more then.

Estephanie described how learning the context to "Imagine" changed her perspective on the song.

Ruth: Can you describe class today to me? [*Referring to the class when Ms. Beckman discussed "Imagine."*]

Estephanie: It started off kind of a little bit noisy, and people were just getting into class and stuff, so, like, they weren't fully focused. And then Ms. Beckman kind of quieted us down. And then we learned about John Lennon. And then a lot of people thought differently about the song, after they heard the backstory about it. And then, I think a lot of people, they think more unnegative, not negative, about the song. And then we sang that song. And then . . . I rushed down to lunch.

Ruth: [*Laughs.*] Ok, so, how did you feel about the song "Imagine" before today?

Estephanie: Before today . . . I don't personally love the song. That is not one of my favorite songs, but I would sing it, because, I don't know, it just, like, it . . . It's not, like, one of the best songs, but I'd sing it, though, because . . . it's part of chorus, I guess.

Ruth: So watching the video today, did it change how *you* felt about the song?

Estephanie: Yeah, it did. It's like, there's a lot more meaning I think to it now, that we know . . . and, yeah.

David Elliott, music educator and author of the book *Music Matters*, described how learning the social contexts surrounding a piece of music encourages students to delve into the interplay of the music, the makers/creators of the music, and the practices involved in creating the music. Investigating the contexts of a piece of music also involves examining the network of beliefs from which "these products [musical works] spring and through which they are being perceived."[3] When students can explore a work of music in this way, they become involved in an encounter with humans from perhaps unfamiliar times and cultures and can begin to view music as a process, rather than as a static object.[4] Students in this study confirmed this idea. Ms. Beckman's exploration of the contexts of "Imagine" definitely produced deeper engagement and participatory behaviors in class.

GROOVE

In their interviews, students described songs they liked as having elements that caused them to feel an emotion, mainly something akin to excitement. They contrasted this emotion with a song that made them feel "tired," which meant a general lack of emotion, or even boredom. The students generally agreed that "He Still Loves Me," performed during the January concert, was a favorite. During the interviews following the concert, the students described their performance of that song as being emotional: they were feeling it. They experienced a sense of pride for that song in particular during the concert. Gregory described his feelings during that moment in the concert thus:

> *Ruth:* Now, you told me your favorite song in the concert was "He Still Loves Me." Can you explain to me why?
>
> *Gregory:* Because it's like . . . the most exciting song. Most of the other songs are kind of quieter, like, tiring to me. And "He Still Loves Me" is one of the only songs that really kept me awake. I enjoyed that song.
>
> *Ruth:* Do you think the other kids feel the same way as you?
>
> *Gregory:* Yeah, most of 'em, yeah.
>
> *Ruth:* So what is it about that song that is more exciting?
>
> *Gregory:* Um . . . . That's a hard question.
>
> *Ruth:* Yeah. [*Both laugh.*]

Other synonyms the students used for this "tiring" quality of a song were "slow," "dull," and "quiet." By contrast, a song that was "exciting" was also described by the students as being "jumpy," "upbeat," "techno," "having attitude in it," and "crazy." These qualities do not refer to tempo or volume but rather *groove*. Both songs that the students generally considered favorites throughout the year, "He Still Loves Me" and "Man in the Mirror" (by Michael Jackson), were slow in tempo compared to other songs in the students' repertoire, but had a *groove*. The students described how the element of groove in a song inspired them to move in some way. In one of the opening quotes for this chapter, Blossom described songs that she liked. Her full statement was, "I like to listen to pop songs that have attitude in it a little bit. They're not just slow . . . they're songs you can dance to." In an individual interview a few months later, Blossom also described how the groove of "He Still Loves Me" was connected to dancing, singing louder, and the tendency of students to "be themselves" while singing this song.

Ruth: All right, let's talk about the concert first. So, on your sheet, you put your favorite part about the choir was "He Still Loves Me." Can you tell me why?

Blossom: I think because when everybody was singing it, everybody got louder than the other songs, because it was more crazy . . . it was more techno, I guess, or something. So, it's like the music that we listen to right now. And not too slow or anything. So then everybody could just start being themselves about it.

Ruth: Would you guess—like, on these sheets—would you guess that most kids wrote "He Still Loves Me" as their favorite song out of the concert?

Blossom: Yeah.

Ruth: And do you know why? Can you guess why?

Blossom: It's a song that you can dance to. Like Ms. Beckman told us . . . like, we wanted to start singing, just start moving around, so then more people would want to just be their selves.

Estephanie compared "He Still Loves Me" to another song the choir was singing, "True Colors" by Cyndi Lauper.

Ruth: So do you have any ideas about . . . how [everyone came to like "He Still Loves Me"]?

Estephanie: Well, I think it's more, like, like . . . upbeat, and stuff. Like, everybody just, like, having fun with it. Not like "True Colors." I like that song, but it's more, like . . . slower. Yeah . . . slower, sadder kind of song.

Interestingly, Ms. Beckman's arrangements of the two songs "True Colors" and "He Still Loves Me" had very similar tempi, yet Estephanie described "True Colors" as being slower and sadder. While this character-ization also relates to the lyrics of the two songs, the choir's arrangement of "He Still Loves Me" had a groove that "True Colors" did not. So what *is* "groove," and does this concept link with the terms the students were using to discuss the music in choir?[5]

Janata, Tomic, and Haberman studied young adults' experiences with groove in music.[6] First, the young adults in their study filled out a survey describing attributes of groove. For them, groove consisted of the degree to which the music made them want to move and was connected to the rhythm of the music. The more the music grooved, the more the young adults associ-ated a positive emotional state with the music.[7]

In the study by Janata et al., factors that did not necessarily influence participants' perceptions of the groove were the tempo (songs with differ-ent kinds of tempi could groove), the familiarity of the piece of music, and the lyrics (either the presence of lyrics or the gender of the vocalist). Janata et al. also found that the genre of music most likely to produce groove for the participants was R&B/soul (with a slightly stronger rating for slower tempi), but groove could also be found in the rock, jazz, and folk genres that had a faster tempo. Groove in Western European classical music was not tested.

Do the students' preferences for songs that groove mean that music teachers should mainly select popular music repertoire that *does* groove, at least in the students' perceptions? No. Does it mean that teachers will not be able to support their students' engagement with other kinds of music, such as Western European concert music or the Carnatic music of South India, for example? No. A skilled music teacher can craft interesting and challenging musical encounters and performances for students that engage them cognitively, emotionally, and behaviorally through multiple strategies.

One lesson that music teachers can learn from the students' interest in music that grooves is that they should search for and include creative ways to encourage students' internalization of music from any context through purposeful movement. Depending on how the music is made and performed, the teacher can craft movement activities that help students reflect these aspects. For example, students can craft movement that reflects a tala cycle in a piece of Carnatic music; the faceting or interplay of rhythmic layers in Agbekor drumming from the Ewe people of Ghana; the harmonies, form, and phrase length of Duke Ellington's "C Jam Blues"; and the pitches in the opening melody of the 2nd Movement of Haydn's "Surprise" Symphony #94. Additionally, music teachers can learn the important lesson that school instruction focusing on popular music that grooves must include an arrangement that grooves and a teaching process that honors the popular music paradigm.

ARRANGEMENTS OF POPULAR MUSIC FOR SCHOOL USE AND THE POPULAR MUSIC PARADIGM

Hip-hop and R&B were the genres of music that the students in this study mentioned most often as containing desirable lyrics and groove; but, at times, the students felt that a song lost its groove when it was arranged for use in school. When asked if there was anything she would change about the music she sang in choir, Blossom stated, "Well, to have more instruments playing . . . so then we can sing other songs too . . . instead of changing up a lot of things."

During a choir class, several students pointedly requested for the addition of instruments (tambourine, guitar, and drums) to their rendition of "He Still Loves Me." Their current arrangement included only piano. One student also suggested collaborating with the orchestra and band classes to make music. These requests were not efforts to reproduce the music exactly as it was heard on the radio, but rather to more closely align the choir arrangement's level of groove to the groove of the original song.

Janata et al. found that the groove of a piece is related to the "contrast or interplay of rhythmic patterns across different instruments/drum sounds."[8] The element of groove in music is not generally part of the way in which music teachers are trained to analyze music in their university music classes. During the Tanglewood Symposium proceedings in 1967, a panel discussion entitled "Pop Music Panel" featured Gene Bruck, the then-42-year-old classically trained musician and music journalist; Mike Stahl, the then-21-year-old guitarist in the band Coconut Groove; and Paul Williams, the then-19-year-old creator/editor of the rock and roll magazine *Crawdaddy!*[9]

The conversation between these three people highlights rock/pop music as a unique musical paradigm.[10] As Stahl and Williams explained the reasons rock/pop is valuable and how it can be understood and evaluated, Bruck and others who commented during the session responded with curiosity but did not go beyond the perspective that rock/pop is not as "complex" and therefore not as valuable as Western European concert music. Bruck asked, "Do you think the number of [rock] performers will grow? After all, there isn't that much professional competence required to be a rock 'n' roll musician, or is there?" Father O'Connor, another participant in this session, stated,

> When the Jefferson Airplane came along, I loved it! But there's a concentration problem that I have because of the simplicity of the textures. Now you've spoken of this music [rock], both of you, as gradually becoming more complex; and yet it, it seems to me . . . this music, however, as our culture has become more complex, has seemed to become extremely simple.[11]

While the questions from Bruck and Father O'Connor illuminated the ways in which they understood and evaluated music, Williams and Stahl described the paradigm for understanding and evaluating rock/pop music. Stahl stated,

> I think rock today is completely different. . . . As part of the Coconut Groove, I know when we sit down and listen to a song, we say, "Boy, I like that sound; it hits me right in the ear." Now it agrees with Coconut Groove. . . . The beat doesn't have to be the hard rock, but it does have to have something that will stick in your mind. It has to catch you. Trying to find a sound for a group is very difficult today. You can't be imitators. Anybody can imitate, but you have to be original to make it.[12]

Stahl used the terms "sound" and "beat" to describe something that is valued in rock because it is original and "hits right in the ear." This description is similar to Ms. Beckman's students' descriptions of music they liked as "jumpy," "upbeat," "not slow," and "makes me want to dance": the groove.

Williams also described an element of the rock/pop paradigm and how rock/pop music can be studied and valued:

There is as much complexity in it [rock 'n' roll], if you mean by complexity that the implications are on a great many levels at once and you continue to go back and get new implications and new discoveries in the music . . . there are implications in a rock 'n' roll song which can be close to infinite, and which can be really beautiful and can operate on a social level.[13]

The element of the rock/pop paradigm Williams identified here is how this music is understood and valued as a poetic reflection of social experiences. Ms. Beckman's students demonstrated a deeper engagement with unfamiliar music once they knew about the social contexts of the song. The conversations from Tanglewood in 1967, as well as the perspectives of Ms. Beckman's students, give insight into the importance for music teachers to learn to think about music, teach music, and make music within the rock/pop paradigm. When teachers transfer this music into the school setting with strategies and arrangements that downplay the reasons that students value a piece of music, students disengage.

In Ms. Beckman's classroom, the students reacted strongly and positively to their choir's performance of "He Still Loves Me." Pedagogically, Ms. Beckman created strong connections to the rock/pop paradigm. The commercial arrangement (meant for school choir) of "He Still Loves Me" that the class began learning did not include Beyoncé Knowles' solo found in the original recording of the song. Ms. Beckman rearranged this song at her students' request to incorporate this solo.

This was a powerful inclusion of the students in the curricular decisions surrounding this song, demonstrating a facet of Ladson-Billings' *conceptions of knowledge*.[14] The solos and resulting performance became a community experience for the group, one that the students consistently mentioned as their favorite moment of choir class up to that point. In John's evaluation of the concert, he wrote that his favorite moment was "in 'He Still Loves Me,' when we were on the risers, we sang so well, I felt so good that I wanted to start dancing on the risers."

LYRICS

Lyrics also played a role in how students in Ms. Beckman's classroom felt about a song. Students described undesirable songs for choir class as those that contained lyrics that were "sad" or "romantic." Students stated that other undesirable lyrics in choir class were those that seemed too babyish. These were songs that the students did not like due to their perceived connection to students younger than themselves. As John stated, "The types of music I don't like are stuff like . . . we're up here in 7th grade and we [shouldn't be] singing those songs like we sang in music class in kindergarten." Williams gave additional insight into how to understand the role of lyrics within the pop music paradigm. He stated,

> The words are a part, but not necessarily a literal part. You won't understand a rock 'n' roll sound by reading the lyrics. . . . As for lyrics, it would take a long, long time, you know, to explain everything. On the back cover of one of the Beatles' albums, the lyrics were actually printed to make it easier for people. Their song, "Fixing a Hole," purposely comes close to being nonsense, because that's part of the feeling they are trying to get out. [*Williams reads the lyrics of "Fixing a Hole." Bruck replies, "It's a long way from nonsense. We've had great experience with nonsense verse, and that's hardly it."*] Well, it's literal, but it's also meant to be silly in a certain sense. It's meant to give a feeling of easiness. I think you get more out of listening to the track musically without the words than just reading the words. Neither is valid alone. It's the whole thing that communicates.[15]

Reflect 3.2

Practice evaluating music with the rock/pop paradigm that Williams and Stahl described. With your group, make some decisions on how to listen to (and evaluate) the Beatles' "Fixing a Hole" from *Sgt. Pepper's Lonely Hearts Club Band* album. Will you research the historical context first? Will you read the lyrics first? Will you listen to the song while reading the lyrics? Will you search out a video of a performance? As you listen to the music, focus on the groove, the musical textures, the interplay of the groove with the lyrics, and the context. As you analyze and describe these elements, think about how your relationship with the song changes. What do you believe is the "meaning" of the song in light of these elements? Examine the chord progression and the melodic line. What is the form? Does using these "traditional" analysis tools add a layer to your evalua-tion? Do you find yourself using the words "simplistic" or "complex" to describe the song? Discuss these questions with your group.

SUMMARY OF MUSICAL CONDITIONS INFLUENCING ENGAGEMENT

Music teachers since the 1967 Tanglewood Symposium have recognized that popular music engages students outside of school. However, it is a mistake to assume that simply the act of bringing this music into the classroom can produce student engagement. The students in this study were initially excited about singing music in choir that was enjoyable to them outside of school, but if a song did not retain elements of its unique groove, or if the students did not connect with the lyrics, they began to disengage when singing. Students (dis)engaged for additional reasons related to the instruction surrounding a song. This will be discussed in the next chapter.

Take Action 3.3

Examine the repertoire you are currently teaching in your music classes. Do you have any pieces that are currently popular with your students outside of school?

- Identify four students in the class who can form a focus group to assist you in analyzing this piece of music and in creating engaging, challenging instruction surrounding this piece.
- With your focus group, play the piece as performed by the original artist. Ask your students what they like about this song. Listen carefully. Ask probing questions. What connects with them about the lyrics? About the groove? About the context?
- Ask the students what they would like to learn about this piece. Would they like to learn to read the melody in traditional notation? Would they like to learn the chord progression?
- Use YouTube to find several arrangements of this song done by school groups. Play these for your focus group. Which arrangements do they like? Why?
- Now, use the ideas of your students to formulate a plan for teaching this piece. If you plan to perform it, how can you retain the essential elements that the students discussed while arranging the piece for a larger ensemble? Can you include any guest artists? Can you even contact the original artist? Can you add instruments from the original? How can you make this arrangement groove? How can you tailor the arrangement to be unique and meaningful for your group?

NOTES

1. "PS 22 Chorus 'Viva la Vida' by Coldplay at McMahon Inauguration," YouTube video, 4:04, posted by PS 22 Chorus, January 8, 2009, www.youtube.com/watch?v=3GgMlUa5Zx0.

2. Travie McCoy, Philip Lawrence, Bruno Mars, and Ari Levine, "Billionaire," edited by Mark Brymer, New York: Hal Leonard (2010), sheet music.

3. David Elliott, *Music Matters: A New Philosophy of Music Education* (New York: Oxford University Press, 1995), 156.

4. Ibid., 158.

5. Sometimes, the students I interviewed would refer to the groove as a "beat."

6. Petr Janata, Stefan T. Tomic, and Jason M. Haberman, "Sensorimotor Coupling in Music and the Psychology of the Groove," *Journal of Experimental Psychology: General* 41, no. 1 (2011).

7. Janata et al., "Sensorimotor Coupling," 57.

8. Ibid.

9. *Crawdaddy!* was the first US magazine dedicated to rock critique.

10. See Carlos X. Rodriguez, ed., *Bridging the Gap: Popular Music and Music Education* (Reston, VA: MENC, 2004) for discussion on teaching within the popular music paradigm.

11. Robert A. Choate, ed., "Pop Music Panel," in *Documentary Report of the Tanglewood Symposium* (Washington, DC: Music Educators National Conference, 1968), 106.

12. Ibid., 104–105.

13. Ibid., 106–107.

14. Gloria Ladson-Billings, *The Dreamkeepers: Successful Teachers of African American Children* (San Francisco, CA: Jossey-Bass, 1994).

15. Choate, "Pop Music," 105.

Chapter 4

Challenging, Clear, Interesting

Student Perspectives on Instruction

It was new, it was a challenge, it was interesting. It was hard, and it was something to do.

—John

Well, I really like "Man in the Mirror," but sometimes when we sing it too much, it gets me bored, and I want to learn new music.

—Alice

For music teachers, crafting challenging, engaging musical learning experiences is sometimes made simpler when the students' and teacher's culturally learned ways of making music, learning music, valuing music, and interacting in a classroom align. If such cultural congruence is present, the teacher's interpretations of students' reactions to classroom pedagogy tend to be accurate since this is often how the teacher herself learns best. However, if cultural congruence is not present and the teacher does not have the tools to assess students' reactions to instruction accurately, the teacher can make false assumptions leading to adjustments in instruction that can produce a cycle of disengagement and lowered musical achievement.

To reverse a cycle of student disengagement, teachers may use these false assumptions to form guesses about the students' instructional preferences and their motivations to learn music. This chapter begins by examining these false assumptions, or myths, and how they form in the classroom. Next, the students in the study will discuss their views on engaging instructional practices in the classroom. Based on the students' ideas, the chapter continues by analyzing the following question: How can a music teacher instruct in a way that aligns with students' culturally preferred ways of learning while maintaining a high level of achievement, challenge, and student engagement?

55

MOTIVATED TO LEARN MUSIC? FALSE ASSUMPTIONS (MYTHS) IN THE MUSIC CLASSROOM

False Assumption #1: Some students enter the music classroom without much motivation for making music. False Assumption #2: Some students do not want to learn music from the Western European tradition, nor do they want to learn music from traditions outside their own time and place. While these statements might be true about a single person, they cannot be haphazardly applied to groups of students based on their ethnicity, their behaviors in the music room, or their musical preferences outside of school. These assumptions are a form of deficit thinking, or assigning negative characteristics to students based on their membership in certain ethnic or social groups. John teaches us how these assumptions can form if a teacher (or in this case, a student) interprets students' behavior solely through a white-normed cultural lens.

John, who had arrived at Clark Middle School from an all-white schooling experience in Iowa, used the ideas and discourses available to him to make sense of his classmates' behaviors.[1] He puzzled over his classmates' disengagement, and formed the following guesses:

> But some kids don't try, and I don't know why. . . . I don't know why some kids are in this class. Maybe they just want to get out of another class or study hall because it's boring. I don't know why kids don't sing or participate. (November 2010 interview)

> Some of the kids, I'm pretty sure, just don't want to be here. I'm pretty sure there are a couple kids in here who just didn't want to be in study hall and couldn't play an instrument in band if they wanted to, so they came here or something. I'm not sure. (January 2011 interview)

> I mean, they don't really want to sing. They just want to be here and they want to play around. They don't really want to do any work, they want to just have fun and joke around . . . they don't find any of it fun. . . . I mean, I don't think they really want to sing. (April 2011 interview)

While John had identified his *own* disengagement in music class as a result of a lack of challenging instruction, he guessed that perhaps some of his classmates were not motivated to sing for internal reasons. In the same way, teachers in music classrooms may assume that some of their students are not motivated to learn music. As John reasoned, they too might assume these students just want to "have fun and joke around."

At Clark Middle School, John's perceptions were not accurate. The other students in the study each stated that they enjoyed singing in choir. At the end of the year, every student in 7th-grade choir chose to be in choir again in 8th grade. The following statements from the students were typical:

The first year we [my cousins and I] came [to the United States from Mexico] . . . we like to sing and dance. And, [when] my cousins came over, we'd put on loud music. And then, we would practice, and then we would make dances and sing. (Alice)

Well, [in choir] we get to pick songs that we like to sing as long as they're school appropriate. And . . . it's fun. (Jacobi)

[I joined choir] because I wanted to sing. (Mila)

[I thought] in choir I would get to sing. (Ángel)

These statements demonstrate that the students' initial motivation to enroll in choir was because they wanted to sing. John interpreted his classmates' disengagement behaviors (their choice not to sing in class) as a lack of motivation to sing and make music in choir (False Assumption #1). Once music teachers subscribe to the assumption that their students are not initially motivated to learn and make music, they can easily subscribe to False Assumption #2. Within this logic, they assume that some students (who *are* motivated to learn/make music) do not want to learn music from the Western European tradition or any other unfamiliar music.[2]

For music teachers who agree with this logic, the act of including popular music would seem to provide motivation for the students to sing or play instruments in music class. Unfortunately, these myths, when acted upon in the music classroom can actually produce a cycle of disengagement among the students. Teachers may attempt to explain this cycle by assuming the students do not want to make music as a result of their home enviroments. Furthermore, they may abandon attempts to provide challenging instruction encouraging deep engagement, instead focusing more on obtaining low levels of behavioral engagement (compliance) and using rote learning to do so.[3]

So, what did the students in this study want from their musical instruction in school? What made learning potent, interesting, joyful, and relevant for them? And, how can teachers develop the skills necessary to provide students with such instruction? The students describe their ideas in the following section.

Reflect 4.1

Discuss with your group the assumptions you hold about your students' motivation for participating in music class.

- Why do you believe your students are enrolled in your class?
- Do you believe they all want to sing/play/create music? What evidence do you have?
- Can you think of a way to garner your students' feelings about singing/ playing music in general? How can you find out what they like to do, musically, outside of class?

INSTRUCTION THAT PROVIDES A SENSE OF ACHIEVEMENT

The students described how important a sense of achievement was for their engagement and gave examples of instructional strategies that helped them gain this sense. Gregory reflected on a key moment in his math class when he realized he understood a concept he had not grasped previously.

> *Ruth:* I want you to think about a time where maybe you didn't know something she [his math teacher] was trying to teach at first. . . . But then the way she taught it . . . kind of made you like it.

> *Gregory:* Mm-hmm. Like, I didn't know. . . . We were doing a unit about geometry, and I didn't know what ratios and scale factors and stuff are, and she would explain it to me in this most simple way, so it would be easy for me to understand what to do and how to do it. So, I never knew what ratio and scale factor was, but now I get it really good.

Gregory felt a clear sense of achievement in his math class, and he appreciated his teacher's clear, understandable instruction. Estephanie described how relevant subject matter and a teacher's enthusiasm for that subject matter enhanced her sense of achievement.

> Social studies makes me want to fall asleep, because I like history, but when it's my history, like I'm learning about my culture and stuff. He [the social studies teacher] makes the class more fun, like, he connects with the kids it seems more. And also he gets more into the subject, like starvation. Like, I didn't really know much about that. A lot of people didn't think it was that big of a deal. But then once he started talking about it, he made us recognize how bad the world can be, and how bad it is getting and stuff, so . . . It made a lot of kids, like, wanting to not throw away their garbage on the ground, like . . . And, like, population, and stuff like that. Like population, teen pregnancy, all that . . . global warming, stuff like that. A lot of teachers, they . . . they taught about it, but they never actually got into it, how much he does, and makes us actually realize, "Oh, this is getting pretty bad."

Estephanie described how her social studies teacher incorporated an element of sociopolitical consciousness into the class, arousing her interest in the material he was teaching. She also described how she enjoyed learning through the class discussions. Both Estephanie and Gregory described how having a sense of achievement in class was engaging and empowering to them. When they felt pride in learning something new or achieving a high level of performance, they were "feeling it" and enjoyed participating in class.

In choir class, the students described their strongest sense of achievement as taking place during their concerts on January 12, 2011, and May 18,

2011. They sang four songs in each concert. Following the January concert, Ms. Beckman discussed their performance with them in class. Marina, a soprano in the choir, thanked Ms. Beckman for not giving up on them when they were reacting negatively to some of the songs and for helping them do their best. Shayla seconded this, "You never gave up on us. Thank you."

John stated in an individual interview that he was inspired and impressed by the solos from members of his class during this concert. John described their performance on "He Still Loves Me" as "the perfect moment, just what we had been trying to do the whole year." He stated that he had not liked the song until this perfect moment. In this interview, he used the word "we" to locate himself within the group, something that he did not do often; more often, he used the term "we" only when he was referring to himself as part of the group of students who sang in class. John's quote illustrates the power of group achievement to foster a sense of identity among the members of the group, underscoring the importance of the Culturally Relevant *conception of social relations* that encourages learning and achieving in community.

John, Estephanie, and Gregory each developed a sense of achievement through different means. Gregory felt successful when his teacher helped him gain a new skill through clear, understandable instruction. Estephanie recognized her deeper understanding of—and growing interest in—the subject matter her teacher delivered in a passionate and relevant way. John felt his choir achieved as a group when they gave an emotional, high-quality performance. Each student linked a sense of achievement to the *outcomes* of his or her classroom experiences. The path to this sense of achievement also involved successfully meeting a challenge encountered during instruction.

CHALLENGING INSTRUCTION

Although the students felt that having fun while learning was important, they also linked the concept of fun to working hard to meet a challenge. The students felt that a desirable challenge in choir class would result in success with something they did not know or could not do before. However, if they perceived that an instructional challenge was too difficult and their attempts to meet the challenge were unsuccessful, this caused them to disengage out of frustration. For them, a challenge had to be coupled with instruction to help them meet the challenge successfully. In addition, if a segment of instruction presented no challenge, or was too easy, the students "got bored" and disengaged, most often by not doing what the teacher asked of them. In choir class, this disengagement mainly took the form of not singing.

The students reported that they would welcome challenging experiences in music that included exploring musical skills and knowledge from a broad range of categories outside of singing. The students discussed their desire to

learn about Western European–based terminology, note reading, and solfège.
For example, Jacobi described what he was hoping choir would be like when
he moved to Lake City:

> *Jacobi:* I was hoping it was going to be like, we'd get to go around town sing-
> ing different concerts . . . singing in different concerts, yeah . . . and we'd learn
> about them things up there [*points to a wall in the classroom where different
> musical terms and symbols are posted*].
>
> *Ruth:* Okay. So you were hoping that you would learn about some of the music
> terminology that's up there?
>
> *Jacobi:* Yeah. Because I never got it when I was little, in all my different music
> classes. So I wanted to learn more about them.

Jacobi discussed his interest in singing in different concerts "around town"
and learning a broad range of musical skills. Alice described how she enjoyed
learning solfège and also participating in the unit on piano that Ms. Beckman
taught.

> *Ruth:* Is there anything else you would like to learn in class?
>
> *Alice:* Well, she [Ms. Beckman] used to teach us the piano, and I think that was
> pretty interesting. And how she did, "Do, Re, Mi, Fa, So, La, Ti, Do." And how
> to play on the piano, that was fun.

Ms. Beckman recognized her students' interest in exploring a broad
range of musical experiences. When she began the year with a new group
of 6th graders, she taught extensive units on piano (as she had a piano lab in
her classroom), which the students enjoyed. In 7th and 8th grades, however,
she had her 6th-grade students from the year before in addition to students
who transferred into her class and had not received her instruction in 6th
grade. This range of skill levels and knowledge presented a difficulty. It
was hard to teach to the specific challenge level of each of the students:
some might feel overwhelmed, while others might feel the instruction was
too easy.

Ms. Beckman strove to find ways to "build bridges or a scaffolding that
[met] students where they [were]," thus engaging in the Culturally Relevant
practice of helping students get where they want and need to be to participate
fully and meaningfully in the construction of knowledge in the classroom.[4]
Ms. Beckman instructed in a way that she felt would neither frustrate her students by being too difficult nor bore them due to a lack of challenge. In order
to do this, she attempted to keep her "skills" instruction segments short, well
paced, and applicable to the songs the students were learning.

Three of the students in this study discussed a moment of disengagement caused by their perceived lack of competence to meet a new challenge. Gregory and Estephanie felt that using sheet music (which they did for several class periods in February 2011) was "confusing." Jacobi felt that learning the Spanish lyrics to one of the choir songs, "Oye," was difficult.[5] However, the students in this study all expressed a desire for more challenging instruction in choir. For example, Alice would get bored in music class if a song was "too familiar." She stated that activities such as writing about her experiences, standing still to sing, and always talking about how to make a song better were "usual" or "boring" in choir class.

Alice: Well, I really like "Man in the Mirror," but sometimes when we sing it too much, it gets me bored, and I want to learn new music.

Ruth: Ok. Do you think that that happens to a lot of the kids? They get bored and then they stop singing?

Alice: Yeah. Well . . . it depends. Because a lot of people like it, and they sing it each time. But a lot of people, they like it . . . but singing it over and over again gets them bored.

Alice felt that "knowing" a song too much, as in knowing how to sing it all the way through at a basic level, made it boring to continue to sing it. John also described how, at times, he would get to know a song and disengage mentally in choir class by thinking about something else while he was singing because he was bored. He thought that maybe some of the other students felt the same way, but he did not have an explanation as to why students would not sing if they were bored.

For John, "knowing the song" was a negative state in choir class if it did not produce mental engagement. In the following interview segment, John compared his experience in school choir with his experience during the same school year with Lake City's Boy Choir festival.

John: And I mean, [one of our songs], it has this steady pattern, but occasionally a part will break off the pattern a little bit. And you know, that's confusing the first couple times you try it, but it's a challenge, so that you work harder to do it, and pretty soon you get it down.

Ruth: Okay, so . . . a challenge, that might make a difference for those kids that are getting bored?

John: Yeah, it's motivating. It's motivating. . . . I mean, a challenge makes it more interesting. You've got more stuff to do, it's harder to do it, so you actually have something to do and concentrate on, instead of this just . . . I mean, like, some of these songs . . . halfway through some of these songs, by now,

I'll be sitting there, I'll be thinking of someone else—something else—and my ears will be hearing the lyrics—so I'll be thinking of something else, but I'm automatically singing it, because I know it by heart. I don't even have to look up at the board and see the words.

Ruth: So . . . what I noticed was . . . when the [songs] were all new to everybody, everybody was paying attention and really trying.

John: I know. It was new, it was a challenge, it was interesting. It was hard, and it was something *to do*. . . . It keeps coming back to challenges and new, interesting things. . . . And then something new, so then we're . . . then they continue to sing.

John described his level of interest as being heightened by the pace of the instruction, the challenges he experienced, and the difficulty of the music. He linked his experience with challenge and achievement in the festival choir to his experience in school choir, concluding that his classmates might feel a lack of challenge when they disengage. John's festival choir experience took place over a weekend, and he described how he learned three or four songs to sing during that weekend, the same amount of music that his choir usually learned in a few months.

The tradition at Clark Middle School was to present two concerts each year, one in January and one in May. In general, students prepared four songs for each concert. This was a constraint based on the hour-long time frame of the concerts and provided the choir, band, and orchestra each time to perform. The students reported that they became bored with the songs they were preparing for the concerts once they were familiar with the songs, often when the concert was still a long way off. They found it difficult to choose to participate when the motivation for doing so was low.

Ms. Beckman often inserted a variety of musical lessons into the classroom schedule at these points, and engagement improved. When lessons returned to practicing songs for the concert, participation through singing decreased. Ms. Beckman assumed that pushing the students for too long on a song during class would frustrate them, causing disengagement. To avoid frustration, she would stop work on a song while engagement was still strong, and switch to another song.

In her experience, frustration from repeating a certain passage would increase nonparticipatory behaviors and this certainly appeared to be the case when students disengaged as they became more familiar with a song. However, the students reported the desire for a challenge and the desire to achieve at increasingly higher levels both as a group and individually. For them, focusing on a challenging musical learning task for an extended period of time was enjoyable and engaging if they knew they were achieving musically. In fact, during multiple class periods throughout the year, students requested that Ms. Beckman continue instruction on a segment of music so that the choir could master the segment before moving on. On one occasion, Ms. Beckman introduced a new piece of music, and after working on one phrase, she prepared the group to move on. One student requested that the choir continue work on that phrase so they could "get it."

Elliott described how the pursuit of music in schools can remain engaging and thus enjoyable for students when they continually experience self-growth.[6] Elliott explained that when students can perceive a musical challenge and meet that challenge successfully, self-growth takes place. If students in music classes do not perceive they are achieving within a cycle of ever-increasing challenges, they become either frustrated because they do not have the know-how to meet the challenge or bored because their know-how is greater than the challenge. When the challenge and the know-how spiral upward together, resulting in an exhilarating experience of self-growth and accomplishment, the participants experience "flow" or enjoyment.

Elliott drew on philosophical standpoints that claim that humans have natural tendencies to apply conscious energy to achieve understanding. Elliott stated how the experience of flow is different than other pleasurable activities in that the learner has applied a consciousness to the challenging task before him and that this manifests as a feeling of being successful and capable. Students who are in a more constant state of flow seem to have overall higher levels of self-confidence and self-esteem and also seem to transfer this self-confidence to other academic pursuits.[7] Elliott's description of students as humans who desire absorbing, demanding, and self-fulfilling activities aligns with CRP. When teachers believe that each student has this desire, and design instruction based on this belief, they guard against deficit thinking and can craft challenging and interesting instruction.

Reflect 4.2

Crafting challenging, engaging instruction is not a simple task. Think of a time in your own classroom when you could sense your students' deep engagement in the learning. Describe the instruction in detail for your group.

- What were the students learning?
- How did they demonstrate their engagement?
- Can you identify the area of challenge, how the students met the challenge, and how the students sensed their own achievement?

HIGH ACHIEVEMENT IN A PLURALISTIC
MUSIC CLASS: CRAFTING CHALLENGING
AND INTERESTING INSTRUCTION

The students' perspectives on engaging instruction align with CRP. As Ladson-Billings explained, teachers whose students achieve have several key practices in place.[8] First, these teachers treat their students as competent and expect them to demonstrate competence. In whatever subject matter students are learning, they are intellectually challenged and provided with the scaffolding to meet the challenges successfully. In order to do this, the teacher must know and recognize the students' experiences, knowledge, and skills and be able to use these as a foundation for learning. Without this knowledge of students, teachers are in danger of holding low academic expectations and providing disengaging instruction. The level of expectations that a teacher holds for her students is critical, because, as Perry described,

> A child's belief in the power and importance of schooling and intellectual work can be interrupted by teachers and others who explicitly or subtly convey a disbelief in the child's ability for high academic achievement, and the child having a rightful place in the larger society—unless a counternarrative about the child's identity as an intellectual being is intentionally passed on to him or her.[9]

Teachers' deficit thinking, or negative perceptions regarding students' abilities, may lead to lowered expectations and to instruction more characterized by rote learning that is not cognitively challenging. This may result from teachers' inabilities to conceptualize their students' strengths, incorporate the knowledge they bring, and include them in the construction of their learning. Lowered expectations and nonchallenging learning environments provided by the teacher can combine with the students' perception of racism and result in low levels of student engagement.[10]

Additionally—and rather logically—the focus of Culturally Relevant teachers is students' learning and achievement. Ladson-Billings stated, "The message that the classroom is a place where teachers and students engage in serious work is communicated clearly to everyone."[11] For learning and achievement to be the focus of a classroom, a structure that provides fast-paced, engaging opportunities to extend students' thinking and abilities must exist.[12]

Ladson-Billings described achievement in academic subject areas where the teachers practiced CRP.[13] In these classrooms, CRP resulted in students' success in standardized tests as well as in other areas within the classroom, including the ability to pose and solve sophisticated problems. Culturally Relevant teachers recognize that academic success has meaning in the world as it is today and seek to provide their students with experiences that will allow them to achieve this success.

The application of Ladson-Billings' theory of academic achievement to the area of music includes obtaining knowledge about and performing music from the Western European classical canon. This is the knowledge that presently allows students to audition for most music schools and enter into music teacher education programs, should they so desire. Importantly, the students in this study described not only their willingness, but also their desire to make music from within the Western European tradition.

Teachers can teach Western European concert music in a Culturally Relevant way. As teachers introduce a piece of music from this tradition to students, they can ask them to explore the social and musical contexts and to compare the Western European paradigms with popular music, folk music, and other music the students study. They can find ways to creatively foster relevant connections between students' experiences and the structure, content, and context of Western European music. To do this, the music teacher can present a reason for learning that arouses the students' curiosity, providing the students with a sense of excitement, puzzlement, and energy for the learning task.[14] If a teacher assumes that her students can see a reason for a musical task without making it explicit, she forgets that

> the questions at the heart of . . . any group for whom there is not a predictable or rational relationship between effort and reward in the social, education, or economic spheres, are these: Why should one make an effort to excel in school if one cannot predict when and under what circumstances learning will be valued, seen and acknowledged? Why should one focus on learning in school if that learning doesn't, in reality or in one's imaginary community, have the capacity to affect, inform, or alter one's self-perception or one's status as a member of an oppressed group?[15]

Each learning experience takes place in a unique context composed of students, teacher, and cultures. The music teacher is both an artist and a scientist as he or she studies the students, builds relationships, discovers what challenges and interests the students, encourages a team environment for learning, and crafts musical learning experiences that are both contextualized and meaningful.[16] Through skillful instruction in a variety of musical cultures, music teachers can engage in an open dialogue that empowers all in the classroom as they evaluate, critique, and discuss their ideas about the music they study. As teachers structure their music classes around excellence and success, they can intentionally provide a variety of opportunities for students to demonstrate their varied musical strengths and learn new and interesting musical skills and practices.

Take Action 4.3

Find a piece of music you are considering teaching your students. Examine this piece, answer the following questions, and discuss them with your group.

- What is the context? Is it important politically or socially?
- Musically, how does it "speak" to you? Is there a key moment that really hits your ear?
- How did the original musicians of this piece create it?
- What is the challenge of this piece? What sense of achievement will your students have after working on this piece?
- Can you craft a dynamic, scaffolded sequence of instruction for this piece? Include a measurable goal that you can accomplish with your students. How can you include your students' interests and ideas in this instruction?
- Implement this sequence of instruction in your classroom. Document the students' engagement levels throughout. Where did the peaks and valleys occur?
- If you cannot find any interesting context, challenging content, or musical moments that hit you, do you think this piece is still worth teaching? Why or why not?

NOTES

1. Shernaz B. García and Patricia L. Guerra, "Deconstructing Deficit Thinking: Working with Educators to Create More Equitable Learning Environments," *Education and Urban Society* 36, no. 2 (2004): 151.

2. Note that this assumption also implies (falsely) that students from within particular groups are not familiar with music other than popular music.

3. See Brenda McMahon and John P. Portelli, *Student Engagement in Urban Schools: Beyond Neoliberal Discourses* (Charlotte, NC: Information Age Publishing, 2012). This important book highlights the negative effects of deficit thinking on student engagement and how deficit thinking permeates the perspectives of teachers who experience low levels of student engagement in their classes.

4. Gloria Ladson-Billings, *The Dreamkeepers: Successful Teachers of African American Children* (San Francisco, CA: Jossey-Bass, 1994), 96.

5. Jim Papoulis, *Oye!* ed. Francisco Núñez (New York: Boosey & Hawkes, 2004).

6. See David Elliott, *Music Matters: A New Philosophy of Music Education* (New York: Oxford University Press, 1995), especially p. 116.

7. See Elliott, *Music Matters*, especially pp. 119 and 131.

8. Ladson-Billings, *Dreamkeepers*.

9. Theresa Perry, "Up from the Parched Earth: Toward a Theory of African-American Achievement," in *Young, Gifted, and Black*, ed. Theresa Perry, Claude Steele, and Asa G. Hilliard (Boston, MA: Beacon Press Books, 2003), 79.

10. Gary E. Bingham and Lynn Okagaki, "Ethnicity and Student Engagement," in *Handbook of Research on Student Engagement*, ed. Sandra L. Christenson, Amy L. Reschly, and Cathy Wylie (New York: Springer, 2012), 83.

11. Ladson-Billings, *Dreamkeepers*, 124.

12. Ibid., 125.

13. Gloria Ladson-Billings, "Toward a Theory of Culturally Relevant Pedagogy," *American Educational Research Journal* 32, no. 3 (1995): 475.

14. Beverly J. Armento, "Principles of a Culturally Responsive Curriculum," in *Culturally Responsive Teaching: Lesson Planning for Elementary and Middle Grades*, ed. Jaqueline J. Irvine and Beverly J. Armento (Boston, MA: McGraw-Hill, 2001), 30.

15. Perry, "Up from the Parched Earth," 11.

16. Ladson-Billings, *Dreamkeepers*, 125.

Part II

DISENGAGEMENT: INTERPRETATIONS, CYCLES, AND INTERVENTIONS

Chapter 5

Students' Engaged Musical Behaviors
Talking, Laughing, Singing, Moving

They like, feeling both of them. I think in both videos, they feeling both of the songs. In the first one, they had movements to the song.

—Jacobi

Human beings interpret each other's behaviors daily. In the classroom, teachers interpret their students' behaviors in order to adjust lessons and reinforce learning. Students interpret their classmates' behaviors and decide how to react. When a teacher's interpretations of the students' (dis)engagement behaviors align with the students' intent, the teacher is more equipped to effectively facilitate students' deep engagement and therefore learning in the classroom. Ms. Beckman understood that engagement in the classroom is not the predictable result of any pedagogical formula: all classrooms contain sets of relationships, experiences, and ways of knowing that constantly evolve, evading easy answers. As Britzman wrote,

> Trying to teach is deeply unsettling and conflictive because experience itself . . . is a paradox, an unanticipated social relation, and a problem of interpretation. . . . The practice of teaching . . . is, first and foremost, an uncertain experience that one must learn to interpret and make significant. . . . And while, of course, familiarity with the teacher's work does matter, it is not a direct line to insight.[1]

Britzman concluded that the act of teaching involves seeing oneself as a researcher of students' perspectives and seeing the difference between these perspectives and one's own in order to avoid simplifying or suppressing complex issues that arise in teaching.[2] Ms. Beckman chose to participate in this study in part to understand the meanings behind her students' (dis)engagement behaviors. This chapter describes the alignment of students' and Ms. Beckman's interpretations of behaviors that signaled engagement,

71

including the cultural congruency between the students' interactional styles and the teacher's expectations for classroom participation.

The students did not use the terms "engagement" or "disengagement" to describe their behaviors. Through the course of this study, the students came to refer to a high level of engagement as "feeling it," which meant that all the students in the choir were interested in the musical task, singing together, enjoying themselves, and meeting challenges with success. "Blanked out," a term first used by Gregory in a focus group discussion, meant that students were not attentive to the musical task, and were bored or frustrated. Table 5.1 lists the behavioral concepts extracted from the student interviews that signaled "feeling it" and "blanked out" for them in choir class. The students discussed behaviors under the following dimensions of (dis)engagement: cognitive, affective, vocal behaviors (singing), vocal behaviors (talking/laughing), and other physical behaviors.

Table 5.1   Behavioral Concepts that Signaled Dimensions of Engagement in Choir Class for Students

		Properties of "Feeling it"	Properties of "Blanked out"
Cognitive		• Concentrating • Focused • "Staying on task" • Working hard	• On autopilot • Bored • Checked out
Affective		• Good mood • Excited • Positive feelings toward teacher, other students • Connecting with others • Having fun • Liking song	• Tired • Sick • "Not wanting to be there" • Frustrated • Not wanting to sing • Not liking song
Vocal Behaviors—Singing		• Singing as if "into it" • Singing well • Singing loud • Putting forth effort when singing	• Not singing • Singing as if tired • Soft singing
Vocal Behaviors—Talking/Laughing		• Talking in class (on topic) • Laughing together • Celebrating the musical success of others	• Talking (off-topic or irritating to other students) • Goofing around • Laughing
Other Physical Behaviors		• Listening • Dancing • Standing/sitting still/straight • Grooving to a song • Doing what the teacher asked • Celebrating the musical success of others	• Not listening • Goofing around • Touching/messing with other kids • Sitting still/daydreaming • Acting crazy

COGNITIVE ENGAGEMENT, AFFECTIVE ENGAGEMENT, AND ENGAGEMENT THROUGH SINGING

In this study, the students and Ms. Beckman exhibited a high level of agreement in their interpretations of student engagement in class and which behaviors signaled engagement. The students reported that they signaled a high level of cognitive engagement in three specific ways. If they were cognitively interested or curious about the instruction or song they were singing, they concentrated (focused on singing), stayed on task by singing, and persevered through the instruction on the song. This finding coincides with research studies in flow theory and engagement theory, which suggest that cognitive engagement is highest when concentration, enjoyment, and interest are simultaneously elevated.[3]

The students reported that if they experienced affective engagement, they were in a good mood, felt excited, and had positive feelings toward the teacher, their peers, and the music they were learning. They also felt a sense of fun and a connection with others in the class. The students described behaviors that demonstrated engagement in the following ways: singing as if "into it," putting forth effort when singing, talking about the topic in class, talking and laughing together, and celebrating the musical success of their peers.

The students' engaged behavior of singing with effort was hard to miss in the Clark Middle School choir classroom. Students who engaged as they sang moved their mouths and produced the melodies and lyrics of the piece they were rehearsing. Chapter 3 described how qualities of the music students sang supported their engagement. As chapter 4 described, if the students could sense their achievement and were meeting interesting challenges successfully, they continued to engage by singing. This chapter describes how the students at Clark demonstrated engagement through other musical behaviors in the classroom that sometimes combined with their singing: talking, laughing, moving, and celebrating each other's musical success.

ENGAGED VOCAL BEHAVIORS: TALKING AND LAUGHING

In addition to singing, Ms. Beckman sometimes requested that the students engage in other classroom learning activities, including classroom dialogue with her and the other students. In these cases, students participated in multiple kinds of musical learning, such as listening to and analyzing music (including recordings of themselves) or studying the historical, political, and musical contexts for songs they were learning.

Ms. Beckman purposefully varied the interactional styles during class discussions, providing cultural congruence for students in classroom interactions, a key feature of a classroom environment that fosters engagement.[4] She explicitly defined her expectations for vocal interaction during these times and made it clear to the students which style of interaction she wanted them to use and why. Sometimes she asked them to listen to a classmate speak and then to respond one at a time. At other times, she wanted a more spontaneous discussion, and students interjected ideas as they came.

The following excerpt from a classroom session on November 22, 2010, provides an example of a moment when both the teacher and the students interpreted vocal behaviors of talking and laughing as a demonstration of student engagement. Ms. Beckman introduced them to a multimovement jazz piece composed by Mary Lou Williams titled *Zodiac Suite*.[5] She explained the characteristics of each zodiac sign, and the students listened to portions of each of the 12 pieces, identifying qualities of the music that might have represented those traits. The students interjected comments that overlapped with Ms. Beckman's, and the discussion was spontaneous, engaged, and on topic. Ms. Beckman's inclusion of this cultural style of interacting highlighted an important way in which her classroom supported cultural congruency for both herself and her students.

Ms. Beckman: [*Begins by describing a free jazz performance taking place during the evening.*] This is all in celebration of Mary Lou Williams. Lake City has been studying and celebrating her life. She would have been a hundred years old this summer, if she had lived. Obviously she didn't. She is actually on that poster over there that says "Women Composers." And this is a picture of her here too. [*Holds up the picture. Students try to find her on the poster, and Ms. Beckman helps them locate her.*]

Student: Oh, I see her!

Another student: Oh, I see her!

Another student: Oh, I see it! She old!

Ms. Beckman: And she was one of those women . . .

Student: Wait, when she die?

Ms. Beckman: She died in 1981. She was one of those really, really amazing composers. But she didn't ever become really recognized as a composer. She never became as famous as she should have been because she was a woman. And jazz was kind of a man's world . . . still kind of is in a lot of respects. Yes, very much so. So today, in honor of her, I picked my most favorite thing that she did and I thought I'd share it with you. . . . Do you know what the zodiac is? [*Several students offer explanations, linking the zodiac to when a person is born and the horoscope.*] The first [sign] on the zodiac chart is the Aries. How many people . . . ? [*Students who are Aries raise hands.*] Okay, so we've got John and Gregory? John and Alli and Gregory. So, what do we know about the Aries? Well, here's what they say. [*Ms. Beckman describes traits of Aries.*]

Student: We should do Taurus.

Ms. Beckman: Oh, we will, my dear. Here's what Mary Lou Williams did. She took these personality traits, and she made a piece of music out of it.

Student: Oh no she didn't!

Ms. Beckman: So here's what she thought Alli would sound like if she were a piece of music, what John would sound like if he were a piece of music. And we want to see if these two things match. It's jazz, so you're going to hear piano, maybe drums, maybe bass. And you want to see, "Yes, I hear this [the character traits]. Or, no." So see what you think. This is Aries.

Student: I want to know what I am.

Ms. Beckman: We'll get to it.

Student: I hear the drums.

Ms. Beckman: Energetic?

Student: I can't catch a beat.

Ms. Beckman: There it is. Does it sound like it's moving forward, like it's a little impatient? Courageous? Maybe we don't know quite yet? Confident. Confident? It does sound confident.

[Piano comes in.]

Student: I hear the piano.

During this class period, Ms. Beckman demonstrated her cultural competence by interpreting students' vocal contributions to the discussion as behaviors that highlighted their positive engagement. When Ms. Beckman first named the jazz musician and composer Mary Lou Williams in her introduction to the lesson, her students responded in different ways. Another teacher might have taken the students' comments, "Oh, I see her!" and "She old!" as either disrespect toward the composer or as unwelcome interjections to the lesson. Ms. Beckman understood these contributions as demonstrations of the students' attention to the topic of study and as comments on what they were noticing.

Immediately following the comment "She old!" a different student asked, "When did she die?" Ms. Beckman acknowledged and answered the question, recognizing this question as further engagement in the topic and as a student's desire to know more. This question does not frustrate Ms.

Beckman as an interruption, and she continues with her instruction. Another example of this engagement occurs after Ms. Beckman connects Mary Lou Williams to the discussion surrounding the zodiac. She stated, "Here's what Mary Lou Williams did. She took these personality traits, and she made a piece of music out of it." One student exclaimed, "Oh no she didn't!" demonstrating her surprise and delight at Williams' composition and also her awareness that this piece of music was unique, something they had not done in class before. Ms. Beckman recognized this comment as a signal of the students' interest in hearing the music and moved seamlessly into the first part of the recording.

In this music class session, Ms. Beckman presented a musical learning activity that she hoped would be of high interest for her students, and the students demonstrated a high level of engagement throughout the class period with on-topic and enthusiastic comments such as "that's raw [*meaning* excellent, good, cool]!" This class period was characterized by such comments and engaged, overlapping talk from the students.

Depending on her goals for a class discussion, Ms. Beckman also used different interactional styles. For example, if she wanted more reserved students to speak at length, she asked students to engage in a more white-normed pattern of interaction: raise hands to elect to speak, speak one at a time, and respond to the comments of the previous speaker. Her accuracy in interpreting her students' engaged interactional behaviors, as well as her ability to select and use multiple interactional styles, demonstrates her desire to make the classroom structure a comfortable and inviting space for her students.

When the students and Ms. Beckman discussed their interpretations of students' talking in class, they strongly agreed on which instances of talking signaled student engagement. For them, this was not a source of conflict but an area of congruency. The lack of conflict surrounding the interpretations of multiple interactional styles may indicate that Ms. Beckman and her students had successfully navigated a critical aspect of classroom relationships influenced by cultural expectations. Sheets described such interpersonal conflicts (that were on the whole absent from Ms. Beckman's classroom) as predominant in many classrooms and consequential for classroom learning.[6] When they occur, the students and teacher are so affected that they cannot engage with academic content. Their focus remains on interpersonal conflict, resulting in poor relationships, and issues of content never become salient. As Irvine also described, teachers' false interpretations of students' culturally situated behavioral styles can lead to a cycle of conflict where teachers impose "unenforceable rules and prohibitions" and students exert effort to maintain their cultural integrity.[7] For Ms. Beckman and her students, the inclusion of multiple interactional modes provided a climate of respect and congruence that contributed to a strong relationship between them.

Reflect 5.1

Can you think of an example of classroom instruction in your music class when you wanted students to elect to speak with a hand raised, speak one at a time, and purposefully respond to either a point made by another student or a question from you? What factors about this discussion necessitated this interactional style?

Can you think of an example of classroom instruction when students interacted in an overlapping, spontaneous vocal style? What sort of instructional sequence works well with this vocal style? What are the other interactional styles that your students use at home? How and when could you incorporate these?

ENGAGED PHYSICAL BEHAVIORS: MOVEMENT AND DANCE

Ms. Beckman clearly explained to the students which physical behaviors she expected of them, especially during their concerts. The following statement describes her behavioral standards for performances:

> Well, I expect them to not embarrass themselves by standing out as the one person who is not doing what everyone else is doing. I expect them to not ruin it for everybody else. You know, I saw a concert at the beginning of my break. It was the Clear Valley schools, their middle school and high school. There was no expectation for how they stood. They had their arms crossed, they're laughing, they're talking, and it was embarrassing! And then you look at these other kids who are doing a good job, and you feel so sorry for them, because they're not getting any attention at all. So yeah, I always expect them to . . . I have three things. One, your hands. Make sure they're at your side, no, not in front, not in back. And two, your feet are at the front of the risers so that everyone is standing kind of straight, in a row. Because otherwise you'll get kids leaning on the back, or getting in someone else's space or whatever. And then the three thing is that your head is facing forward and straight. You know, so you're not looking around or talking or anything like that. So yeah, they know that that's expected.

Ms. Beckman explained to the students during class how following her three standards for behavior during their January concert would create a professional presentation. She wanted her students to be seen in the highest possible light for their achievements during concerts, and she gave them tools to accomplish this. The students wanted to look professional and to command the audience's attention, and they trusted her judgment on how to accomplish this.

During the January concert, as Ms. Beckman predicted, the students commanded the audience's attention with their physical behaviors, the quality of their singing, and the obvious pride they felt in their accomplishments. The most enthusiastic applause of the concert came after "He Still Loves Me." While only a few students moved expressively to the music, the power of their singing (which demonstrated mastery of intonation, dynamic contrast, and two-part harmony) produced a successful concert experience from which the students and their parents took pride.

When Ms. Beckman's students moved expressively to the music or stated that dancing was fun for them, Ms. Beckman let them know that she felt dancing *was* an appropriate behavior for choir class and for performances. However, it was not a behavior that she herself was comfortable with. She told them, "You want to dance? That's cool! I can't dance." Ms. Beckman wanted the students to express themselves through the music but was not comfortable modeling it for them. She said, "It's just not me. And that's where I run into the issue. Just not a mover. I'm not a dancer . . . and you know, I've thought for years . . . I wish it wasn't like that."

Some of her students were not "movers" either, and this characteristic crossed racial constructions. As Gregory described for me, even around his family, he did not express himself physically with music because he was "shy." Even if all of the other students in choir were moving expressively, he would choose not to; it was just not something with which he was comfortable.

During a focus group session on January 10, 2011, John, Estephanie, Mila, and Gregory discussed the meanings they attached to movement and dance in choir class. During this session, the students compared two choirs singing "Viva la Vida" by Coldplay: a girls' junior high group with physical behaviors similar to those requested by Ms. Beckman and the PS 22 Chorus of 5th graders from Staten Island, New York. The students in the PS 22 Chorus moved expressively and individually while singing, often looking at each other. Because the students had described in their interviews how songs with a "groove" or songs that they liked to listen to contained an element that made them want to move and that this movement was desirable, I expected the students to interpret the behaviors exhibited by the PS 22 students as signals of deep engagement. In making this assumption, I did not anticipate that some of the students might interpret the movements of the PS 22 Chorus as demonstrations of disengagement.

John was the most outspoken during this session. Estephanie and Gregory would sometimes exchange looks while John was speaking and would attempt to interject their thoughts when they disagreed with him. The following excerpt is about how the students began to compare the two choirs:[8]

Estephanie: But the [PS 22 students], they were all squirming, and it looks weird. Like, they were all not moving the same way, so it kind of looks like . . . a little bit different.

Mila: [PS 22 students] were singing, but it was like they were looking around at other students, so I probably would pick the first [choir we watched, if I had to join one].

Ruth: You would pick the first one to join, too? What about you? [*Looks at Gregory.*]

Gregory: The first one.

Ruth: The first one. Why?

Gregory: Because it was just a better choir.

Ruth: Better . . . better in what way?

Gregory: It was more organized than the other one.

Ruth: It was more organized. This one [PS 22] seemed more disorganized?

Gregory: Mm-hmm.

John: The other group [Blach Middle School] looks more like an adult choir. It looks like they're adults. They know what they're doing, and they're doing it correctly and well.

Ruth: Ok, and you didn't feel like the second one [PS 22] did?

John: They just look like they're just little kids that are out there having fun. Running around singing songs. It's like, if everybody does what they want to do to have fun, like they're dancing all over the risers . . . it'll look crazy. So, you can sing the songs you enjoy and stuff like that, but you don't want to be dancing around, talking with your friends the whole time.

All four students in this focus group stated that they felt that the PS 22 Chorus exhibited less-than-desirable behavior when compared to a choir that stood still, with their eyes on the conductor and hands at their sides. Even though the students in the focus group described the PS 22 Chorus as having "more flow" (Estephanie) and looking like they were having "more fun" (John), they still discussed the importance of looking organized, looking like "you know what you're doing" and looking "like adults" (John). The students in this focus group (most vocally, John) discussed their preference for visually presenting themselves like "adults" and connected this with the concept of professionalism.

Further into the focus group discussion, John, Mila, and Gregory were sure that at least two of the students on another PS 22 video were not participating by singing—they were goofing around.[9] John described how he saw at least four students who were not singing, including one who was "just sitting there." He went to the screen to point them out, but the one student he pointed to, it could be argued, *was* participating by singing.

In the end, Estephanie and Gregory stated that they would consider joining a choir like PS 22, because they sounded good and it seemed they were
having fun. John remained unconvinced, but admitted he was a "maybe." He
conceded that the PS 22 students acted like they enjoyed the songs they were
singing. For him, this did not mean that they were participating "correctly,"
and he would not necessarily want to be associated with this group. Mila
stated that she definitely would not join. She stated that the PS 22 students
appeared to be "looking around at other students." She felt these students
should have their gaze focused on the teacher.

The students' comments during this focus group discussion aligned with
Ms. Beckman's behavioral expectations for concerts. Ms. Beckman had no
intention to devalue individual, emotional expression through music; in fact,
she had encouraged her students to "feel the music," shown them videos of
the PS 22 Chorus as an example of an excellent choir, and told them that she
was not opposed to movement while singing. However, in the students' experiences, when they followed Ms. Beckman's behavioral expectations for concerts, they received a positive response from their audience, and they believed
that they were acting professionally—like "adults." For most of the students,
their orientation to Ms. Beckman's performance instructions took precedence
over any desire they may have had to move expressively to the music. They
were convinced that these behaviors demonstrated disengagement—a lack of
focus and concentration on the instruction.

In a subsequent focus group session on January 13, 2011, Jacobi, Ángel,
Blossom, and Alice began by viewing two clips of the PS 22 Chorus in
rehearsal and then assessed the engagement level of the group.[10] In this focus
group session, I did not ask the students to compare two groups, but rather
to analyze the PS 22 Chorus alone. My reasoning behind this change in presentation was that I felt I had mistakenly assumed that the students would
analyze the PS 22 Chorus in the same way that I did: as a positive demonstration of engagement enacted through bodily expression. With the second focus
group, I did not make the same assumption and wanted to present a different
mode of analysis in order to access the reactions of the students to the PS 22
Chorus alone.

Before the first clip was shown, Blossom stated that she sometimes listened to the PS 22 Chorus on her own, setting a positive tone for the viewing.
Following the clip, the students agreed that PS 22 Chorus members were all
engaged in the singing and did not identify anyone who was not singing.
Jacobi's first comment was, "They like, feeling both of them. I think in both
videos, they feeling both of the songs. In the first one, they had movements
to the song."[11]

The students guessed that maybe PS 22 members all liked their songs, or
that their teacher had asked them to move expressively and feel the music as

they sang. They thought that maybe the teacher's model of expressive movement and having fun while singing was a reason they engaged or that perhaps
the teacher taught them the meaning of the songs. As Jacobi stated, "Maybe
he brought that song to them the way Ms. Beckman brought 'Imagine' to us?"

Next in this focus group session, the students viewed a videoclip of a
middle school chorus that exhibited body comportment similar to what Ms.
Beckman requested of her students.[12] The students described this group's
body comportment as seeming "stiff and awkward" but also felt that this
group "sounded good." They felt that Ms. Beckman would approve of this
choir's body comportment; Blossom described how she knew that Ms. Beckman wanted them to look "concentrated" and professional.

Next, the students viewed several more choirs and discussed their initial impression of choirs that incorporated movement as "disorganized" or
"sloppy." However, they could also tell that those groups were "feeling it,"
and this was a desirable quality to them. In this way, the students connected
expressive body comportment during choir performances with "feeling it."
The students in this group suggested that they would be more willing to join
a group that was characterized by "feeling it" through movement and also
expressed a desire for their own choir to feel it in this way.

While the second focus group's discussion took a different turn than the
first, all students acknowledged that their teacher's request for a particular
style of body comportment was designed to produce a professional appear-
ance, and that perhaps the teacher of the PS 22 Chorus had made a different request of his students. They felt that the PS 22 students demonstrated
engagement, a desirable quality for them in choir class, but they did not feel
that the expressive movement either *caused* the engagement or was a *result* of
the engagement, simply that it was a behavior that demonstrated engagement.

The differences in the two focus groups' discussions cannot be explained
easily. In addition to the different setup for analyzing the PS 22 Chorus videos, the social interactions that took place among the focus group members
themselves may have influenced the meanings they made.[13] For example, in
the first focus group, John initially set forth a negative response to the PS
22 Chorus, perhaps planting this seed in the other group members' thinking.
However, in the second focus group, Blossom was the first to comment with
a positive remark about her enjoyment of the PS 22 Chorus outside of school.

In addition, valuing one cultural form of body comportment over another
is culturally entrenched and systemically supported. As Crotty stated, "Historical and cross-cultural comparisons should make us very aware that, at
different times and in different places, there have been and are very divergent
interpretations of the same phenomena."[14]

For example, John, the most outspoken advocate of "organized" uniform
body comportment during the focus group session, had been a member of his

Catholic school choir for years before coming to Clark Middle School and had served as a cantor. He was not exposed to expressive movement; it was not a behavior he saw modeled. He was not aware that movement compression, low physical stimulation, and emotional containment might run contrary to the cultures of some students.[15] For some students, however, the incorporation of behavioral norms that include expression through movement, high-energy physical stimulation, and emotional expression offers a way to provide cultural congruency and affirmation in the choir classroom.

Reflect 5.2

- What is your preferred movement response to music? Do you like to move expressively or is this something that you are not comfortable with?
- Do you choose your movement responses based on the setting? In which movement settings might you move expressively and when might you maintain still body comportment?
- Have you ever had a musical experience where you or someone near you chose a movement response that was deemed "culturally inappropriate" by others? How did it feel? For example, I attended a Sting concert in 2005. I assumed that this concert would be similar to my other rock concert experiences, with attendees standing and dancing along to the songs. However, my choice to stand and move was clearly frowned upon, and I moved over to an open aisle area with a friend. It felt lonely. I did not feel that I was a part of the rest of the group.
- Watch the videos that the students watched in this chapter. What are your responses to the movement? How do you perceive the "professionalism" of each choir?

CONTEXT FOR ENGAGED BEHAVIOR: CELEBRATING THE MUSICAL ACHIEVEMENT OF PEERS

Both Ms. Beckman and the students in this study reported that behaviors that celebrated the musical success of classmates were desirable demonstrations of engagement. In rehearsals, the students celebrated each other's musical efforts with applause or with verbal remarks. The strongest example of this came during the choir's January 2011 concert.

During their performance of the song "He Still Loves Me," the choir experienced what the students described as a high point for them regarding engagement. During this moment, they all worked together as a choir to produce a high-quality product of which they were proud. Several of the individual solos resulted in vocal cheering and applause from the audience, and the whole class took pride in the success of the soloists. The cheering and clapping of the audience, the two inspirational solos from choir members, and the electricity generated by all of the students singing together in harmony produced a memorable experience for the choir.

Estephanie described her favorite part of the concert. She replied, "When we had the solos. When Callie and Shayla sang, because they were really good. And it tied the whole concert together." Ángel also discussed this moment.

Ruth: What was your favorite part in the concert?

Ángel: When . . . they sing the solo.

Ruth: Why did you like that?

Ángel: Because they sing, they clap too.

Ruth: The audience clapped and really liked it too?

Ángel: Yeah.

Ruth: So that was kind of cool . . . ?

Ángel: Yeah.

Jacobi and John also remarked that this was a particular moment of pride and cohesiveness for the whole class. For John, who had described his feelings of disconnection with his classmates, the choir's performance of "He Still Loves Me" provided him with a feeling of success and group identity with his choir. In this excerpt, John referred to his classmates and himself as "we," thereby including himself as a member of the group. He stated,

> It was just, like, the perfect moment, the highest moment of the year for our choir. It was, like, . . . working as a team, doing what we were supposed to do, doing it well, doing it loudly enough that everybody could hear. Just what we had been trying to do the whole year. Final success, at long last. I mean, everybody. . . . I mean, the *solos* . . . you got to have some guts to get up and do a solo . . . and those two . . . they were also really good singers. . . . It was amazing. It was just amazing.

The students' responses to the January 2011 concert suggest a strong link between peer encouragement, relationships, and engagement in the classroom. This finding demonstrates how the Culturally Relevant classroom feature of working together as a team (instead of competing against each other) can function in a music classroom. The students in this study celebrated and were inspired by the solos that their classmates sang, even though they themselves were not singing during that moment.

This moment of celebration within the choir also highlights how Culturally Relevant choirs need not focus on competition to produce a quality vocal performance. The students were proud of their achievements as a group, and they received many accolades on their accomplishments following the concert. Ladson-Billings described how the Culturally Relevant teachers she studied supported excellence by fostering this type of collective effort. She stated,

> [In such classrooms] there is little reward for individual achievement at the expense of others. Even when individuals achieve on their own—inside or outside of the classroom—the teachers frame that achievement in a group context. They say things like, "Look what that member of our class did. Aren't we proud of that? Don't we have some brilliant people in our family?"[16]

The students discussed how their peers' successful solos produced a sense of community and achievement for the group, reflecting the positive effects of Ms. Beckman's efforts to foster a team attitude in this way.

The moment of community during the January 2011 concert also illuminates another major point: a Culturally Relevant choir can be a place where students' solo work (demonstrating technical skill) can be recognized and celebrated. In contrast, within a competition-oriented choir classroom, solos can be "won" based on a one-dimensional value system where students with soloing strengths are seen as more valuable than the other students. This produces a classroom climate where students are divided and competitive with each other, instead of supportive.[17]

However, in Ms. Beckman's classroom, this was not the case. Ms. Beckman modeled positive ways of encouraging and celebrating the musicality of all the students in her class. She invited those who wanted to sing solos to attempt them during class, instead of singling out only those some might deem "most talented." She offered individual singing assistance on her lunch hour or after school to students who wanted it, demonstrating that she felt they were each talented musically and worthy of her time. Ms. Beckman often highlighted the strengths of the students in her choir, including their musical strengths, interpersonal strengths, and leadership traits, with words of encouragement. This classroom climate supported moments of community, as experienced during the January 2011 concert, when students saw the success of the soloists as the success of the whole group and celebrated this as a team.

In this chapter, the students of Clark Middle School give three important lessons for music teachers on the topic of physical demonstrations of engagement in class. First, they need a teacher who can recognize multiple interactional styles as valid. Competent teachers can use these styles successfully during instruction, demonstrating that they value their students' home patterns of interaction and also that they are willing to move between interactional styles, teaching their students to also become competent in this skill. Second, students might internalize both their teacher's verbal instructions regarding body comportment and the teacher's behaviors during music making. Music teachers can explore how to make expressive movement an integral part of the way students internalize music as well as how they perform music. Finally, students do not need to exist in competition with each other to achieve musically. As the teacher assists all of his students in developing musical skills, he can highlight each one in his or her area of strength. As students celebrate each other's strengths, they can develop a sense of community and identity within their group.

Boykin described how white-normed cultural participation structures in classrooms serve to maintain inequitable power structures within schools and within society as a whole. When classrooms and teachers reinforce the white-normed cultural characteristics of containing emotion, silently engaging in tasks without communicating verbally with others, enforcing inflexible time boundaries, or promoting individualized competition, they can serve to disempower and alienate students for whom these ways of behaving are not congruent with their home discourses.[18] In contrast, a culturally competent music teacher can validate, use, and build upon his or her students' valued ways of engaging in class to strengthen classroom community and elevate musical achievement.

Take Action 5.3

Plan to include a new mode of interaction in your classroom discussions. For example, if you typically include a spontaneous, overlapping style, examine your instruction for a segment when your students might benefit from either a one-at-a-time style when you call on the students to contribute or a choral response style when you ask all of your students to respond at once. You might try asking students to respond with a brief written statement and share in pairs. Discuss this with your group. Were you able to include students who might not contribute otherwise? How did this help you identify which styles are most comfortable for your students?

Also, make a plan to find out what movement response styles your students enjoy. Could you create a survey or have a class discussion? How can you explore and include additional movement styles in your classroom? Keep in mind that students have already internalized the instruction on body comportment that you have given them along with their own comfort levels with movement. Include your students in planning how to do this.

NOTES

1. Deborah P. Britzman, *Practice Makes Practice: A Critical Study of Learning to Teach*, rev. ed. (Albany: State University of New York Press, 2003), 5–6.

2. Ibid., 238–39.

3. David J. Shernoff and Mihaly Csikszentmihalyi, "Flow in Schools: Cultivating Engaged Learners and Opti Learning Environments," in *Handbook of Positive Psychology in Schools*, ed. Rich Gilman, E. Scott Huebner, and Michael J. Furlong (New York: Routledge, 2009), 131–45.

4. See Gloria Ladson-Billings, *The Dreamkeepers: Successful Teachers of African American Children* (San Francisco, CA: Jossey-Bass, 1994); Jacqueline J. Irvine, "The Critical Elements of Culturally Responsive Pedagogy: A Synthesis of the Research," in *Culturally Responsive Teaching: Lesson Planning for Elementary and Middle Grades*, ed. Jacqueline J. Irvine and Beverly J. Armento (Boston, MA: McGraw-Hill, 2001), 2–17; Beverly J. Armento, "Principles of a Culturally Responsive Curriculum," in *Culturally Responsive Teaching: Lesson Planning for Elementary and Middle Grades*, ed. Jacqueline J. Irvine and Beverly J. Armento (Boston, MA: McGraw-Hill, 2001), 27.

5. Mary Lou Williams, *Zodiac Suite* [Recorded by Geri Allen, Buster Williams, Billy Hart, and Andrew Cyrille on *Zodiac Suite: Revisited*, 2006, (first released in 1945 by Mary Records), Compact Disc] See chapter 2, page 27, for a discussion on Ms. Beckman's use of the lesson on the *Zodiac Suite* as a way to build community.

6. Rosa Hernández Sheets, "Urban Classroom Conflict: Student-Teacher Perception: Ethnic Integrity, Solidarity, and Resistance," *The Urban Review* 28, no. 2 (1996): 165–83.

7. Irvine, "Critical Elements," 8.

8. The first clip was the first minute of "'Viva la Vida,' Choir, Blach Middle School," YouTube video, 3:33, posted by Michael Shorts, October 6, 2010, www.youtube.com/watch?v=yDyyrdhAxMw. The second clip was the first minute of "PS 22 Chorus, 'Viva la Vida' by Coldplay at McMahon Inauguration," YouTube video, 4:04, posted by PS 22 Chorus, January 8, 2009, www.youtube.com/watch?v=3GgMlUa5Zx0.

9. "PS 22 Chorus, 'Forever Young' by Alphaville," YouTube Video, 3:01, posted by PS 22 Chorus, June 26, 2009, www.youtube.com/watch?v=KlfzbmPS3n4.

10. "PS 22 Chorus, 'Just Dance' by Lady Gaga," YouTube Video, 3:12, posted by PS 22 Chorus, June 15, 2009, www.youtube.com/watch?v=h0FPZolbYns.

11. Following "Just Dance," the students also watched PS 22 singing "Forever Young."

12. "Woodlands Middle School Chorus, 'Velvet Shoes,'" YouTube video, 2:44, posted by eabhorselvr, July 29, 2008, www.youtube.com/watch?v=VrgBAZdZF9c.

13. Michael Crotty, *The Foundations of Social Research: Meaning and Perspective in the Research Process* (London, UK: SAGE Publications, 2003), 72.

14. Ibid., 64.

15. A. Wade Boykin, "Afrocultural Expression and Its Implications for Schooling," in *Teaching Diverse Populations: Formulating a Knowledge Base*, ed. Etta R. Hollins,

Joyce E. King, and Warren C. Hayman (Albany: State University of New York Press, 1994), 247; Theresa Perry, "Up from the Parched Earth: Toward a Theory of African-American Achievement," in *Young, Gifted, and Black*, ed. Theresa Perry, Claude Steele, and Asa G. Hilliard (Boston, MA: Beacon Press Books, 2003), 75.

16. Ladson-Billings, *Dreamkeepers*, 76.

17. James R. Austin, "Competition: Is Music Education the Loser?" *Music Educators Journal* 76, no. 6 (1990): 21–25; Alfie Kohn, *No Contest: The Case Against Competition*, rev. ed. (Boston, MA: Houghton Mifflin, 1992).

18. Boykin, "Afrocultural Expression," 248.

Chapter 6

Guessing Wrong

How Students' Behavior Can Be Misinterpreted in the Classroom

I don't really sing. Because . . . I'm tired. I don't want to sing . . . and I was talking.

—*Ángel*

During periods of disengagement in Ms. Beckman's classroom, both the teacher and the students agreed that disengagement was taking place. However, the students sometimes attached meanings to their classmates' disengagement behaviors that contrasted with their interpretations of their *own* behaviors. Ms. Beckman's interpretations also differed from the meanings made by the students.

STUDENTS' INTERPRETATIONS OF THEIR OWN DISENGAGED BEHAVIORS

If the eight students in the study were "blanked out" cognitively, they usually reported that boredom was their predominant mental state. They sometimes described this state as being "tired" or "not feeling like being there." This state of boredom manifested a variety of behaviors in individual students, including going on "autopilot" (complying with the instructions to participate while allowing their minds to focus on thoughts outside of the instruction); "checking out" mentally and not complying with instructions to sing but remaining quiet; or demonstrating behaviors such as off-topic talking, not singing, singing as if tired, soft singing, or "goofing around."

When the students described what "goofing around" meant to them, they described both vocal and physical behaviors. Vocally, this meant they were teasing or joking with their peers or distracting those around them by talking to them. Physically, this could mean moving around in a distracting way, touching or playing with something they were not supposed to, or touching/play-fighting with peers.

At times, even compliant behaviors from the students, such as singing when asked or refraining from talk during a song might not demonstrate engagement but rather "disengagement manifesting as passive compliance."[1] For example, John reported that sometimes his choice to sing, while compliant with the teacher's instructions, was not the result of a high level of engagement. John stated,

> I mean, some of these songs . . . halfway through some of these songs, by now, I'll be sitting there, I'll be thinking of someone else—something else—and my ears will be hearing the lyrics—so I'll be thinking of something else, but I'm automatically singing it because I know it by heart. I don't even have to look up at the board and see the words.

John described how he sometimes checked out mentally, even as he continued to demonstrate behavior that did not draw Ms. Beckman's attention or cause her to attempt to get him back on track. Estephanie and Alice also reported that there were times when, even if they were not engaged cognitively, they were in compliance with participatory behavioral expectations.

In contrast, some students who "blanked out" might also more actively reject the "status quo" regarding compliance[2] by choosing not to sing, instead talking or laughing with their classmates during songs. During Gregory's interview following the class period on December 9, 2010, he described how some students, including him, were "goofing around."

> I think the people were goofing around a lot, and . . . a lot of talking. And we didn't sing like . . . as loud, and we weren't . . . like, everybody wasn't focused. It was just some people [participating], like the people who really cared about it. . . . I would like the class to go better, but . . . I don't think I did anything bad, though.

Gregory, along with Jacobi and Ángel, saw goofing around as a natural response to relieving boredom when they disengaged in class. Gregory stated that he did not feel that he had "done anything bad," even though Ms. Beckman mentioned to him that he also was "goofing around" during this class period. When Jacobi disengaged, he often moved around, talking and laughing with students near him. He was quiet about it, not directly challenging the teacher with disrespectful statements. Ángel also disengaged by talking and goofing around quietly with his peers in class. He described his disengagement during one class period in this way:

Ruth: Can you tell me about your song "Stand Together" today? How did it sound?

Ángel: I don't really sing. Because . . . I'm tired. I don't want to sing.

Ruth: So you didn't really sing along on that one because you were tired?

Ángel: Yeah, and I was talking.

Ángel linked the concept of not singing with feeling tired, not wanting to sing, and talking (lack of behavioral engagement). Even when his teacher asked him to sing, his engagement levels formed the context for his choice not to sing and therefore not to comply with his teacher's request.

While some students may make a determination about their level of involvement in an activity by assessing the formal demands or rules governing the setting (i.e., the teacher's request for certain behaviors) following a white-normed pattern of behavior, other students may make their determination to participate based on different cultural patterns: the social effects of the situation or the individual level of commitment to the activity.[3] In the home communities of many students, children are taught to trust their own instincts and to follow leaders based on their own judgment.[4]

Additionally, within some African-American cultural styles of communication, a valued facet is "truth-telling" or "telling it like it is."[5] This is seen as signifying courage, honesty, and unwillingness to compromise one's integrity and is in contrast to some European-American cultures in which "one is to avoid insults and hurting people's feelings, or where there is a preference for indirect communication or concealing the ulterior motive."[6]

Throughout their interviews, students explained that their own disengagement was not because they did not like singing or Ms. Beckman but due to other factors affecting their engagement. When they examined the disengagement behaviors of their classmates, they sometimes felt that the reasons behind their classmates' behaviors mirrored their own: they were uninterested cognitively or affectively in class. However, at times, students interpreted some of their classmates' disengagement behaviors as signals of something other than disengagement, as the following section explains.

STUDENTS' INTERPRETATIONS OF THEIR CLASSMATES' DISENGAGED BEHAVIORS

The students mentioned how they found the disengagement behaviors of other students irritating and distracting at times, even if they themselves exhibited similar behaviors. The students who generally complied with instructions to sing even when they were not engaged cognitively discussed their feelings about the behaviors of other students most often. Estephanie described how it affected her when Ms. Beckman did not receive full participation from all of the students.

Ruth: What do you think she meant by "best singing"?

Estephanie: To give your full effort and to sing out loud, and stop being so quiet, kind of. Like, stop thinking it's like a joke and actually sing. Because a lot of people, like Gregory, he's always laughing at things, and I think he's, like, ruining it for us kind of because he's always laughing, and then Ms. Beckman gets distracted. And then she can't really do her job because he's sitting there like, "ha, ha, ha, ha." Like, joking around.

Ms. Beckman requested that students participate by doing their best singing at all times during class. For Estephanie, as well as other students, doing their "best singing" meant becoming engaged with the song and the instruction. "Best singing" went beyond singing on "autopilot" to singing with a level of concentration and interest. Participating by doing one's best singing would demonstrate that the learner is "personally absorbed in and committed to participation in the processes of learning and the mastery of a (chosen) topic, or task, to the highest level of which they are capable."[7]

Interestingly, the members of the group who chose not to sing varied from class period to class period—it was not an identifiable or predictable group. The students who were not singing did not have a motivation or desire to engage that was strong enough to "drive the individual to take advantage of particular learning opportunities."[8] During her interview, Estephanie did not suggest that the students exhibiting disengaged behaviors might be reacting to the instructional contexts in the classroom but instead felt that students were not complying with instructions to participate because they "thought it was a joke." She located the responsibility to comply with instructions to sing with her classmates, regardless of their engagement levels. In this way, Estephanie linked the students' behavioral compliance (whether cognitively engaged or not) with Ms. Beckman's ability to "do her job."

John, like Estephanie, felt that some students did not want to be in choir. He assumed that the students who demonstrated active disengagement behaviors simply did not want to learn or "do any work." For John, his familiar cultural discourses were also serving as a barrier to understanding his classmates and keeping him from forming deeper relationships with them.

While John started the year with the view that some of his classmates were "delinquents," toward the end of his last interview on April 11, 2011, he began to wonder if perhaps the other students who demonstrated disengagement might be experiencing what he also felt was a lack of challenging instruction. As John became aware of his own reasons for disengaging in class, he began to realize that his classmates' behavior also reflected disengagement. He then viewed his classmates in a different light.

Blossom had an awareness shift similar to John's during the course of our interviews. In her initial interview on November 29, 2010, she guessed that perhaps some of her classmates did not want to be in choir and did not like singing.

> *Blossom:* I think [Ms. Beckman] is doing a pretty good job, but the kids . . . some of them I know, they don't want to be in this class. Their parents just signed them up, thinking it was good for them. But they know that they didn't like this class—that they'd rather be in band or orchestra, or even study hall.
>
> *Ruth:* Okay, so you think maybe they're in here because their parents signed them up and they . . . would choose not to if they could?
>
> *Blossom:* Yeah. Because some of them don't even sing. They just talk to their friends a lot.

While Blossom herself sometimes chose to not sing due to cognitive disengagement, she initially did not assume that her classmates chose not to participate for the same reason. Later in the school year, however, Blossom noticed that sometimes the whole class became cognitively disengaged and did not participate in singing. She felt that when the majority of students did not participate, then perhaps Ms. Beckman missed the reason that some students "didn't want to be there," and that this was something within her power as a teacher to address. Blossom contrasted this phenomenon of whole-class disengagement with the disengagement of a single student who was just having a bad day.

> Like, [Ms. Beckman] . . . I don't think she really knows us that much. Because so many kids slack off. Not saying, like, just any of the kids . . . but, like, everybody, they slack off at once. So she doesn't really have time to know what's going on and stuff . . . even though she tries a lot to make kids help her, but some kids don't even care what she says, and just ignore her. . . . Sometimes I just want to sing, because we all get it . . . but some of us don't even care. That's the thing. Sometimes she doesn't understand that people don't even want to be here, so they don't do anything. She should, at times, ask how we are doing. And then, like, ask the whole class. Say, if most of the class was happy, then she'll try to get the rest of the students to be more cooperative. Then, if most of the class is bored or bad or something, just ask them why. And then, if she tries to make it feel better, just start singing songs.

Blossom perceived that perhaps when the "whole class slacks off at once," their disengagement with instruction made them "not want to be there." Throughout their interviews, students reinforced that this type of disengagement was not because they did not like singing or Ms. Beckman. Blossom suggested that in a class period where the majority of students exhibited disengagement, Ms. Beckman might open a conversation with them, probing them for any elements of class that were promoting a feeling of boredom or "not wanting to be there." Blossom also suggested that Ms. Beckman might use her own positive enthusiasm to "make it feel better" and to lead the class in "just singing songs."

While Ms. Beckman did ask the students to tell her their reasons for disengagement, Blossom suggested that she question them specifically about feelings of boredom. Blossom's statements reflect research on increasing student engagement, which indicates that teachers who can encourage their students to express their dissatisfaction with classroom instruction during periods of disengagement can discover their students' perspectives and revise instruction effectively.[9]

The act of (dis)engagement during singing was a complicated process that involved cognitive, affective, and behavioral elements for the students. Often, students could not explain the reasons behind a particular moment when they (dis)engaged because it involved a subconscious reaction to the context. Throughout the school year, as the interviews continued and students examined examples of deep engagement and strong disengagement, they began to more clearly identify and articulate behaviors that signaled their level of engagement.

Reflect 6.1

With your group, describe the cycle of disengagement in your music classroom. How can you tell when a majority of your students are beginning to disengage from your instruction? What behaviors do they exhibit? What do you think might be triggers of this initial disengagement?

MS. BECKMAN'S INTERPRETATIONS OF STUDENTS' DISENGAGED BEHAVIORS

When the students demonstrated their disengagement through nonparticipatory behaviors, Ms. Beckman recognized that these behaviors signaled their disengagement and would attempt to reestablish engagement among the students. She adopted a stance of curiosity toward the students' disengagement, often by asking the students to tell her why they were choosing not to sing. The students could identify feelings for her, such as, "I am tired or hungry or distracted, and I don't want to sing," but at that moment they could not explain the reason for their disengagement. Ms. Beckman felt their behaviors might mean a number of things, and she implemented instructional methods based on these ideas.

Ms. Beckman wanted her students to feel happy, welcome, and comfortable in her classroom. She sought to build connections with them and to reassure them that they were each important to her and to the choir's success as a whole. To that end, she expected them to participate, especially in singing, and reiterated to them that their voices mattered to the group—that their efforts in rehearsal directly affected the quality of the concert. She told them, "You don't think you're very important, do you? You think that if you stop singing, it's not going to matter. You're wrong. It matters a lot. Whoever told you that you weren't important? Because it wasn't me. I need your voice."

If students chose not to sing, she encouraged them with reminders that they were important and that the choice not to sing would affect their peers, their teacher, and their performance. In many cases, this strategy did result in heightened participatory behaviors from the students. As Ladson-Billings described, emphasizing the importance of each student's contribution to the class is a Culturally Relevant practice related to creating a team environment in the area of social relations within the classroom.[10]

Ms. Beckman also knew that at times, her students were affected by personal circumstances that caused them to be uncomfortable emotionally with singing. To address this, she might not require full participation from students who were not singing for this reason.

An additional meaning that Ms. Beckman attached to her students' disengagement behaviors was that perhaps these behaviors were not indicative of disengagement but signaled a need for self-awareness. She reasoned that maybe the students were unaware of how their disengagement behaviors made them look and sound.

To increase their awareness of their behaviors, Ms. Beckman spent time in class having the students view videos and listen to audio recordings of themselves. The students analyzed how they sounded as a choir, how they looked while singing, and compared themselves to other choirs. Ms. Beckman used this strategy to encourage an "open classroom, student responsibility approach" rather than taking on an authoritarian approach to the classroom and assuming that her students "lack[ed] self-control and [were] always talking to their neighbors."[11]

When Ms. Beckman sought to understand why her students were disengaged, she did not characterize her students in negative ways. Even when she encouraged them to analyze their participatory behaviors with the goal of improving singing, she attributed the tendency toward subconscious behavior to all humans, including herself. She stated, "We all do stuff unconsciously, and we don't know that we're even doing it. And I'm wondering if some people are not singing, but they don't even realize that they're not."

INTERPRETATIONS OF (DIS)ENGAGEMENT IN MS. BECKMAN'S CHOIR CLASSROOM

The students' and teacher's interpretations of *engagement* behaviors aligned in this study—they all interpreted such behaviors as signals of a high level of engagement. When the students as a whole exhibited behaviors that they reported as signals of engagement, Ms. Beckman recognized their behavior as such, even if the behaviors were outside of the white cultural norms for classroom behavior (raise your hand, don't speak unless called on). When students demonstrated an interactional style that involved overlapping talk or calling out but were engaged, Ms. Beckman navigated these interactions and participated in them fluidly.

Ms. Beckman had the difficult job of assessing the reasons behind a student's disengagement behaviors and deciding on a course of action, often on the spur of the moment.

She knew that her students liked her and wanted to be in choir, as they clearly demonstrated by continuing to sign up for her class each year. She believed that she was providing sufficient student choice in the classroom, enabling their interests to be the focus.

She felt that perhaps the students might not recognize their importance to the group, might not be aware of their participation levels, or might be affected by a personal issue related emotionally to singing. She did not, however, connect their disengagement behaviors with students' desires for conditions that heightened the challenge and interest levels of their learning in class. When the students exhibited behaviors signaling either engagement or disengagement, this affected the flow of the classroom, producing a series of effects. Chapter 7 will discuss the effects of (dis)engagement in the classroom.

Take Action 6.2

Follow Blossom's advice. First, teach a sequence of instruction for a new piece of music. Include the strategies from the first part of this book: design the lesson to be challenging, include ways to give the students a connection to the context of the music, provide a clear goal and scaffolding to meet that goal, include students' ideas, and invite their contributions to the learning.

If you sense a moment when the students begin to disengage, ask them to talk about it with you. What are they feeling? Are they feeling bored (a strong signal of disengagement)? What causes them to feel bored? Invite their feedback and ask questions. Discuss what you learned with your group. How will this help you in designing instruction?

NOTES

1. Ruth Deakin Crick, "Deep Engagement as a Complex System: Identity, Learning Power and Authentic Enquiry," in *Handbook of Research on Student Engagement*, ed. Sandra L. Christenson, Amy L. Reschly, and Cathy Wylie (New York: Springer, 2012), 675.

2. Ibid., 676.

3. Barbara J. Shade, "Understanding the African American Learner," in *Teaching Diverse Populations: Formulating a Knowledge Base*, ed. Etta R. Hollins, Joyce E. King, and Warren C. Hayman (Albany: State University of New York Press, 1994), 179.

4. Kathryn H. Au and Alice J. Kawakami, "Cultural Congruence in Instruction," in *Teaching Diverse Populations: Formulating a Knowledge Base*, ed. Etta R. Hollins, Joyce E. King, and Warren C. Hayman (Albany: State University of New York Press, 1994), 10.

5. Barbara J. Shade, Cynthia Kelly, and Mary Oberg, *Creating Culturally Responsive Classrooms* (Washington, DC: American Psychological Association, 1997).

6. Ibid., 23.

7. Deakin Crick, "Deep Engagement," 679.

8. Ibid.

9. Johnmarshall Reeve, "A Self-Determination Theory Perspective on Student Engagement," in *Handbook of Research on Student Engagement*, ed. Sandra L. Christenson, Amy L. Reschly, and Cathy Wylie (New York: Springer, 2012), 149–72.

10. See Gloria Ladson-Billings, *The Dreamkeepers: Successful Teacher of African American Children* (San Fransisco, CA: Jossey-Bass, 1944), Ch. 4, "We Are Family," especially pp. 76–77.

11. Shade et al., *Creating Culturally Responsive*, 51.

Chapter 7

Spiraling Downward

The Effects of (Dis)engagement, Misunderstanding, and "Behavior Talk"

When I was watching you, some of you just really, really didn't cut it. You were up there talking, making faces, distracting other people, laughing . . . how is that fair?

—Ms. Beckman

Classroom cycles of engagement and disengagement spiral throughout the course of a year, a week, or even one class period. As time progresses in a classroom, these cycles are enacted when contextual conditions produce a level of (dis)engagement and a set of effects including new contexts with new resulting levels of (dis)engagement.[1] As described in part I of this book, contextual conditions affecting engagement in classrooms include teacher-student relationships, peer relationships, academic content, and instruction surrounding the learning tasks. The students respond to their surrounding contexts, demonstrating varying levels of (dis)engagement.

These cycles are often confusing and frustrating for a teacher. While one lesson seems to flow and produce high levels of engagement, another (seemingly similar) lesson results in disengagement. The eight students in this study shared their perceptions of the effects of both engagement and disengagement on teacher-student interactions, relationships, behaviors, and emotions. This chapter discusses the intricacies of their thoughts during the cycles of engagement and disengagement.

EFFECTS OF POSITIVE STUDENT ENGAGEMENT: THE PROCESS OF ESTABLISHING ENGAGEMENT

During the opening of each choir class in Ms. Beckman's classroom, various conditions influenced the students and the teacher, creating the classroom context. The students usually entered the classroom each day with an interest in what Ms. Beckman had on the agenda, displaying neutral or positive cognitive engagement. They also entered with positive feelings about their relationship with Ms. Beckman, displaying affective engagement. They engaged by finding their seats, listening to her as she started class, and watching her for cues about the first segment of instruction.

The students' knowledge of Ms. Beckman and their moods and experiences outside of the classroom influenced their engagement levels more strongly at the start of class than later in the class period. This impacted how Ms. Beckman constructed the context for the next segment of class. If this context included conditions where the students were cognitively interested, emotionally excited, and stimulated to go from a neutral mode of engagement to a positive mode, the interaction generally continued to flow in what both her students and Ms. Beckman considered a positive direction.

The effects of student engagement included positive flow in classroom sequences, heightened musical achievement, positive mood contagion, group unity/connectedness, and continued positive levels of engagement. Figure 7.1 depicts the process of engagement in Ms. Beckman's classroom, demonstrating how the conditions supporting engagement resulted in a series of effects including a tendency toward deeper engagement.

POSITIVE FLOW IN CLASSROOM INTERACTIONS AND HEIGHTENED ACHIEVEMENT

When engagement levels are high in a classroom, one important effect is that the class flows in a positive direction with a continued focus on learning, resulting in heightened student achievement.[2] In Ms. Beckman's classroom, during periods of deep student engagement, the flow of the class period continued in a positive manner. Ms. Beckman's instructional style invoked a sense of fun and enthusiasm, and she did not need to pause to address disengagement behaviors during the learning tasks. Students generally followed her instructions, attended to any new information she provided, and attempted any skill she requested. An example of these positive effects occurred on February 10, 2011, a class period characterized by high levels of student engagement.

Toward the end of this class period, Ms. Beckman began to introduce the final song of the class period, "Billionaire," by Travie McCoy.[3] The students

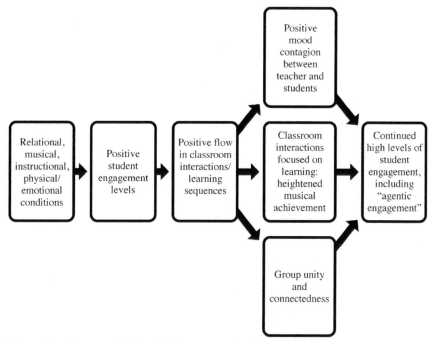

Figure 7.1   Process and Effects of Engagement in Choir Class

demonstrated interest in learning this song, and Ms. Beckman smiled and described some of the popular venues at which the song had been recently used. As she was setting up the lyrics, one of the students commented on a scarf that was hanging on a tree outside the school, visible from the choir room's window. Several students joined in the commentary on the scarf, joking and laughing about whose scarf it might be.

This classroom interaction was not related to any instruction and could have been construed as disruptive by Ms. Beckman, resulting in a segment of teacher talk regarding staying on task. However, Ms. Beckman smiled, looked at the scarf, and quipped, "When we're done [with this song], we can play, 'Whose scarf is that?' That would be a fun game." Then she promptly started the music for "Billionaire," while students laughed at her comment and one student said, "Oooh, she sounded sarcastic!" When it was time for the students' to begin the song, the scarf was forgotten and all of the students sang.

This type of interaction occurred regularly during periods of engagement, demonstrating how the flow of the classroom continued positively. Ms. Beckman addressed any off-task behavior quickly and with humor, cracked jokes and made the students laugh, and encouraged the students by complimenting their singing as they learned new portions of music. The students mirrored this positive mood, laughed at Ms. Beckman's jokes, and continued to exhibit engagement behaviors.

The energy and emotion of this type of context were positive for both students and teacher. As a result, more time was spent on teaching and learning in class, rather than on addressing disengagement and getting back "on task." Heightened musical achievement was often a result of high levels of engagement in Ms. Beckman's classroom as well.

As research in engagement theory and CRP has suggested, student engagement is a causal factor in learning and achievement.[4] During periods when the students were engaged and learning was happening rapidly in Ms. Beckman's classroom, they began to exert their own agency proactively toward learning tasks. Reeve made a distinction between this type of "agentic engagement" and cognitive/behavioral engagement that is maintained by external coercion or a controlling style of classroom management. Reeve described agentic engagement in this way:

> Agentic engagement refers to students' intentional, proactive, and constructive contribution into the flow of the instruction they receive. . . . Conceptually, agentic engagement is the process in which students try to create, enhance, and personalize the conditions and circumstances under which they learn.[5]

Reeve found that agentic engagement, when added to the dimensions of behavioral, cognitive, and affective engagement, strongly supported student achievement and learning. When students exhibited agentic engagement, learning was a wholly predictable outcome and resulted in a tendency toward continued engagement and increased achievement for students.

Reflect 7.1

- Describe to your group a time when you found yourself exhibiting agentic engagement in a classroom environment. What were the conditions that supported your agentic engagement?
- Describe a time when your students exhibited agentic engagement. Were all students engaged in this way, or just some?
- What information do you still need in order to support agentic engagement in your classroom?

GROUP UNITY/CONNECTEDNESS

In Ms. Beckman's choir classroom, deep engagement affected the students' feelings of connectedness with their classmates. The students in this study felt an elevated level of connectedness with their choir when they all engaged at high levels, further promoting a strong sense of achievement and success. John's description of the choir's performance of the song "He Still Loves Me" during the January concert demonstrated how this experience resulted in feelings of achievement as well as group connectedness for him (see chapter 5, page 83, for John's statements). These feelings of connectedness also surfaced when a member of the choir demonstrated a musical achievement and the class celebrated with him or her. The students clapped and cheered for a classmate who sang a solo or attempted a new skill in class.

Ladson-Billings described the sense of community that was present in the Culturally Relevant classrooms she studied.[6] In Ladson-Billings' study, as in Ms. Beckman's classroom, these moments of connectedness in relationships were a *condition* and also an *effect* of engagement. As Ms. Beckman encouraged the students to observe and celebrate the success of their peers, the students experienced a deeper sense of self-efficacy and motivation to succeed, resulting in a further desire to encourage their peers. As Schunk and Mullen described, "Similarity to others is a cue for gauging one's self-efficacy. Observing others succeed can raise observers' self-efficacy and motivate them to try the task at hand because they are apt to believe that if others can achieve, they can as well."[7]

When engagement levels were high in Ms. Beckman's classroom, the effects included a positive flow of classroom happenings and interactions, heightened musical achievement, positive mood contagion, and group connectedness. All of these effects in turn became conditions that encouraged further engagement for students. For Ms. Beckman, these effects resulted in her own "flow" and feelings of self-efficacy, increasing the frequency of actions that supported students' autonomy and agency in learning. This suggests that "flow" is also important in the life of a teacher. In essence, the

Reflect 7.2

Think about the cycles of student engagement and disengagement in your classroom.

- When your students are engaged, how does this motivate your own agentic engagement in the classroom (your motivation to design creative lessons, explore new resources, try new instructional strategies)?
- When your students disengage, how does this affect you? Do you tend to withdraw from the process of agentic engagement by putting less energy into lesson planning and enthusiastic instruction? If so, discuss with your group some strategies for recognizing and breaking this cycle in your classroom.

causal effects of an engaged classroom are positive: the teacher provides conditions that continue to support engagement and the students are more likely to continue to engage and apply a level of agency to their learning activities, acting creatively in the classroom environment to question, research, and personalize their learning.[8]

EFFECTS OF DISENGAGEMENT

This section of the chapter discusses the effects of disengagement in Ms. Beckman's classroom, beginning with a description of how Ms. Beckman's mood was affected by disengagement. This discussion accomplishes two purposes: to describe how frustration in the teaching act can trigger a sequence of events and to identify the point of frustration as a signal that a cycle of disengagement is beginning. The chapter continues with an analysis of the effects of classroom interactions—such as behavior talk—that followed periods of disengagement.

While this chapter focuses mostly on the effects of disengagement, this does not signify that students were predominantly disengaged in Ms. Beckman's classroom. In fact, the converse was usually true: her students were often very engaged. The detailed analysis of the effects of disengagement is designed to be comprehensive in its scope to assist practicing teachers and teacher educators in understanding the range of disengagement effects in classrooms. Figure 7.2 depicts the process and effects of disengagement in the choir classroom. Disengagement resulted in a disrupted classroom flow, teacher frustration, teacher instructional interventions including "behavior talk," negative mood contagion, fractured group relationships, and continued disengagement.

"BEHAVIOR TALK"

In Ms. Beckman's classroom, periods of high student engagement produced a positive, uninterrupted flow in classroom interactions and instruction. However, as is the case with any teacher, when the students demonstrated disengaged behaviors and Ms. Beckman could sense low engagement, she experienced frustration. Ms. Beckman responded to this frustration by initiating interactions designed to reestablish engagement such as shortening or changing an activity, giving students a choice in the classroom activities, or asking students to analyze and take responsibility for their disengagement behaviors. These strategies often followed her initial intervention, "behavior talk."

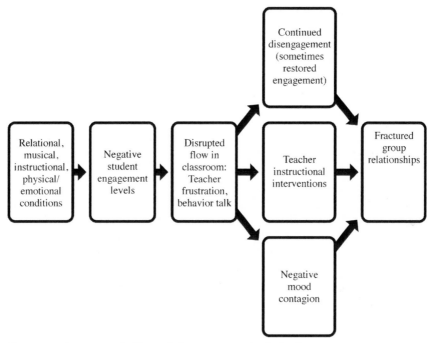

Figure 7.2   Process and effects of disengagement in choir class

Behavior talk was a segment of classroom talk that was not necessarily directly related to the musical learning at hand but more often directed at drawing students' attention to disengaged behaviors and searching for a means to redirect this behavior back into participatory mode. Behavior talk was a flexible strategy that Ms. Beckman adjusted based on her perceptions of what was needed to reestablish engagement. She directed behavior talk to the whole class (as opposed to one student) and intended that it would briefly draw attention to the disengaged behaviors and redirect the flow of the class back to the task at hand. The length of the behavior talk varied and might be combined with one or more of the instructional strategies listed above.

During periods of student disengagement in class, time spent on behavior talk affected the amount of time spent on the learning task, consequentially lowering the amount of learning and achievement taking place. The phenomenon of lowered achievement as a result of disengagement is well documented in research in the field of engagement theory.[9] While this effect occurred in Ms. Beckman's classroom as a result of the time spent outside of the learning tasks, behavior talk also became a condition affecting students' choices to reengage, their thinking about themselves, and their thinking about their classmates.

The effects of the behavior talk on the students varied. At times, segments of behavior talk and the instruction that followed had a positive effect on student effort and participation. Gregory described how he was motivated to care and try in class by Ms. Beckman.

> Before class starts, sometimes, like . . . I think it was last Thursday, [Ms. Beckman] started talking to people, and it made everybody feel bad about what they were doing. . . . And she told us to stand up and sing, and everybody was singing really loud. They were singing really good. And I think that was probably the best thing that happened, so I think she should do that again.

When Ms. Beckman engaged in behavior talk, she did not label which students were the target of the behavior talk, but she did not shy away from addressing the undesirable behaviors directly. In this way, she demonstrated her intent to alleviate the disengagement, rather than ignore it and continue on.

The following examples of behavior talk demonstrate Ms. Beckman's desire to establish engagement and acknowledge that a group of *some* students was exhibiting disengaged behaviors. Ms. Beckman tacitly invited the students to determine whether or not the talk applied to them as individuals through her use of the phrase "some of you," as demonstrated in this classroom excerpt:

> I'm wasting time waiting for you. The one thing that is standing in your way right now is your lack of self-control and your lack of discipline. Because when I was watching you, *some of you* just really, really didn't cut it. You were up there talking, making faces, distracting other people, laughing . . . how is that fair?

During this segment of behavior talk, as in other segments, Ms. Beckman was careful not to characterize the whole class as being nonparticipatory. She used the language "some of you" to refer to the group of students she was addressing. She knew that the whole class would hear the behavior talk but that it did not necessarily apply to all of them. Therefore, it was up to the students to determine if she was addressing them as "one who didn't cut it," or if they were "doing what they were supposed to do." In the following example of behavior talk, Ms. Beckman again used the phrase "some of you" to refer to students who were not participating:

> [*The students begin to sing "Man in the Mirror."*] You know this one! Sing it out! [*During the first verse, several students goof around. One gets sent out. He complains that another student made him laugh. Ms. Beckman continues with the song.*] You're not going to get to see your concert today [*a reward she had promised them at the end of class*]. I'm so sorry, you won't have time. You

know, I don't know what's wrong with *some of you*, but I really hope you get it together. We're not going to put up with this anymore. You're old enough, you should be close enough to 8th grade that this isn't happening. So whatever your problem is, fix it. We are sick of it. (italics added)

The term "we" constructed a group of students, who, along with the teacher, were there to participate. Ms. Beckman did this to encourage her students to become leaders in the classroom by participating positively, and she did this under the assumption that her students might be disengaging because they were not aware of when they were talking off-topic or not singing. In this way, she suggested that a group of students aligned with her expectations and did what they were supposed to do. Ms. Beckman's use of the phrase "Some of you" suggests a group that, in contrast, did not follow the rules, was not self-aware, and did not follow directions.

The students also categorized their classmates, creating in their minds a group of students who were "wasting their time" and a group of students who were "leaders." Each student interpreted who belonged to which group differently. This produced a divide in some students' minds, where some of their classmates were seen as being helpful to accomplishing the goals of the group and some were seen as inhibiting the progress of the group.

Reflect 7.3

What style of behavior talk do you employ in the classroom? Discuss with your group. Do you see any oppositional groups forming among your students, possibly hindering a community relationship in the classroom? Can you identify any causes of this?

EFFECTS OF BEHAVIOR TALK ON HOW STUDENTS THOUGHT ABOUT THEMSELVES

The students placed themselves into either the group that was "doing what they were supposed to do" and "leading" or the group that was the focus of the behavior talk. Gregory and Jacobi sometimes included themselves in the group that was "not doing what they were supposed to do" or "doing really bad" in class. Gregory stated,

Sometimes *we would do really bad* one day in this class. And then, Ms. Beckman will talk to us about something. Like, she wanted us to sing louder. One day, she talked to us about how to do it and stuff, and then we were a lot louder, and I think that made a lot more people care about this class. (italics added)

While Gregory again acknowledged that behavior talk could have a positive effect on engagement behaviors, he identified himself with the group that was "doing really bad one day in class," even though he was not named by Ms. Beckman in the instance he described. Jacobi also identified himself with the group of students who were not participating:

> The reason why I didn't participate is because, when she was, like—in the beginning of the class, when she was talking about our last class, and she was, like, making it seem like *we was bad* and stuff and then I was, like, "All right, then, I'm not just going to sing this today." And plus I didn't feel like singing, plus I didn't want to. (italics added)

Jacobi's use of the phrase "we was bad" signals that he constructed himself as part of the group that was the focus of the behavior talk. This was a factor for Jacobi when he chose not to participate. In contrast, some students heard the behavior talk and thought, "She means those other students, not me," thus separating themselves from the group of students being reprimanded. For example, Ángel does not associate himself with the group of students at whom the behavior talk is directed, even though he exhibited the same behaviors:

Ruth: If you could change one thing about this class, what would it be?

Ángel: Um . . . like, the kids sometimes don't listen to the teacher.

Ruth: Is it all the kids, do you think? Or is it just some?

Ángel: Some.

Ruth: Why do you think they don't listen to the teacher?

Ángel: Um . . . because *they're bad boys.* . . . I'm just kidding! I don't know. (italics added)

Ruth: When she says, "Do it this way," and they don't do it that way, why do you think they do that?

Ángel: Because sometimes they think that it's boring.

Ruth: Okay. Why do they think it's boring? Is it the problem with the songs?

Ángel: No, because sometimes they want to be . . . like, I don't know . . . fun and talk and . . . yeah.

While Ángel may have picked up on my use of the term "they" and continued with this term, he goes on in the interview to state that he felt that Ms. Beckman should send the "bad" students to Time Out or call their parents. Interestingly, Ángel's classmates often chastised him during class for talking and laughing during times when the class was asked to sing. When asked if he ever chose not to participate, he began by saying, "I don't remember," but later admitted that sometimes he did not sing because he did not want to. In the same interview, he described how the one student he noticed most in class that day was another male who did not sing. He said he would just ignore this classmate. Ángel wanted to identify with the group that participated and led in class but would exhibit the same behaviors he identified as "bad" when he was disengaged.

Jacobi and Gregory were the only two students in the study who discussed taking the behavior talk personally. They were also the only two African-American male students in the study. While this sample size does not allow for a generalization that may apply to African-American males, research suggests that the stereotypes often associated with African-American males may have affected Jacobi and Gregory's perceptions.

Steele described how the knowledge of stereotypes regarding groups to which one belongs can influence the perceptions of students, causing stress in situations where they feel they are being viewed through the lens of a negative stereotype.[10] For students under stereotype threat, perceptions that they are being identified as confirming the stereotype can also result in anxiety, depression, and lowered achievement.[11] Milner and Hoy explained the emotional and cognitive effects of stereotype threat in this way:

> The burden is the possibility of confirming the stereotype, in the eyes of others or in their own eyes. . . . It is not necessary that the individual even believes the stereotype. All that matters is that the person is *aware* of the stereotype and *cares about performing* well enough to disprove its unflattering implications. (italics in original)[12]

In this case, the stereotype of black males as exhibiting worse behavior than other students may have psychologically affected Jacobi and Gregory if they felt that they (as African-American males) were in danger of confirming the stereotype. Ladson-Billings and Donner described this as "the call," referring to the way "African Americans almost never are permitted to break out of the prism (and prison) of race that has been imposed by a racially coded and constraining society . . . and reminds one that he or she still remains locked in the racial construction."[13]

This study identifies how behavior talk can sometimes (in a subtle and hidden way) serve to work against the efforts of a teacher to create a classroom environment that promotes cultural competence. While some students who exhibit disengagement behaviors may disassociate themselves from the talk (as Ángel may have), others may experience stress and anxiety if they feel they are under stereotype threat.

Awareness of these factors can assist teachers in understanding both how students may interpret their talk and the importance of applying the Culturally Relevant tenet of cultural competence in their classroom. Culturally competent teachers find ways to affirm the cultural identity of students, connecting their cultural identity to strength, achievement, and leadership.[14] By becoming aware of how stereotype threat operates in students' lives, teachers and teacher educators can formulate new practices that function intentionally to address disengagement *and* affirm cultural identity.

EFFECTS OF BEHAVIOR TALK ON HOW STUDENTS THOUGHT ABOUT THEIR CLASSMATES

The results of the construction of two groups of students (a group that participates and "do what they are supposed to do" and another group that doesn't participate and "don't want to be there") produced a division in Ms. Beckman's classroom. This division was a result of students' frustration with the behavior of their classmates and depended on how the students interpreted which of their classmates were the source of the frustration.

The students sometimes identified particular students that "they couldn't work with," an identification that operated contrary to Ms. Beckman's desire that the class function as a community that supported each other. As periods of disengagement intensified, students' frustration with their classmates also increased. This frustration had an effect on the mood of the students: as the negative feelings surfaced, it was increasingly difficult for students to "feel it" when asked to sing.

Mila: Half of these kids, they think it's funny to mess around with people when they be trying to sing, and Ms. Beckman don't like that, because she has to stop. And then she has to yell somebody name out. And then she has to send them to detention. And that makes her angry. . . . I never act up in her class.

Ruth: Ok. What if she were to take you aside and ask you . . . because you sing most of the time, right?

Mila: Yeah! But sometimes I don't. It's because my stomach be hurting, and I have a headache, and people be making me mad and all that.

Ruth: Ok. So sometimes it has to do with how other kids in the class are acting?

Mila: [*Nods.*]

Ruth: What if all the other kids in the class were acting . . . like, they were all singing and they were all doing their thing?

Mila: Then I will sing! Yeah, I'll sing!

Mila discussed how she viewed herself as "not acting up in Ms. Beckman's class." Even when she did not sing, she did not "mess around with the other kids." When Mila perceived that there was a small group of her peers who were consistently "acting up," this caused her to become frustrated because the teacher had to stop instruction to deal with the misbehavior. For Mila, this frustration also became a source of her own disengaged behaviors. Other students in the study echoed this frustration; however, they each constructed different groups of their peers as "acting up" from day to day. The students pinpointed different classmates in their choir class who frustrated them personally with their behaviors.

The construction of two groups of students did not support either Ms. Beckman's purpose of inspiring cognitive and behavioral engagement or her intention that the students identify themselves and all of their classmates as part of the group. Ms. Beckman promoted group identification during team-building activities and other classroom instruction; however, the oppositional groups that students constructed worked to discourage them from working together to solve their engagement problems; rather, one group was seen as the problem.

Figure 7.3 depicts the cyclical nature of the effects of behavior talk on relationships among the students, demonstrating how the interpretations some students made about the intended audience of Ms. Beckman's "behavior talk" sometimes provided an additional source of disengagement and also hindered group cohesiveness.

Figure 7.3 focuses specifically on how behavior talk created—inadvertently on the teacher's part—one chain of effects related to disengagement (see Figure 7.2 for a comprehensive view of the effects of disengagement). While Ms. Beckman intended her behavior talk to increase student engagement (and sometimes it did), it also had the effect of working against group cohesion, which was an additional cause of disengagement.

The students interpreted Ms. Beckman's "behavior talk" in a variety of ways, thus influencing how they perceived their classmates. Instances of "behavior talk" from the teacher during periods of disengagement sometimes became a conduit to the students' construction of two groups. They felt they were either "able to work with" another student or that the other student was distracting them and inhibiting their ability to participate in class. They began to form negative opinions of particular classmates whom they perceived as slowing their teacher's instruction and prohibiting them from moving on to more interesting classroom material. Stereotype threats may have affected the African-American males in the study due to their concern that they were seen as confirming the stereotype that black males engage in "disruptive" behavior.

The students' perceptions of their classmates also served to foster (dis)engagement by means of mood contagion. When students perceived that their classmates were distracted and disengaged, they began to feel distracted or irritated. The converse was also true: when students perceived a high level of enthusiasm and positive engagement from their classmates, they were motivated to engage positively. In this way, mood contagion also influenced students as they took on the moods and then the behaviors of their engaged or disengaged classmates. The next chapter discusses how to recognize and reverse the disengagement cycle.

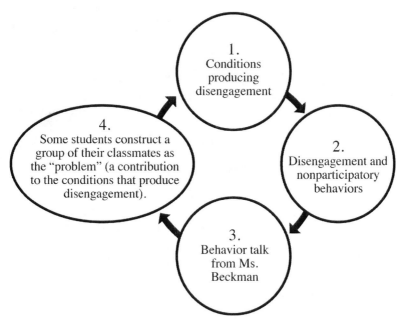

Figure 7.3   Cyclical View of Classroom Effects Involving "Behavior Talk"

Take Action 7.4

Videotape yourself teaching for a day. When you find yourself using "behavior talk" to reengage your students, transcribe that segment of class. Analyze the words you use, the questions you ask, and the students' responses. Do you construct and categorize a group of students (or the whole class) as not participating? What assumptions do you make about the students?

With your teacher group, discuss how you might rewrite your behavior talk to continue to construct the class (including yourself) as a unit. Use the word "I" to refer to any feeling of frustration you want to share with the class, but then use the word "we" to discuss how you can all work together to identify the source of disengagement and alleviate it.

NOTES

1. Johnmarshall Reeve, "A Self-Determination Theory Perspective on Student Engagement," in *Handbook of Research on Student Engagement*, ed. Sandra L. Christenson, Amy L. Reschly, and Cathy Wylie (New York: Springer, 2012), 149–72.

2. Ellen A. Skinner and Michael J. Belmont, "Motivation in the Classroom: Reciprocal Effects of Teacher Behavior and Student Engagement Across the School Year," *Journal of Educational Psychology* 85, no. 4 (1993): 571–81.

3. Travie McCoy, Philip Lawrence, Bruno Mars, and Ari Levine, "Billionaire," ed. Mark Brymer, New York: Hal Leonard (2010), sheet music.

4. Beverly J. Armento, "Principles of a Culturally Responsive Curriculum," in *Culturally Responsive Teaching: Lesson Planning for Elementary and Middle Grades*, ed. Jacqueline J. Irvine and Beverly J. Armento (Boston, MA: McGraw-Hill, 2001); Sandra L. Christenson, Amy L. Reschly, and Cathy Wylie, "Preface" in *Handbook of Research on Student Engagement*, ed. Sandra L. Christenson, Amy L. Reschly, and Cathy Wylie (New York: Springer, 2012), v–ix; Ellen A. Skinner and Jennifer R. Pitzer, "Developmental Dynamics of Student Engagement, Coping, and Everyday Resilience," in *Handbook of Research on Student Engagement*, ed. Sandra L. Christenson, Amy L. Reschly, and Cathy Wylie (New York: Springer, 2012), 21–44.

5. Reeve, "Self-Determination," 161.

6. Gloria Ladson-Billings, "Toward a Theory of Culturally Relevant Pedagogy," *American Educational Research Journal* 32, no. 3 (1995): 465–91.

7. Dale H. Schunk and Carol A. Mullen, "Self-Efficacy as an Engaged Learner," in *Handbook of Research on Student Engagement*, ed. Sandra L. Christenson, Amy L. Reschly, and Cathy Wylie (New York: Springer, 2012), 223.

8. Reeve, "Self-Determination."

9. See Christenson et al., "Preface"; and Jennifer A. Fredricks, Phyllis C. Blumenfeld, and Alison H. Paris, "School Engagement: Potential of the Concept, State of the Evidence," *Review of Educational Research* 74, no. 1 (2004): 59–109.

10. Claude Steele, "Stereotype Threat and African-American Student Achievement," in *Young, Gifted, and Black*, ed. Theresa Perry, Claude Steele, and Asa G. Hilliard (Boston, MA: Beacon Press Books, 2003), 111.

11. Carmen G. Arroyo and Edward Zigler, "Racial Identity, Academic Achievement, and the Psychological Well-Being of Economically Disadvantaged Adolescents," *Journal of Personality and Social Psychology* 69, no. 5 (1995): 903–14; Steele, "Stereotype Threat."

12. H. Richard Milner and Anita Woolfolk Hoy, "A Case Study of an African American Teacher's Self-Efficacy, Stereotype Threat, and Persistence," *Teaching and Teacher Education* 19 (2003): 265, citing Aronson et al.

13. Gloria Ladson-Billings and Jamel Donner, "The Moral Activist Role of Critical Race Theory Scholarship," in *The SAGE Handbook of Qualitative Research*, 3rd ed., ed. Norman K. Denzin and Yvonna S. Lincoln (Thousand Oaks, CA: SAGE Publications, 2005), 279.

14. Gloria Ladson-Billings, *The Dreamkeepers: Successful Teachers of African American Children* (San Francisco, CA: Jossey-Bass, 1994); Ladson-Billings, "Toward a Theory," 476.

Chapter 8

Recognizing and Reversing the Disengagement Cycle
"Classroom Management" and Student Autonomy

A teacher plays a new piece of music for her 2nd grade general music class. The children are seated on the floor and gaze up at her as the music plays. The children begin to move their bodies in various ways as they sit. "I like this music!" one says. "Can we dance?" says another. "No, you may not dance. We are going to listen," says the teacher. Obvious vocal disappointment erupts from the students. They look away from the teacher and begin to talk with each other.

This scenario took place in an elementary music classroom. It is striking how the engagement of the students turned on a dime after only a few interactions. During the following moments of class, the teacher attempted to coerce the students to participate by "listening" and answering questions. She became quickly frustrated by the students' disengaged behaviors. The teacher began to talk louder and faster, and then began to offer negative consequences to students who wouldn't "listen." The students' behaviors became more obvious and forthright, and the disengagement continued throughout the entire class period. At the end, the frustrated teacher and the disengaged students were all relieved that the class was over.

The teacher in the opening scenario did not identify her students' initial question ("Can we dance?") and her answer ("No, you may not dance. We are going to listen.") as the point at which her students began to disengage. Rather, she may have identified it as the moment when the students began to disobey and demonstrate to her that they needed a more controlled classroom management style in order for her to accomplish her lesson plan, an important difference in perception. While the teacher in the opening scenario may have chosen to not encourage students' movement for multiple reasons (possibly including the assumption that "dancing" and "listening" cannot occur simultaneously), this chapter focuses on the music teacher's identification of moments of students' disengagement and selection of strategies to reestablish engagement. The critical moments in the disengagement cycle are the following:

1. The point at which students begin to exhibit disengaged behaviors;
2. The point at which the teacher begins to experience a negative mood (such as frustration) in response to those behaviors;
3. The point at which the teacher must choose an intervention to reestablish engagement; and
4. The point when a teacher can reassess the students' engagement levels to determine if the intervention was successful or if further strategies are needed.

As teachers become aware of these critical moments while they are teaching, they can adopt a stance of curiosity toward their students' disengagement and open up conversations with the students regarding their disengagement. They can then purposefully integrate a pedagogical intervention that can reverse the disengagement cycle.

Reflect 8.1

Think about the last time you experienced or observed teacher frustration related to whole-group behaviors in the classroom. What events took place directly before? What interventions did the teacher (perhaps you) try? How did the class period end?

IDENTIFYING THE MOMENT OF DISENGAGEMENT IN A MUSIC CLASSROOM

In the opening scenario of this chapter, the first three critical moments in the disengagement cycle happened early in the class period and followed each other in rapid succession.

1. The students demonstrated their initial disengagement by vocally announcing their disappointment and then looking away from the teacher and talking with each other.
2. The teacher immediately experienced elevated frustration levels demonstrated by her louder and faster speech patterns.
3. The teacher chose an intervention—coercing the students to comply with her lesson plan by suggesting negative consequences for noncompliance.

Following this sequence of events, the students neither complied with the teacher's requests nor reengaged with her learning activity, and the disengaged behaviors continued and multiplied as the class period went on. The teacher was not able to identify or apply an appropriate intervention for disengagement because she did not identify the students' initial dissatisfaction with the suggested learning activity as disengagement. After this class period, the teacher did not characterize the class period as an example of student disengagement but rather as an example of student deficits: behavioral, academic, and musical.

The study of Ms. Beckman's classroom indicates that teachers who can learn to identify critical moments that signal disengagement can begin to apply interventions in relational, instructional, and musical categories (identified by the students in this study and discussed in part I) that can reestablish engagement. When a teacher can accurately identify when a class moves from being engaged to disengaged, then he or she can begin to reverse the cycle by purposefully choosing to adopt a mode of curiosity (as opposed to reacting in frustration).

Skinner and Belmont studied the link between teacher behavior and student engagement, highlighting the intentional awareness a teacher needs in order to resist the tendency toward frustration during moments of student disengagement.[1] They suggested that teachers could adopt a stance of curiosity as they encourage students to express their negative feelings toward the learning task, acknowledging students' disengagement as signals of boredom or anxiety with the learning task. Learning to identify the point when frustration begins may assist a teacher in opening a conversation with students about what elements are disengaging to them. By adopting effective strategies to reestablish engagement—beginning from a stance of curiosity—the teacher may more successfully redirect students' frustration or boredom to curiosity and persistence.

For example, in the opening scenario, the teacher experienced frustration as the students chose nonparticipation with her "listening" activity. If she had identified this moment as a reason to adopt a stance of curiosity, she might have resisted the feelings of frustration by wondering, "Why do the students disengage when I ask them to listen without moving? It can't be the music. What might happen if I *did* encourage the students to move while listening?"

She could then retain her stance of curiosity and encourage the students to move expressively, giving them guidelines based on the space within the classroom. As she selects this intervention, she can then ask, "Will this adjusted learning activity, based on the students' responses, also meet my goals for the learning activity? How can I adjust similar learning activities in the future based on what has happened in this classroom segment?"

As the students choose to reengage, they also demonstrate agentic engagement. Their motivation to engage through movement is strong, and when the teacher supports their selected response, the cycle of engagement continues.

THE MOMENT WHEN A TEACHER SELECTS AN INTERVENTION TO REESTABLISH ENGAGEMENT: STUDENT CONTROL OR STUDENT AUTONOMY?

Skinner and Belmont described how the teachers they studied instinctively reacted to students' high engagement levels with actions that promoted continued engagement, such as more involvement, more autonomy support, and more consistency.[2] Reeve defined autonomy support as "interpersonal sentiment and behavior teachers provide during instruction to identify, nurture, and develop students' inner motivational resources."[3] Reeve found that student engagement encouraged such actions on the part of the teacher and discussed three conditions that must be in place to enact autonomy support in the classroom: the teacher adopts the students' perspectives; the teacher welcomes the students' thoughts, feelings, and behaviors; and the teacher supports the students' motivational development and capacity for autonomous self-regulation.[4]

In order to meet these conditions, teachers were patient with students, encouraging them to work at their own pace to master skills and complete tasks; provided explanatory rationales for instruction, connecting learning tasks to students' lives in a relevant way; paid attention to students' inner motivational resources, such as their interests, preferences, and psychological needs; used noncontrolling language to help students identify and solve problems; and accepted students' expressions of negative affect as valid reactions to aspects of learning.[5] Reeve also investigated the converse effect: when student disengagement occurs in a classroom environment, the tendency for teachers is to adopt a more controlling motivational style in order to reestablish engagement.[6]

In the opening scenario, the teacher's initial intervention was to apply a more controlling, or "strict" motivational style. The use of a more controlling style has the effect of lowering student engagement, especially "agentic engagement" where the students act upon the learning task creatively. Ms. Beckman, in contrast to the teacher in the opening scenario, recognized that a more controlling, "strict," motivational style would not motivate her students to participate or engage.

Some students in this study thought that Ms. Beckman might address the group of students whom they had constructed as holding up the progress of the group with a more "strict" application of consequences (remember, each student had different ideas about which students belonged in this group). Some students suggested that Ms. Beckman should be a little less "nice": they felt she could more firmly define behavioral expectations and administer consequences with more regularity. Halting the class's flow frustrated them, and they felt that Ms. Beckman couldn't "do her job." As Alice described,

> *Ruth:* If you could change something about this class . . . what would it be?
>
> *Alice:* Probably . . . Ms. Beckman's attitude, because she's too nice, and I think that's why kids want to get away with it, and they don't want to sing, and they have, like, their own attitude.
>
> *Ruth:* What would the expectations be for the kids?
>
> *Alice:* Then they would listen more, they would be . . . respectful. Because a lot of kids, when we're going to perform and videotape, a lot of kids were just sitting down, and they were like, "I don't want to do it. I don't want to stand by her. I don't want to stand up, and I'm not even going to the concert, so I'm not going to be there." They have their own attitude towards her because she's nice.
>
> *Ruth:* So what would Ms. Beckman's attitude be like, then?
>
> *Alice:* Well . . . fun, and more . . . not strict, like being mean. But, like, she's fun already, but she should, like, . . . not be mean, but . . . give them a warning, "That's your first warning, and if you get another one, you're going to go to Time Out. And if you get two times going down to Time Out with me, then you're not going to go to choir for a whole week," or something. And not that strict, so they can know their expectations, like, "I shouldn't do that; it's going to be my first warning."

Alice constructed a group of her classmates whom she felt were "getting away with it" based on their disengaged behaviors. She then described her view of the word "strict" and made it clear that she did not want Ms. Beckman to be "mean." Ms. Beckman also associated the word "strict" with being mean and did not want to turn the kids off to her instruction by being "mean."

> That's a tough one [when the students say they want a "strict" vs. a "not strict" teacher] because it's also the "mean" and "not mean." And if you are not happy, and especially not happy with the teacher, why would you work for that? So, yeah, I struggle with that line a lot.

As Ms. Beckman knew, when the students did not participate because they were disengaged, she could not reestablish engagement with a stronger application of behavioral consequences. The students who used the terminology "strict" often applied this to students who "just didn't care," referring to those students whom they felt were the target of the behavior talk. They felt that "being strict" would encourage "some students" to take the class more seriously and result in more time spent on learning.

The students' interpretations and desires in these instances may have been a result of behavior talk. They had constructed a group of students who were the "problem," and they might have felt that those students needed firmer expectations and consequences. Students in the focus group session on January 13, 2011, described "strict" in much the same way as Alice did—as holding to firm expectations and consequences.

Blossom: She's not strict.

Alice: She's too nice. [*Jacobi raises hand.*]

Ruth: She's not strict. She's too nice. Okay. Do you agree with that? [*Looks at Jacobi.*]

Jacobi: Yeah, like . . . you can't put all your friends by each other. It'd be a lot more quiet.

Blossom: Yeah . . . not giving us so many warnings, because if they haven't really listened the first time, why would you give them a second chance? A lot of people get in trouble.

The difficulty for Ms. Beckman was that she desired for her students to choose to participate and not to be coerced by authoritarian means. In her experience, a firmer application of behavioral expectations with a controlling motivating style would result in stronger disengagement, an assumption in line with research on control.[7] Ms. Beckman realized that, when a majority of students were exhibiting disengagement behaviors in class, it would have been nearly impossible to determine who should get a warning or a consequence and who may have disengaged with behaviors designed to relieve boredom.

The research on engagement theory has demonstrated that environments that support a high level of student autonomy *combined* with structure encourage high levels of engagement.[8] Educational research (and practicing teachers and teacher educators) sometimes construct student autonomy and structure to work in an oppositional way. However, Jang, Reeve, and Deci argued that this view is a result of perceiving structure to be synonymous with control, or at least to contain aspects of control that are oppositional to autonomy.[9] Jang et al. described how teachers provide structure in the classroom by clearly communicating expectations and directions, taking the lead during some instructional activities, providing strong guidance during the lesson, providing step-by-step directions when needed, scheduling student activities, marking the boundaries of activities and orchestrating the transitions between them, offering task-focused and personal control-enhancing feedback and providing consistency in the lesson.[10]

Control is not essential to structure. While structure can be presented in either a control-supportive way or an autonomy-supportive way, teachers who move away from structure entirely create a laissez-faire environment conducive to the kind of chaos that serves to lower engagement.

The research on CRP also underscores the importance of classroom structure in an environment that supports student autonomy. In this body of literature, effective teachers demonstrated warmth and care toward students while simultaneously requiring students to meet high academic and behavioral standards.[11] To do this, teachers aroused students' curiosity for the learning task, communicated the purposes for learning activities, included multiple modes of learning, encouraged students' use of comfortable communication patterns, created space for the students to relate to each other in meaningful ways, and encouraged choices and decisions while learning.[12]

Reflect 8.2

Think about a teacher from your own schooling days who provided you and your classmates with a strong classroom structure that also included support for student autonomy. Contrast this with a teacher who provided a strong classroom structure based on student control. What made the difference? Discuss with your group.

A CLASSROOM MANAGEMENT MYTH IN MUSIC EDUCATION

A common myth in music education (and education in general) is that students in racially diverse settings require a firmer classroom management style that includes maintaining a higher level of control than is needed in white, middle-class classrooms. Texts, conference sessions, and personal conversations in which teachers discuss their experiences in "urban" or increasingly "rural" settings often include statements such as "It is a battlefield," "Students come to school without knowing the expectations for behavior," "You must make sure the students know you are the one who makes decisions in the classroom," and "Your expectations must be clear and your consequences swift."

Based on the perceptions of the students in Ms. Beckman's classroom, the following conclusions refute the classroom management myth stated above:

1. In Ms. Beckman's racially diverse classroom, low-level instruction, weak relationships between students, and uninteresting music promoted disengagement. This is the same in white-normed classrooms.
2. Students with more white-normed behavioral responses to disengagement may continue to disengage but still appear compliant. Students who demonstrate different, more active disengagement behaviors may result in the teacher's assumptions that these students "just don't know how to behave" or that they need stronger classroom management.
3. A laissez-faire approach to classroom pedagogy (creating a classroom environment where students make all of the choices) can lead to frustration and student disengagement.
4. Students are aware of their disengagement behaviors. However, teachers must also recognize these behaviors as signals of disengagement. Then, they can ask their students specific questions regarding the instructional, musical, or relational contexts for their disengagement as they choose an appropriate intervention.

As music teachers become more culturally competent, they can adjust their perceptions of student disengagement behaviors in their classrooms. Hubbard studied white women who were effective teachers of black students, focusing on their classroom management styles.[13] He found that the classroom climate these teachers established began with certain attitudes and dispositions they possessed.

The teachers in Hubbard's study interpreted their students' behaviors, especially those that might be viewed as disruptive, through the lens of cultural ways of interacting. For example, talking out in class was at times perceived as a student's right to enter into a discussion instead of being disruptive or rude.[14] Students also assisted in developing rules and procedures in the classroom and were trusted to self-correct distracting behaviors as well as to maximize their time spent on educational tasks.[15]

These teachers did not let misbehavior slide, however. They assertively addressed any form of disrespect in the classroom and let the students know that they were being firm and consistent with an eye toward the student's achievement and the achievement of the class. Clear instruction was given on what disrespect looked like and the message was unmistakable: "I am your teacher. I am committed to making sure you learn. I care about the quality of your learning."[16]

CHOICE IN THE CURRICULUM: STUDENT AUTONOMY?

Ms. Beckman gave her students choices related to the songs they were singing during most class periods. She described how she felt that these choices would demonstrate her respect for their voices in class and also promote engagement. The types of choices she gave them included selecting which songs they learned in class; the order of songs to rehearse for the day; which songs to sing during the concert; and which part to learn in a song. For example, if there was a segment of a three-part harmony, she might offer the altos a choice between two of the parts. The students appreciated that Ms. Beckman invited them to participate in selecting songs. Inviting this type of student voice in the curriculum is an important facet of CRP and had a positive effect on engagement in Ms. Beckman's class.[17]

However, other types of choice had a stronger influence on the students' disengagement than Ms. Beckman would have liked. When Ms. Beckman provided the students with choices pertaining to which of their rehearsed songs were to be sung at the concert, she hoped this would be motivation for engagement, especially for singing. This happened during a class session on January 3, 2011, just a week before their concert; Ms. Beckman took a class vote on which of their four songs were to be sung in the concert. There was general agreement that they should sing two of the songs, but only about half of the students voted to sing the other two. One student said, "Just make us do all four!" Ms. Beckman said that her preference was that they would sing all four, and discussion on this continued.

While Ms. Beckman may have been intending to encourage the students to take ownership, she found that gaining consensus was difficult. The student who implored Ms. Beckman to have them sing all four songs demonstrated her frustration with this type of curricular choice: a choice that allowed for the possibility that some students might not want to sing all of their prepared songs. In their interviews, students expressed frustration with Ms. Beckman's desire to promote student engagement by garnering their opinions on which songs they liked and therefore wanted to sing in class or during the concert. Alice described how she felt that class time was wasted on this activity and that Ms. Beckman should just do the songs she liked, exercising her authority and judgment for the good of the students.

> *Ruth:* So, was there anything that Ms. Beckman could maybe do that might help with [student participation during singing]?
>
> *Alice:* Well, I like to tell Ms. Beckman my opinions, but at the same time, like when I say it, they [other students] are like, "No, that's not a good idea! Why would we want to dance?" . . . She takes people's opinions . . . she should have

her own opinions . . . and first take hers, and if hers doesn't work, then probably she should ask the kids that don't really talk because they're kind of shy to talk out loud, because they are worried about what other people might think about their opinions.

Alice described her desire for Ms. Beckman to trust her instincts and choose music based on her own estimations about what would foster musical achievement for the group but that also fit with her own interests.

In February 2011, Ms. Beckman gave the altos a choice for a particular lyrical pattern to sing when the song they were learning split into three parts. They would sing one part, the other part would be given to the other 7th-grade class's altos. She demonstrated the two parts for them, and someone from the alto section picked one. Ms. Beckman asked them all to sing the new part, but multiple students chose not to participate.

Up until this moment in class, students had been fully participatory, learning a complicated portion of the song in two-part harmony in about eight minutes. In this example, Ms. Beckman invited the students to choose their part, feeling it would motivate them to sing, but nonparticipation resulted. Only one student made the decision for the whole group, and when that occurred, other students may have lost their buy-in.

In the same way that structure can be a tool to support either autonomy or control in the classroom, student choice can also be a pedagogical tool that supports either engagement or disengagement. While some forms of student choice support autonomy and therefore engagement, other forms do not.[18] For students, the mere act of choosing is not valuable by itself; the value resides in the relationship of the options presented in the choice to the students' personal goals. The options must "involve an opportunity for a meaningful realization of the individual's desires or preferences."[19]

The students in this study reported that they desired instruction similar to the pedagogy described in the literature on engagement theory and CRP. The students appreciated Ms. Beckman's willingness to let them have meaningful input into the curriculum, such as choosing songs that were relevant to them, but demonstrated apathy (and sometimes continued disengagement) when the choice involved meaningless options in which they had no personal stake.

Refer one more time back to the opening music classroom scenario. Student engagement is more than a matter of addressing one pedagogical decision, that is, a teacher not allowing the students to dance. However, if the teacher had identified the question "Can we dance?" and the answer "No, you may not" as the moment at which disengagement began, she might also have been able to identify her frustration as an emotional response to that disengagement. With this awareness, she could adopt a stance of curiosity,

Take Action 8.3

With a partner, take turns analyzing video segments of each other teaching a lesson to a pluralistic group of students. Answer the following questions:

• Was there a moment during the lesson when the students began, as a group, to exhibit disengagement behaviors?
• Was there a moment following this disengagement when I began to experience frustration?
• What interventions did I try?
• How did the level of engagement change following the intervention?

Now, go back and examine the interactions prior to the disengagement. What do you think caused the disengagement: instruction, music, relationships, or something else? Identify several short-term and long-term strategies to build engaging pedagogy for that particular type of lesson. If the lesson did not yield a moment of disengagement, analyze how the instruction, music, and relationships supported the engagement. If this was a practice lesson in a cooperating teacher's class, how did the classroom climate established by that teacher support continued engagement as you taught? As always, even in a lesson that ran smoothly, look for places where engagement wavered or achievement levels could be enhanced.

select an instructional intervention, and evaluate the success of that intervention. In this way, she could more accurately design engaging lessons in the future and react more effectively to moments of disengagement in her classroom.

NOTES

1. Ellen Skinner and Michael Belmont, "Motivation in the Classroom: Reciprocal Effects of Teacher Behavior and Student Engagement Across the School Year," *Journal of Educational Psychology* 85 (1993): 571–81.
2. Ibid., 578.
3. Johnmarshall Reeve, "Why Teachers Adopt a Controlling Motivating Style Toward Students and How They Can Become More Autonomy Supportive," *Educational Psychologist* 44 (2009): 160.
4. Johnmarshall Reeve, "A Self-Determination Theory Perspective on Student Engagement," in *Handbook of Research on Student Engagement*, ed. Sandra Christenson, Amy Reschly, and Cathy Wylie (New York: Springer, 2012), 162.
5. Ibid.
6. Reeve, "Why Teachers Adopt a Controlling Motivating Style."

7. Reeve, "A Self-Determination Theory," 162.

8. Hyungshim Jang, Johnmarshall Reeve, and Edward Deci, "Engaging Students in Learning Activities: It Is Not Autonomy Support or Structure but Autonomy Support and Structure," *Journal of Educational Psychology* 102 (2010): 588–600.

9. Ibid.

10. Ibid., 589.

11. See Michele Foster, "Effective Black Teachers: A Literature Review," in *Teaching Diverse Populations: Formulating a Knowledge Base*, ed. Etta R. Hollins, Joyce E. King, and Warren C. Hayment (Albany: State University of New York Press, 1994), 225–42; and Gloria Ladson-Billings, *Dreamkeepers*.

12. Armento, "Principles," 28.

13. Terrance M. Hubbard, "It's About More Than 'Just Be Consistent' or 'Out-Tough-Them': Culturally Responsive Classroom Management" (PhD diss., Ohio State University–Columbus, 2005), 164.

14. Ibid., 167.

15. Ibid., 164.

16. Ibid.

17. Gloria Ladson-Billings, "But That's Just Good Teaching! The Case for Culturally Relevant Pedagogy," *Theory into Practice* 34, no. 3 (1995): 159–65.

18. Idit Katz and Avi Assor, "When Choice Motivates and When It Does Not," *Educational Psychology Review* 19 (2007): 429–42.

19. Ibid., 432.

Chapter 9

Lessons to Learn

Music Education, Culturally Relevant Pedagogy, and Student Engagement

My brother—he raps and I sing along sometimes. Sometimes, we'll practice songs just for fun . . . we'll take turns on the lyrics . . . we'll sing together. We laugh a lot because it's fun, I guess.

—*Blossom*

I like singing. . . . I remember once I was in the shower singing. Then my sister had recorded me, and they sent it to a friend at school. Then it just got around at school! It was funny.

—*Jacobi*

I sing with my friends. . . . I had friends in choir, and I wanted to sing.

—*Mila*

Friendship, making music, laughing, dancing—school music (and school in general) can, and should, be a place where joy and pleasure coexist with deep engagement and musical achievement. Yet, in the United States, students of color are dropping out of school music programs at disproportionately higher rates than their white counterparts. This trend signals, in part, a lack of interesting, relevant, and challenging instruction, resulting in students' disengagement from music class.

In this study, the process of (dis)engagement in Ms. Beckman's classroom was complex: it had effects on both students and teacher and was influenced by multiple conditions unique to the classroom context. Over the course of the school year, the students' (dis)engagement trajectories sometimes intersected and sometimes were unique. As in all classrooms, these similarities and differences created a context influenced by relationships, emotions, and learning needs that produced levels of (dis)engagement.

This book identifies key aspects of the conditions, behaviors, and effects of (dis)engagement that mattered to the students in the study and to their teacher, bringing music education discourses, CRP, and engagement theory into conversation with each other. The students' perspectives demonstrate how cultural norms factor into students' and teachers' interpretations and actions in the classroom. The resulting findings demonstrate not only the complexity of (dis)engagement but also the usefulness of describing and comparing students' and teachers' perceptions and interpretations for understanding this complexity.

The perspectives and experiences shared by the students of Clark Middle School provide practicing teachers and teacher educators an insight into pedagogical practices that can more effectively serve their students. Without these insights, teachers' assumptions regarding their students' behavioral cues and learning needs may misalign with the students' actual perceptions and intents, causing misunderstanding, lowered achievement, disengagement, and fractured relationships. These misunderstandings are sometimes exacerbated when the classroom contains a broad spectrum of cultural norms. This chapter provides a review of the students' perspectives as given earlier in this book, and then suggests several ways in which the field of music education can respond.

REVIEW OF THE STUDENTS' PERSPECTIVES

The students reported that the teacher-student relationship was the foundational element contributing to their engagement. The teacher-student relationship was the main conduit through which the students filtered all other pedagogical strategies. Ms. Beckman's beliefs about herself, her students, and social relations in the classroom formed the basis for this relationship. These beliefs aligned with two of the tenets of CRP: conceptions of social relations and conceptions of self/others.

The students reported that they were engaged by instruction that was challenging, interesting, and relevant to their lives and future goals. They were engaged by musical instruction in a wide range of musical styles and genres. However, if a popular song that they liked outside of class did not present a "challenge," they disengaged. This finding aligns with CRP in the area of academic achievement, as well as research in engagement theory and "flow" theory.

Students reported that when they were highly engaged, they were "feeling it" and exhibited behaviors related to staying on task such as singing with feeling, working hard, contributing to class discussions, focusing attention on the task, and persevering to the end of the task. Cultural norms and expectations also played a role both in students' behavioral choices in the classroom and in the teacher's interpretations of those choices. During classroom discussions in which students were engaged by the content and instruction, they often chose to participate by interacting spontaneously with their teacher and each other, signaling their engagement in ways that were representative of cultural diversity. Ms. Beckman's assumption that the students were demonstrating engagement during these times aligned with the students' intent, demonstrating her cultural competence—a central tenet of CRP.

While teacher and student interpretations of behaviors in the classroom aligned during periods of engagement, when students disengaged, differing interpretations were more likely. Students reported that when they found the classroom context disengaging, they "blanked out." Some continued to comply with requests for participation but went on "autopilot." Some "tuned out" by not participating, either zoning out mentally or thinking about other things. Some engaged themselves in other activities: talking, laughing, or "goofing around." The students reported these behaviors as signals of their own disengagement, but sometimes interpreted their classmates' similar behaviors as a signal that they "did not care and were not there to sing."

The students' interpretations were influenced by teacher "behavior talk." Through their interpretations, the students constructed a group of the classmates who were perceived as holding up the progress of the class. Ms. Beckman interpreted the students' disengagement behaviors differently than her students: she felt that perhaps the students did not feel important to the group or that they were not aware of how their behaviors affected the group.

The students interpreted expressive body movement in varied ways. Their interpretations were influenced by instruction regarding body comportment in their choir class: some linked it to engagement while others linked it to a level of disengagement.

The effects of student engagement included positive flow in classroom sequences, heightened musical achievement, positive mood contagion, group unity/connectedness, and continued positive levels of engagement. Disengagement resulted in a disrupted classroom flow, teacher frustration, teacher instructional interventions including "behavior talk," negative mood contagion, fractured group relationships, and continued disengagement. This finding links to CRP under the tenet of conceptions of self and others and cultural competence. The perceptions that students developed of their peers during periods of disengagement demonstrated differing understandings of behaviors and affected peer relationships negatively.

WHAT CAN WE LEARN FROM THE STUDENTS ABOUT TEACHER-STUDENT RELATIONSHIPS?

This study implies that, in order to cultivate strong teacher-student relationships, there is a need for teacher education programs to continue to find ways for prospective teachers to explore and practice a central tenet of CRP: the teacher's *conceptions of social relations*. These beliefs cannot easily be taught or learned in a teacher education classroom. Ms. Beckman demonstrated her openness to learn from her students and to share her life with them. Part of her openness was due to her own willingness to learn from others throughout her life.

As students learn to understand and consider the perspectives of others, they can also begin to practice what Gilroy described as "nonracial humanism."[1] This type of human identity differs from manifestations of colorblindness and includes the idea that, while racism has played a significant factor in past and present oppression and inequalities, there are essential experiences that bring humans together. Nonracial humanism views these commonalities and differences as unique aspects of humanity, not as a display of a hierarchy of values.[2]

For many teachers who experience conflict with students in a pluralistic setting, the source is often their own lack of intercultural understanding and their lack of desire and skill in building relationships with their students.[3] The following are ways in which teachers can build strong relationships with students. These strategies can be incorporated into teacher education programs and professional development for practicing teachers. Teachers cultivate strong relationships by

1. taking responsibility for initiating positive relationships;
2. becoming culturally competent as they begin to view their own experiences and understandings as culturally situated instead of "the norm";
3. caring for students with humility and caution by working to understand students' culturally situated understandings and values;
4. constructing an environment where students are seen as equal contributors with the teacher to the musical learning; and
5. focusing care for students on their musical achievement.[4]

WHAT CAN WE LEARN FROM THE STUDENTS ABOUT CHALLENGING MUSICAL INSTRUCTION?

The students highlight the pedagogical need to create a strong structure of challenge and achievement in the music classroom, including musical goals that the students cocreate and that they perceive as relevant. Music teachers need to do more than form a strong relationship with their students and choose enjoyable repertoire that connects to their lives. These facets of pedagogy are key, but they are not enough. Within the traditional model of choir and band instruction in the United States, preparing for a small number of concerts each year may not be enough to maintain challenge and relevance. Teachers can create further opportunities for students to sing or play. These opportunities must be meaningful, well planned, and challenging to students.

When disengagement does occur, music teachers can examine the level of challenge as a key contributor. This study aligns with research in CRP, demonstrating that relationships between teachers and students must not only be warm and caring but also simultaneously focus on high achievement. As Antrop-Gonzalez and De Jesus concluded, "Minoritized students will not benefit from forms of caring that [are disconnected from] the expectation of academic excellence."[5] Teachers can be seen as tough or even harsh when pushing students to succeed, yet this is a critical element of CRP for students' success.[6]

Primary motivation for students to engage exists when they can sense a purpose in the instructional activity. Applying this to music, students should readily sense a reason for singing or playing a particular song each time they do so; otherwise "it is going to be difficult for students to pay attention, to be fully engaged in the learning tasks, and to relate their prior understandings to new ideas."[7] For every teacher, part of the art of teaching is giving the students a challenge that does not cause a level of frustration and, therefore, disengagement. Even seasoned teachers cannot teach to students' appropriate challenge levels by chance but must continue to examine their work in this area reflectively.

The following short list of recommendations for music teachers and music teacher educators can be applied in a variety of ways because different groups of students will have different interests and resources:

1. Students and their teachers can use pedagogy outside of the traditional school music models. For example, students within large school ensembles can participate in a wide variety of musical activities in addition to singing or playing an instrument—including units on composition, improvisation, music history, the other arts, and musical technology.
2. Music teachers can form collaborations across disciplines or within the music discipline by working with other teachers or fostering relationships with musicians from outside of the school setting, such as recording artists, university groups, among others. Music students from band, orchestra, and choir and other large-group ensembles can collaborate across classes to work in small ensembles and develop greater musical independence.

3. Music teachers can research, design, and implement new music courses in addition to large ensembles. Courses such as music composition, rock ensemble, music technology, or any other nontraditional ensembles are options.[8]

WHAT CAN WE LEARN FROM THE STUDENTS ABOUT STUDENT AUTONOMY?

It is important for music teachers to include students in the crafting of instruction, thereby supporting student autonomy and "agentic engagement."[9] This study highlights the balance in the art of teaching between including the students in crafting the learning (autonomy) and facilitating the students' learning needs with a sense of structure, efficiency, and challenge. This is not a simple task, and for a teacher who is isolated in his or her own classroom without feedback, self-reflection in this area can be difficult. This suggests that teachers should be able to work with a mentor or coach who can provide feedback on their instruction, assist in developing a goal-oriented means for learning this way of instruction, and model lessons for the new teacher.

To support autonomy, teachers can invite students to describe their own ideal musical learning contexts and incorporate students' input by (1) purposefully fostering a relevant "now" connection between their students and the musical content, and (2) highlighting links between a musical task and a meaningful goal for the students. In addition, the use of student choice in the classroom must support student autonomy, not offer a selection between meaningless options. The following short list is a starting point for encouraging students' autonomy in the classroom:

1. Throughout the course of a class period, students can be invited to act upon the learning, influencing the direction it takes by asking questions that shape the outcomes. They can be encouraged to draw upon their own experiences, knowledge, and interests throughout each class period.
2. Students can participate in selecting musical content for study. The teacher can work with a group of students to look for musical content that considers the following questions: What musical challenge will this content offer the group? How can the group master this challenge and demonstrate achievement? What goals can the group set for learning this content? Will the group take pleasure in working with this content and meeting the goals?[10]
3. A group of students can assist in providing analysis of the group's progress toward musical goals. They can review video or audio recordings and offer self-evaluations that can be incorporated into the learning process.

WHAT CAN WE LEARN FROM THE STUDENTS ABOUT (DIS)ENGAGEMENT BEHAVIORS AND THE IMPORTANCE OF CRP?

It is important for music teachers to develop an awareness of the cultural norms influencing how students respond to their environment. Students choose their behaviors purposefully, if unconsciously. With a strong relationship in place between the students and the teacher, the teacher can view the students' disengaged behaviors as signals of boredom rather than a sign of a deficit. When teachers engage in deficit thinking, their logic is, "The students are disrespectful, and they do not want to learn. Therefore, the engagement problems in this classroom are theirs alone."

Ms. Beckman did not engage in this type of deficit thinking. She maintained a stance of curiosity regarding her students' disengagement but did not recognize that the level of challenge and interest in the curriculum were a source of disengagement. This book demonstrates the importance of CRP as a resource to accurately identify the sources of students' disengagement as well as the culturally normed behaviors indicating their disengagement.

Ms. Beckman demonstrated a sensitivity to students' culturally situated ways of interacting both verbally and nonverbally, as well as an awareness of variances in preferences for certain styles of learning. In her classroom, differing interpretations occurred around the notion of body comportment. This finding begs the question: Does a Culturally Relevant music teacher need to be comfortable expressing himself or herself physically through movement?

A hierarchy that values a more restrained emotional body comportment stems from historical systems and assumptions, whereby the culturally preferred styles of expression of some students are devalued, often by people who are unaware that they are doing so.[11] Music teachers can, if willing, expand their own culturally situated interactional and musical behaviors. Teachers and prospective teachers can intentionally seek out musical learning that expands their areas of comfort and expertise, learning to develop new perspectives, friendships, and ways to value multiple cultural norms for behavior, interaction, and music making. For example, a teacher with a low level of comfort with expressive movement can still model risk taking and the willingness to try new, possibly uncomfortable styles of movement. In this way, students will be encouraged to become risk takers as well.

CONCLUDING THOUGHTS

The students in Ms. Beckman's 7th-grade choir, interviewed for this study, desired Culturally Relevant teaching. They wanted a teacher who cared about them. This meant someone who was willing to listen to them, to keep them safe from ridicule, and who believed they were capable. But it also meant someone who pushed them to achieve even when they felt they could not. The students wanted an engaging curriculum that was relevant and interesting.

Maintaining the traditional view of music teachers as the sole crafters of instruction and reproducers of musical knowledge prevents teachers from inviting students to become coparticipants in their musical learning and thereby blocks many opportunities for deep engagement. When teachers develop CRP that involves the perspectives of their students, they can begin to work together with their students to develop musical contexts that move music education into a new place where cross-cultural classrooms showcase students' strengths in limitless areas of music making.

Take Action 9.1

With your teaching group, look back through chapter 9. Identify two goals that you want to work toward, based on the student perspectives in this book. Create a plan to reach these goals.

NOTES

1. Paul Gilroy, *Against Race: Imagining Political Culture Beyond the Color Line* (Cambridge, MA: The Belknap Press of Harvard University Press, 2000).

2. As a starting point, see Barbara J. Shade, Cynthia Kelly, and Mary Oberg, *Creating Culturally Responsive Classrooms* (Washington, DC: American Psychological Association, 1997). This book, a valuable resource for music teachers and music teacher educators, provides guidelines on ways for teachers and teachers-to-be to reflect cultural preferences, values, and ways of behaving in the classroom.

3. Rosa Hernández Sheets, "Urban Classroom Conflict: Student-Teacher Perception: Ethnic Integrity, Solidarity, and Resistance," *The Urban Review* 28, no. 2 (1996): 165–83.

4. Ruth Gurgel, "Building Strong Teacher-Student Relationships in Pluralistic Music Classrooms," *Music Educators Journal* 101, no. 4 (2015): 78. This article provides more detail on building strong cross-cultural relationships.

5. Rene Antrop-Gonzalez and Anthony De Jesus, "Toward a Theory of Critical Care in Urban Small School Reform: Examining Structures and Pedagogies of Caring in Two Latino Community-Based Schools," *International Journal of Qualitative Studies in Education* 19, no. 4 (2006): 424.

6. Gloria Ladson-Billings, *The Dreamkeepers: Successful Teachers of African American Children* (San Francisco, CA: Jossey-Bass, 1994); and Eric Toshalis, "The Rhetoric of Care: Preservice Teacher Discourses that Depoliticize, Deflect, and Deceive," *The Urban Review* 44, no. 1 (2012): 1–35.

7. Beverly J. Armento, "Principles of a Culturally Responsive Curriculum," in *Culturally Responsive Teaching: Lesson Planning for Elementary and Middle Grades*, ed. Jaqueline J. Irvine and Beverly J. Armento (Boston, MA: McGraw-Hill, 2001), 30.

8. These examples are only a small set of ideas. Music teachers around the world are implementing creative pedagogical practices based on their students' interests and experiences. See Ann C. Clements, *Alternative Approaches in Music Education: Case Studies from the Field* (Lanham, MD: Rowman & Littlefield, 2010) for more examples.

9. Johnmarshall Reeve, "A Self-Determination Theory Perspective on Student Engagement," in *Handbook of Research on Student Engagement*, ed. Sandra L. Christenson, Amy L. Reschly, and Cathy Wylie (New York: Springer, 2012), 149–72.

10. For additional ideas regarding including students in planning instruction, see Bernadette Scruggs, Patrick K. Freer, and David E. Myers, "Constructivist Practices to Increase Student Engagement in the Orchestra Classroom," *Music Educators Journal* 95, no. 4 (2009): 53–60.

11. Shernaz B. García and Patricia L. Guerra, "Deconstructing Deficit Thinking: Working with Educators to Create More Equitable Learning Environments," *Education and Urban Society* 36, no. 2 (2004): 150–68; and Ruth Gustafson, "Drifters and the Dancing Mad: The Public School Music Curriculum and the Fabrication of Boundaries for Participation," *Curriculum Inquiry* 38, no. 3 (2008): 267–97.

Appendix A

Research Questions

The following questions guided this research study:

1. What aspects of pedagogy do students perceive as factors contributing to (dis)engagement?[1]

    a. How do students' perceptions compare to their teacher's perceptions?

2. What behaviors do students report as signaling their cognitive and affective (dis)engagement?

    a. What meanings does the teacher attach to these behaviors?
    b. What meanings do the students attach to their classmates' behaviors?

3. What are the effects of (dis)engagement on teacher and student interactions, relationships, behaviors, and emotions?

4. How do the (dis)engagement perceptions held by the student and teacher participants align with CRP?

A set of assumptions underlies these questions:

1. The students I interviewed had elected to be in their 7th-grade choir class. The class itself was an elective, and the students stated in initial interviews that they were not compelled by their parents or other forces to choose choir class.

2. A high level of engagement over time in music classrooms will heighten students' desire to continue to seek out additional experiences in school

music. I base this assumption on research done in flow theory, engagement theory, and CRP. When a person participates in an activity that produces flow, he or she tends to seek out that activity again.[2] Activities that produce flow have multiple similarities with classroom learning tasks that produce engagement and that are categorized as Culturally Relevant, including learning activities that are intellectually challenging and interesting.[3]

3. While a teacher may teach with the intent to engage her students, the students' interpretations of their teacher's pedagogy will ultimately determine their level of engagement. These interpretations are filtered through cultural expectations as well as how the students perceive their relationship with the teacher.[4]

4. A high level of engagement among students in a music classroom is an underlying indicator of effective teaching.[5] Examining students' perceptions of conditions producing engagement, therefore, might serve as a means to open up an avenue of research into how pedagogy can be improved to better serve all students in music classrooms.

NOTES

1. In this book, the word "pedagogy" refers to the teacher's choices of curricular materials and the methods used to teach, as well as his or her attitudes and beliefs. It is, as Nieto describes, the "how" and "why" of teaching. Two different teachers may use similar methods, but differing beliefs and attitudes of the teachers may filter through those methods, resulting in very different outcomes for students (Sonia Nieto, "Lessons from Students on Creating a Chance to Dream," *Harvard Educational Review* 64, no. 4 [1994]: 392–426).

2. Mihaly Csikszentmihalyi, *Flow: The Psychology of Optimal Experience* (New York: Harper & Row, 1990).

3. Terrance M. Hubbard, "It's About More Than 'Just Be Consistent' or 'Out-Tough Them': Culturally Responsive Classroom Management" (PhD diss., Ohio State University–Columbus, 2005); Gloria Ladson-Billings, *The Dreamkeepers: Successful Teachers of African American Children* (San Francisco, CA: Jossey-Bass, 1994); Nieto, "Lessons."

4. Jacqueline J. Irvine, "The Critical Elements of Culturally Responsive Pedagogy: A Synthesis of the Research," in *Culturally Responsive Teaching: Lesson Planning for Elementary and Middle Grades*, ed. Jacqueline J. Irvine and Beverly J. Armento (Boston, MA: McGraw-Hill, 2001), 2–17.

5. Sandra L. Christenson, Amy L. Reschly, and Cathy Wylie, "Preface," in *Handbook of Research on Student Engagement*, ed. Sandra L. Christenson, Amy L. Reschly, and Cathy Wylie (New York: Springer, 2012), v–ix.

Appendix B

Methodology and Procedures

In this study, I examined the phenomenon of student engagement in a 7th-grade choir class. The purpose of this qualitative phenomenological study was to identify and compare students' and their teacher's perceptions of (dis)engagement in a 7th-grade, racially diverse, middle school choir class. Phenomenological research seeks to foreground the experiences of individuals from their own perspectives, with the possible outcome of challenging the structural or normative assumptions usually associated with a particular phenomenon.[1]

In studying students' perspectives on engagement, I was guided by the phenomenological principles of minimum structure and maximum depth.[2] Due to the focus on students' perceptions of (dis)engagement, a phenomenological standpoint is appropriate, given that "one of the goals of phenomenology is to allow the participants to define the issues that are salient to them with regard to their lived experiences."[3] This appendix will explain the methodology used for data collection and analysis in this study, tracing the path from my research questions to my analytical procedures.

INTERVIEWING PROCEDURES FOR
INDIVIDUAL STUDENT INTERVIEWS

When school began at Clark Middle School in September 2010, I distributed consent forms in both English and Spanish to all 67 members of Alicia Beckman's two 7th-grade classes and received student and parental consent forms from eight students in one of the classes. Since those eight students represented an approximately proportional sample of racial diversity represented within the school, I formalized this group of students as the research participants and began conducting interviews, beginning in October 2010.

The purpose of the individual interviews with students was to understand their perspectives on engagement and classroom practices consistent with CRP.[4] Because the establishment of rapport and empathy is key in gathering a depth of information, especially when participants have a strong personal stake in the issues they are asked about,[5] I included a portion during the initial interviews in which I asked students to tell me about their home lives, their experiences with music outside of school, their families, and their hobbies. I asked them to describe their history with school music as well as other aspects of their schooling in order to gain a background for further discussions.

The students' individual interviews took place immediately following their choir class, during their lunch hour, and lasted for approximately 25 minutes each. The students brought their lunches to their interviews, and we were able to use the choir classroom as no other classes were taking place and the teacher was supervising a study hall in another location in the school. I interviewed students on a rotating schedule. When I finished one round of interviews, I started another round, proceeding in the same order. There were times when I did have to adjust the order of students interviewed, because a student I had planned to interview was absent. I continued through three rotations of interviews and chose to conclude the interviews in May 2011 because the themes the students discussed were beginning to repeat in the interviews, and I felt that saturation of data had been reached.

To address the first three research questions of this study, I designed some of the interview questions to ascertain which aspects of CRP they experienced in music class and how these aspects affected their engagement levels in class. In all three interviews with students, I asked questions that were related to the events in the class period the student had just taken part in or class periods from the week before. My goal was to elicit discussion from the students about how their engagement levels were influenced (or not) by interactions, relationships, and events that took place in their music class. I sought to allow the interview to unfold as a conversation about a class period that had just taken place and encouraged the students to discuss events that were salient to them and their experiences with engagement. I listened to the students and then asked clarifying questions based on events and ideas that the students talked about.

The fourth research question of this study asks: How do the students and teacher participants' perceptions of engagement align with CRP? To examine this alignment, I used the following questions based on the theory of CRP as a guide when starting an interview or focus group session. I also used them when formulating clarifying questions during discussions with the students and with the teacher.

1. Do the students and the teacher feel they are achieving excellence in the field of music? Ladson-Billings (1994, 1995a, 1995b) describes Culturally

Relevant classrooms as setting high standards and providing the means for students to achieve excellence.

2. Do the students feel they are able to work collaboratively with the teacher and their peers, or do they feel a spirit of individualized competition? Does this matter to them? CRP encourages collaborative work as opposed to individual competitiveness in classrooms.

3. Do the students and their teacher feel that the pedagogy and the classroom interactions acknowledge students' voices and allow them to be creative contributors to the classroom? Or do they feel that their interests, experiences, and knowledge are not represented? CRP encourages teachers to view their students as individuals with funds of valuable knowledge and experiences that can add to the classroom learning instead of being viewed by the teacher as empty vessels to be filled.

4. What are students' perceptions about how the teacher views them? Culturally Relevant teachers view themselves as colearners with their students and do not attempt to exert complete control over students. These teachers also seek to get to know each student instead of only focusing on those deemed "talented."

5. How do students view the curriculum used in the music classroom in light of cultural competence? CRP encourages students to become competent in multiple cultures, not just the dominant culture.

6. Do the students feel that the curriculum reflects issues that are important to them? Do the students feel that the music classes encourage them to voice their ideas and feelings about these issues? CRP gives students ways to name and respond to the social and political nature of their worlds.

The individual interviews of both the students and the teacher were audiotaped during this research. These audio recordings were used to create verbatim transcriptions, which participants reviewed for clarity and to make any corrections they deemed important. Only one student offered a correction, and that pertained to a change in the number of siblings he had—his mom had given birth since the initial interview had taken place.

PROCEDURES FOR FOCUS GROUPS

I divided the eight students I interviewed individually into two focus groups of four, with two males and two females in each. Each group met with me twice during the course of the 2010–2011 school year, once during the fall and once during the spring. Each focus group session was held in the choir room and lasted approximately 30 minutes. I provided pizza for the students since the sessions were held over their lunch period. The purpose of the focus group sessions was to elicit students' collective perceptions of remembered common events (the music classes) as they related to engagement and CRP. I used a semistructured format for the focus group sessions during which I presented the students with descriptions or videos of events from the choir classes in which they had all participated and I encouraged students to interpret those events as they saw them.

In addition, the students and I viewed videos of other school choir groups (available on YouTube) and discussed various aspects of these groups' performances. I chose videos of choral groups that I felt demonstrated varying levels of engagement behaviors that the students discussed in their individual interviews. My intention was to provide additional ways in which students could discuss what deep engagement in a music class looked like and felt like for them. The focus group data proved to be a source of rich detail of the experiences of students, providing a unique view of students' perceptions of engagement in music classrooms.

In conducting both individual interviews and focus group sessions, I sought to recognize several important factors. First, individual interviews serve to gain valuable individual perspectives and interpretations of classroom interactions and community happenings. However, certain themes that are important to students might not emerge in a one-on-one conversation because such conversations are affected by the identities of the coparticipants;[6] therefore, I sought to provide a space for collective discussions surrounding themes that were important to the students regarding engagement. I also hoped to create spaces where students could collectively make sense of their experiences. Madriz offers a similar view about conducting focus groups with women:

> The shared dialogues, stories, and knowledge generated by the group interview have the potential to help such women to develop a sense of identity, self-validation, bonding, and commonality of experiences. Focus groups tend to create environments in which participants feel open to telling their stories and to giving their testimonies in front of other women like themselves.[7]

As the researcher figure, I strove to create the type of environment described by Madriz by stepping back as much as possible in order for students to converse with each other naturally.

INTERVIEWING PROCEDURES FOR INDIVIDUAL INTERVIEWS WITH MS. BECKMAN

I formally interviewed Ms. Beckman two times over the course of the school year. Ms. Beckman and I also had many informal, open-ended conversations before or after class periods. I often took field notes from these short informal conversations that also became part of the data. The purpose of the two formal interviews was to elicit her perceptions of classroom events and to compare her perceptions to CRP. During the formal interviews, my goals were to understand her perceptions regarding factors influencing students' engagement in the classroom, students' engagement behaviors in class, and the effects students' (dis)engagement had on her. To provide a springboard for these topics, I presented Ms. Beckman with an incident from class or a perception held by one of her students, which we would then discuss.

To learn about her background of music and teaching, I began the first formal interview by asking Ms. Beckman to talk about her path to becoming a music teacher; her childhood experiences with her family; her goals as a teacher; and her thoughts about her work, her students, and music in general. This portion of the interview was also important to understanding Ms. Beckman's beliefs regarding social relations, knowledge, and herself as a teacher. Thus, these portions of Ms. Beckman's interviews related to the fourth research question of this study, which asks: How do the students and teacher participants' perceptions of engagement align with CRP? To that end, the semistructured questions in Ms. Beckman's interviews were also designed to elicit descriptions of how she constructed her lessons as well as ideologies informing her practice.

CLASSROOM OBSERVATIONS AND VIDEOTAPING

I observed, took field notes, and videotaped classroom sessions the research participants took part in as a way to provide a reference point to the classroom happenings they spoke about as we discussed their perspectives on engagement. The observations took place over eight months (from October 2010 to May 2011), the same period of time during which I conducted interviews. During those eight months, I observed one section of 7th-grade choir, twice weekly, for 50 minutes at a time. During classroom observations, I took field notes but did not interact with the teacher or the students. I was introduced to the class as a researcher. To the greatest extent possible, I sat behind the students or off to the side of the classroom.

The teacher was the only one captured visually on videotape, as per district protocol, and I turned the camera off if students moved around the classroom in such a way that capturing them on tape was unavoidable. None of the videotaping (intentionally) altered the choir experience for the students. They were not asked to change seats or alter their participation. The videotape captured classroom interactions, sequences of instruction, and student participation (aurally if not visually). I reviewed the videotapes to transcribe dialogues and to create more detailed field notes. The classroom observations did not serve as data but as a reference point to provide me with an understanding of classroom events students discussed in their interviews.

In addition, I attended the concert this class gave with their 7th-grade counterparts in band and orchestra in January 2011 and viewed the videotape of their concert in May the same year. In their interviews the students discussed moments of (dis)engagement during these concerts, and my familiarity with the events of these concerts provided a context for discussions during interviews regarding these moments.

DATA MANAGEMENT AND MINIMIZING RISK FOR PARTICIPANTS

I employed multiple techniques to identify and minimize risks to the students and the teacher who participated in this research. All data transcription and analysis was done in my home office, from my home computer, which was secured with a password. Audio recordings of interviews were kept on that computer and DVDs of video data were kept in a locked office. Copies of the data were also kept on a locked hard drive. I used the student-chosen pseudonyms when I created the transcriptions. Any reference to another student in class was also changed to a pseudonym. When I presented Ms. Beckman with a student comment from an interview or focus group session for her analysis, I did not even use a pseudonym but kept such remarks anonymous.

In conducting focus group sessions, I encouraged students to respect each other's privacy and sought to lower risk in this way. I informed the students that they were free to stop participating in the interviews, the focus group sessions, or the research as a whole at any time with no consequences. I also informed them that they were free to refuse to answer a question at any time. I did this to reduce the chance that students might publicly reveal comments made in a focus group session by another student, thus producing embarrassment or worries over how a comment would affect their report card evaluation by Ms. Beckman.

There were many risks to Ms. Beckman in this study. To agree to allow a researcher access to her students, especially when this involved the possibility of critique from them, is daunting to any person who prides herself on her work. Ms. Beckman not only agreed to allow me to talk with her students, to interview her, and to videotape her class sessions but expressed her belief that this research would result in important findings for the field of music education. Ms. Beckman continued to reinforce this belief throughout the research process by engaging in discussions with me and continuing to provide me with access to any information that we both felt would be useful.

ANALYSIS OF DATA

I began transcribing, coding, and creating memos as soon as I began interviewing students at the beginning of the school year (October). My analysis procedures involved "constant comparison" of data and further data collection until I felt I had reached a point of saturation, or had collected enough data to provide rich descriptions of the research participants' perceptions of classroom engagement in choir class.[8]

RESEARCHER'S ROLE AND ASSUMPTIONS

In formulating my analysis, I recognized that even the act of choosing what counts as data is influenced by my interpretations. I further recognized that the choices I made when labeling categories and organizing themes arose from the *interpretations* I made of data rather than from the data as an object. Charmaz advised researchers to examine their own situated-ness in this way, stating,

> [W]hat observers see and hear depends upon their prior interpretive frames, biographies, and interests as well as the research context, their relationships with research participants, concrete field experiences, and modes of generating and recording empirical materials. No qualitative method rests on pure induction—the questions we ask of the empirical world frame what we know of it.[9]

I came at this research from my own ways of viewing the world and knew it would be important to continue to identify my own perspectives and assumptions as I asked the research participants to share their unique perspectives with me. I understood the issues of interpretation that could result when examining the perspectives of those with vantage points and discourses that differed from my own. To that end, I strove to become reflexive in examining how my interpretive frames of reference influenced how I both gathered and analyzed data.

An important frame of reference that influenced my perspectives is my participation in the realm of practicing teachers. I have taught in seven schools, and my participation in the teaching and learning community deeply shaped my approach to the research site at Clark Middle School. I chose a teacher to work with whom I deeply respected and who had as many years of experience in the classroom as I did because I did not want my role to become that of mentor or teacher-assistant in the classroom.

I knew that my experience as a music teacher provided a vantage point for the themes in the data, and I strove to be aware that students were most likely coming to the questions I asked from a vantage point I was unfamiliar with. As I transcribed the interviews, I became aware that there were times when I thought a student was saying one thing, but upon closer listening, they were leading to another thing altogether. Fortunately, I had multiple attempts at conversations with the students, and was able to revisit topics with them. I also employed several self-reflexive processes during analysis that assisted me as I strove to faithfully report what the students and teacher perceived and as I reflected on those in light of CRP. These processes are described in the following sections.

CODING AND QUESTIONING

In coding and analyzing the data, I primarily used analysis strategies derived from grounded theory.[10] I found this to be an important resource for defining starting points within the large amount of data with which I was working. My goal was not to generate theory, which is what many grounded theorists generally do, but I found that the tools of grounded theory analysis assisted me in both identifying the thematic strands that were important to the research participants and managing the large amounts of data I gathered over time.

As I began coding for concepts, I searched for the properties and dimensions of particular categories that I believed emerged from the data. For example, when students discussed songs in choir class that they "liked" and singing a song they liked produced a certain level of engagement, I searched for their descriptions of what qualities or properties these songs had. The students described their favorite songs as "connecting" to them and containing particular facets of rhythm/beat and lyrics, which combined to produce positive responses from the students. The dimensions of a song's rhythm/beat ranged for students from "slow" (and this was not a reference to tempo, but rather to a combination of instruments and groove) to "jumpy" (containing an energizing quality promoting interest, excitement, and connection in the students). As in this example, I searched for the dimensions and properties of larger categories that mattered to the participants to establish the links between smaller concepts.

OPEN CODING

Open coding was my first step in identifying concepts in the data. As Strauss and Corbin stated, "To uncover, name and develop concepts, we must open up the text and expose the thoughts, ideas, and meanings contained therein."[11] For me, this involved breaking down the data and labeling the concepts that

I felt were important to the research participants' perceptions of engagement. I remained cognizant of how my own interpretations would inevitably influence what I saw or found as a "meaning" or an important concept. Because of this, I did not attempt to limit my concept identification at first. Only after labeling concepts in all the interviews and field notes did I identify those that I felt emerged as more important.

AXIAL CODING

Once categories began to emerge, I coded intensely around these categories (axial coding). "The purpose of axial coding is to begin the process of reassembling data that were fractured during open coding."[12] In this stage, I began to look for dimensions and properties of the categories that emerged. For example, "good singing" emerged as a theme for students as something that was a result of engagement. The process of axial coding also led to the processes of memoing and diagramming.

MEMOING

Memoing can take many forms in research and data analysis. In this research, it consisted of notes written during the data collection phase and during analysis. These notes assisted me in recording reflective thoughts that I wanted to remember. They also provided a way to become reflexive about how I was labeling the concepts and forming categories.[13]

With the amount of data I had obtained and the themes that I felt were emerging, I could not rely on memory to provide me with the means to formulate an analysis. Memos served as a way to trace my own thinking as I coded, searched the literature, and reflected on my own positioning. I wrote memos during open and axial coding (code notes), during my reading of the literature and thinking about the data (theoretical notes), and as basic reminders to myself of points or concepts I wanted to revisit (operational notes). As I began collecting and organizing memos, I found that they were indispensable in shaping the writing of the final analysis chapters.

DIAGRAMMING

I used diagrams to create visual frameworks of concepts, categories, and their relationships. They varied in form and were in a constant state of flux. These diagrams provided me with visual representations of outlines, themes, and larger categories. These often began as "movable" diagrams, where I had concepts and categories printed out on small paper rectangles that I could move around on larger charts. As I continued to code and analyze, these movable diagrams provided a way for me to explore how the concepts were relating to each other and which concepts were key in examining perceptions of engagement.

TRUSTWORTHINESS

In collecting and analyzing data, I sought to faithfully report what the teacher and the students were telling me regarding their perspectives. I sought to be self-reflexive and systematic about how I compared their perspectives to CRP. As Kincheloe and McLaren have suggested, qualitative researchers in the social sciences must abandon traditional notions of triangulation in pursuit of validity. Objects (or subjects) of study in this field "are far too mercurial to be viewed by a single way of seeing or as a snapshot of a particular phenomenon at a specific moment in time."[14]

Kincheloe and McLaren posited that researchers who are unaware of the processual nature of qualitative research are in danger of producing knowledge that becomes reductionistic.[15] They described the work of a qualitative researcher as "watching the world flow by like a river in which the exact contents of the water are never the same."[16] To that end, I kept in mind that my reporting of the interview data I was gathering was inevitably a result of my own interpretations, and I continued to seek to be true to the words and perspectives of the participants.

I sought to spend enough time at the research site and in conducting interviews to ensure that I gathered a sufficient amount of data to reach saturation of the topics and themes that I believe emerged. More than 340 pages of single-spaced transcriptions resulting from the interviews and focus group sessions served as the primary data sources for this study. I felt that this amount of data provided "counterpatterns as well as convergences"[17] in examining perceptions of classroom events surrounding engagement. As I began to locate themes in the data, I continued to search for theories related to what I saw emerging. I included work from the field of music education, CRP, and literature on classroom engagement theory.

According to Lather, the researcher must demonstrate systematic self-reflexivity, so as to resist molding data to fit preexisting, a priori theory without considering data that provides "counterpatterns."[18] Similarly, Charmaz asked, "Has the researcher revealed liminal and taken-for-granted meanings?"[19] Within my study, I attempted to become self-reflexive about my taken-for-granted meanings within a music classroom. I continued to ask: Could what appeared at first as a counterpattern within the data instead be a construct that was new to my own paradigms? For me, this process involved alternating between themes emerging in the data and the literature that spoke to those themes (and also ran counter to those themes).

Lather described one form of trustworthiness as "face validity."[20] Face validity results from recycling beginning attempts at analysis back through the respondents to gain their thoughts and reactions in order to refine future analysis. Charmaz described this form of validity as the "resonance" of a study. She asked, "Do the analytic interpretations make sense to members and offer them deeper insights about their lives and worlds?"[21]

For me, this meant discussing themes that I believed were emerging in the data with the teacher and the students both individually and in focus groups. For example, I began to ask students for descriptions and examples of what "being strict" as a teacher, a category I felt was emerging, meant for them. A researcher could understand this phrase in many ways, and I had my own preconceived notions of what a "strict teacher" was. The students clarified that they wanted a teacher who was "strict" in the sense that she was consistent with expectations and consequences, meant business in regard to learning, held high standards, and was organized. A "strict" teacher, however, was neither "mean" nor "unfair" and could still have fun, learn from the students, and listen to what the students had to say. In a similar way, I also continued to seek feedback from the teacher during the analytical process.

SUMMARY OF THE DATA COLLECTION AND ANALYSIS

This appendix provides a description of the approach to data collection used in this phenomenological study and the analytical procedures of coding, questioning, memoing, and diagramming. I employed the methodology described in this appendix with the purpose of presenting a written analysis of the research participants' perceptions of engagement in a racially diverse choir classroom. In analyzing the data, my goal was not to provide a complete picture or theory of student engagement in music class. I recognized that the themes and concepts that emerged were always filtered through my lens as the researcher. There may very well be nuances, categories, or interpretations that are underexplored in this study and from which further study may spring. The themes and concepts that emerged from my interpretation of events may exist and emerge in some form in other classrooms as well and provide a starting point for further research on the engagement of students.

WHAT ARE THE LIMITATIONS OF THIS BOOK?

In this study, I examined the interpretations eight students and one teacher made of classroom events in a classroom setting. Because of the nature of qualitative studies, the first limitation of this study is that it is not generalizable. In this 7th-grade choir class, Ms. Beckman and her students had constructed a learning environment and context that was based on her curriculum and pedagogy and on their unique relationships and interactions with each other. I did not seek to generalize the students' experiences based on racial categories. Each participant offered a unique perspective. However, I did seek to open an avenue to explore how cultural characteristics affect what (dis)engagement looks and feels like for students and how teachers may view their students' demonstrations of (dis)engagement in the classroom.[22] I hope that this book inspires further research that garners student perspectives.

NOTES

1. Stan Lester, *An Introduction to Phenomenological Research*, from Stan Lester Developments (1999), www.sld.demon.co.uk/resmethy.pdf.

2. Ibid.

3. Greg Wiggan, "From Opposition to Engagement: Lessons from High Achieving African American Students," *The Urban Review* 40, no. 4 (2007): 322.

4. See Appendix A for interview questions.

5. Lester, *Introduction*.

6. Andrea Fontana and James H. Frey, "The Interview: From Structured Questions to Negotiated Text," in *Collecting and Interpreting Qualitative Materials*, 2nd ed., ed. Norman K. Denzin and Yvonna S. Lincoln (Thousand Oaks, CA: SAGE Publications, 2003), 62.

7. Esther Madriz, "Focus Groups in Feminist Research," in *Collecting and Interpreting Qualitative Materials*, 2nd ed., ed. Norman K. Denzin and Yvonna S. Lincoln (Thousand Oaks, CA: SAGE Publications, 2003), 383.

8. Anselm Strauss and Juliet Corbin, *Basics of Qualitative Research: Techniques and Procedures for Developing Grounded Theory*, 2nd ed. (Thousand Oaks, CA: SAGE Publications, 1988).

9. Kathy Charmaz, "Grounded Theory in the 21st Century," in *The SAGE Handbook of Qualitative Research*, ed. Norman K. Denzin and Yvonna S. Lincoln, 3rd ed. (Thousand Oaks, CA: SAGE Publications, 2005), 507–35; Strauss and Corbin, *Basics of Qualitative Research*, 509.

10. Strauss and Corbin, *Basics of Qualitative Research*.

11. Ibid., 102.

12. Ibid., 124.

13. Strauss and Corbin, *Basics of Qualitative Research*.

14. Joe L. Kincheloe and Peter McLaren, "Rethinking Critical Theory and Qualitative Research," in *The Sage Handbook of Qualitative Research*, 3rd ed., ed. Norman K. Denzin and Yvonna S. Lincoln (Thousand Oaks, CA: SAGE Publications, 2005), 320.

15. Ibid., 320.

16. Ibid., 319.

17. Patti Lather, "Issues of Validity in Openly Ideological Research: Between a Rock and a Soft Place," *Interchange* 17, no. 4 (1986): 67.

18. Ibid.

19. Charmaz, "Grounded Theory," 528.

20. Lather, "Issues."

21. Charmaz, "Grounded Theory," 528.

22. While assigning a racial term as an identification seems fairly simplistic, I remind the reader that racial identities are extremely complex.

Bibliography

Antrop-Gonzalez, Rene, and Anthony De Jesus. "Toward a Theory of Critical Care in Urban Small School Reform: Examining Structures and Pedagogies of Caring in Two Latino Community-Based Schools." *International Journal of Qualitative Studies in Education* 19, no. 4 (2006): 409–33.

Apple, Michael W. *Official Knowledge*, 2nd ed. New York: Routledge, 2000.

Armento, Beverly J. "Principles of a Culturally Responsive Curriculum." In *Culturally Responsive Teaching: Lesson Planning for Elementary and Middle Grades*, edited by Jaqueline J. Irvine and Beverly J. Armento, 19–33. Boston, MA: McGraw-Hill, 2001.

Arroyo, Carmen G., and Edward Zigler. "Racial Identity, Academic Achievement, and the Psychological Well-Being of Economically Disadvantaged Adolescents." *Journal of Personality and Social Psychology* 69, no. 5 (1995): 903–14.

Au, Kathryn H., and Alice J. Kawakami. "Cultural Congruence in Instruction." In *Teaching Diverse Populations: Formulating a Knowledge Base*, edited by Etta R. Hollins, Joyce E. King, and Warren C. Hayman, 5–24. Albany: State University of New York Press, 1994.

Austin, James R. "Competition: Is Music Education the Loser?" *Music Educators Journal* 76, no. 6 (1990): 21–25.

Banks, James A. "Approaches to Multicultural Curriculum Reform." In *Multicultural Education: Issues and Perspectives*, 3rd ed., edited by James A. Banks and Cherry A. McGee Banks, 229–50. Boston, MA: Allyn & Bacon, 1997.

Barsade, Sigal G. "The Ripple Effect: Emotional Contagion and Its Influence on Group Behavior." *Administrative Science Quarterly* 47, no. 4 (2002): 644–75.

Bell, Derrick A. "White Superiority in America: Its Legal Legacy, Its Economic Costs." *Villanova Law Review* 33 (1988): 767–79.

Bingham, Gary E., and Lynn Okagaki. "Ethnicity and Student Engagement." In *Handbook of Research on Student Engagement*, edited by Sandra L. Christenson, Amy L. Reschly, and Cathy Wylie, 65–95. New York: Springer, 2012.

Bonilla-Silva, Eduardo, and David Dietrich. "The Sweet Enchantment of Color-Blind Racism in Obamerica." *The ANNALS of the American Academy of Political and Social Science* 634 (2011): 190–206.

Boykin, A. Wade. "Afrocultural Expression and Its Implications for Schooling." In *Teaching Diverse Populations: Formulating a Knowledge Base*, edited by Etta R. Hollins, Joyce E. King, and Warren C. Hayman, 243–73. Albany: State University of New York Press, 1994.

Britzman, Deborah P. *Practice Makes Practice: A Critical Study of Learning to Teach*, rev. ed. Albany: State University of New York Press, 2003.

Butler, Abby, Vicki R. Lind, and Constance L. McKoy. "Equity and Access in Music Education: Conceptualizing Culture as Barriers to and Supports for Music Learning." *Music Education Research* 9, no. 2 (2007): 241–53.

Charmaz, Kathy. "Grounded Theory in the 21st Century." In *The SAGE Handbook of Qualitative Research*, edited by Norman K. Denzin and Yvonna S. Lincoln, 3rd ed., 507–35. Thousand Oaks, CA: SAGE Publications, 2005.

Choate, Robert A., ed. "Pop Music Panel." In *Music in American Society: Documentary Report of the Tanglewood Symposium*, 104–108. Washington, DC: Music Educators National Conference, 1968.

Christenson, Sandra L., Amy L. Reschly, and Cathy Wylie. "Preface." In *Handbook of Research on Student Engagement*, edited by Sandra L. Christenson, Amy L. Reschly, and Cathy Wylie, v–ix. New York: Springer, 2012.

Clements, Ann C. *Alternative Approaches in Music Education: Case Studies from the Field*. Lanham, MD: Rowman & Littlefield, 2010.

Creswell, John W. *Qualitative Inquiry and Research Design*, 2nd ed. Thousand Oaks, CA: SAGE Publications, 2007.

Crotty, Michael. *The Foundations of Social Research: Meaning and Perspective in the Research Process*. London: SAGE Publications, 2003.

Csikszentmihalyi, Mihaly. *Flow: The Psychology of Optimal Experience*. New York: Harper & Row, 1990.

Csikszentmihalyi, Mihaly, and Isabella Csikszentmihalyi, eds. *Optimal Experience: Psychologic Studies of Flow in Consciousness*. Cambridge, MA: Cambridge University Press, 1988.

Deakin Crick, Ruth. "Deep Engagement as a Complex System: Identity, Learning Power and Authentic Enquiry." In *Handbook of Research on Student Engagement*, edited by Sandra L. Christenson, Amy L. Reschly, and Cathy Wylie, 675–94. New York: Springer, 2012.

Delgado, Richard, ed. *Critical Race Theory: The Cutting Edge*. Philadelphia: Temple University Press, 1995.

Derman-Sparks, Louise, and Patricia Ramsey. *What if All the Kids Are White? Anti-Bias Multicultural Education with Young Children and Families*. New York: Teachers College Press, 2011.

Dixson, Adrienne D., and Celia K. Rousseau. "And We Are Still Not Saved: Critical Race Theory in Education Ten Years Later." *Race Ethnicity and Education* 8, no. 1 (2005): 7–27.

Elliott, David. *Music Matters: A New Philosophy of Music Education*. New York: Oxford University Press: 1995.

Elpus, Kenneth, and Carlos R. Abril. "High School Music Ensemble Students in the United States: A Demographic Profile." *Journal of Research in Music Education* 59, no. 2 (2011): 128–45.

Ennis, Catherine D. "Teachers' Responses to Noncompliant Students: The Realities and Consequences of a Negotiated Curriculum." *Teaching and Teacher Education* 11 (1995): 445–60.

Finn, Jeremy D., and Kayla S. Zimmer. "Student Engagement: What Is It? Why Does It Matter?" In *Handbook of Research on Student Engagement*, edited by Sandra L. Christenson, Amy L. Reschly, and Cathy Wylie, 97–131. New York: Springer, 2012.

Fontana, Andrea, and James H. Frey. "The Interview: From Structured Questions to Negotiated Text." In *Collecting and Interpreting Qualitative Materials*, 2nd ed., edited by Norman K. Denzin and Yvonna S. Lincoln, 61–106. Thousand Oaks, CA: SAGE Publications, 2003.

Foster, Michele. "Effective Black Teachers: A Literature Review." In *Teaching Diverse Populations: Formulating a Knowledge Base*, edited by Etta R. Hollins, Joyce E. King, and Warren C. Hayman, 225–42. Albany: State University of New York Press, 1994.

Fredricks, Jennifer A. "Engagement in School and Out-of-School Contexts: A Multidimensional View of Engagement." *Theory Into Practice* 50, no. 4 (2011): 327–35.

Fredricks, Jennifer A., Phyllis C. Blumenfeld, and Alison H. Paris. "School Engagement: Potential of the Concept, State of the Evidence." *Review of Educational Research* 74, no. 1 (2004): 59–109.

García, Shernaz B., and Patricia L. Guerra. "Deconstructing Deficit Thinking: Working with Educators to Create More Equitable Learning Environments." *Education and Urban Society* 36, no. 2 (2004): 150–68.

Gilroy, Paul. *Against Race: Imagining Political Culture Beyond the Color Line.* Cambridge, MA: The Belknap Press of Harvard University Press, 2000.

Gudykunst, William B., and Young Yun Kim. *Communicating with Strangers*, 2nd ed. New York: McGraw-Hill, 1992.

Gurgel, Ruth. "Building Strong Teacher-Student Relationships in Pluralistic Music Classrooms." *Music Educators Journal* 101, no. 4 (2015): 77–84.

Gustafson, Ruth. "Drifters and the Dancing Mad: The Public School Music Curriculum and the Fabrication of Boundaries for Participation." *Curriculum Inquiry* 38, no. 3 (2008): 267–97.

Howard, Tyrone C. "Hearing Footsteps in the Dark: African American Students' Descriptions of Effective Teachers." *Journal of Education for Students Placed at Risk* 7, no. 4 (2002): 425–44.

Hubbard, Terrance M. "It's About More Than 'Just Be Consistent' or 'Out-Tough-Them': Culturally Responsive Classroom Management." PhD diss., Ohio State University–Columbus, 2005.

Irvine, Jaqueline J. *Black Students and School Failure: Policies, Practices, and Prescriptions.* New York: Praeger, 1990.

Irvine, Jaqueline J. "The Critical Elements of Culturally Responsive Pedagogy: A Synthesis of the Research." In *Culturally Responsive Teaching: Lesson Planning for Elementary and Middle Grades*, edited by Jaqueline J. Irvine and Beverly J. Armento, 2–17. Boston, MA: McGraw-Hill, 2001.

Irvine, Jaqueline J. *Educating Teachers for Diversity: Seeing with a Cultural Eye.* New York: Teachers College Press, 2003.

Janata, Petr, Stefan T. Tomic, and Jason M. Haberman. "Sensorimotor Coupling in Music and the Psychology of the Groove." *Journal of Experimental Psychology: General* 41, no. 1 (2011): 54–75.

Jang, Hyungshim, Johnmarshall Reeve, and Edward Deci. "Engaging Students in Learning Activities: It Is Not Autonomy Support or Structure but Autonomy Support and Structure." *Journal of Educational Psychology* 102, no. 3 (2010): 588–600.

Kincheloe, Joe L., and Peter McLaren. "Rethinking Critical Theory and Qualitative Research." In *The SAGE Handbook of Qualitative Research*, 3rd ed., edited by Norman K. Denzin and Yvonna S. Lincoln, 303–42. Thousand Oaks, CA: SAGE Publications, 2005.

King, Joyce E. "The Purpose of Schooling for African American Children: Including Cultural Knowledge." In *Teaching Diverse Populations: Formulating a Knowledge Base*, edited by Etta R. Hollins, Joyce E. King, and Warren C. Hayman, 25–56. Albany: State University of New York Press, 1994.

Kohn, Alfie. *No Contest: The Case Against Competition*, rev. ed. Boston, MA: Houghton Mifflin, 1992.

Kunter, Mareike, Anne Frenzel, Gabriel Nagy, Jurgen Baumert, and Reinhard Pekrun. "Teacher Enthusiasm: Dimensionality and Context Specificity." *Contemporary Educational Psychology* 36, no. 4 (2011): 289–301.

Ladson-Billings, Gloria. *The Dreamkeepers: Successful Teachers of African American Children*. San Francisco, CA: Jossey-Bass, 1994.

Ladson-Billings, Gloria. "But That's Just Good Teaching! The Case for Culturally Relevant Pedagogy." *Theory into Practice* 34, no. 3 (1995a): 159–65.

Ladson-Billings, Gloria. "Toward a Theory of Culturally Relevant Pedagogy." *American Educational Research Journal* 32, no. 3 (1995b): 465–91.

Ladson-Billings, Gloria. "It's Not the Culture of Poverty, It's the Poverty of Culture: The Problem with Teacher Education." *Anthropology and Education Quarterly* 37, no. 2 (2006): 104–09.

Ladson-Billings, Gloria, and Jamel Donner. "The Moral Activist Role of Critical Race Theory Scholarship." In *The SAGE Handbook of Qualitative Research*, edited by Norman K. Denzin and Yvonna S. Lincoln, 3rd ed., 279–302. Thousand Oaks, CA: SAGE Publications, 2005.

Ladson-Billings, Gloria, and William Tate. "Toward a Critical Race Theory of Education." *Teachers College Record* 97 (1995): 47–68.

Lake City School District. *District Demographics*, 2008. Retrieved May 27, 2009, from the World Wide Web, Lake City School District (2008).

Lake City School District. *District Enrollment*, 2011. Retrieved June 4, 2012, from the World Wide Web.

Lather, Patti. "Issues of Validity in Openly Ideological Research: Between a Rock and a Soft Place." *Interchange* 17, no. 4 (1986): 63–84.

Lester, Stan. *An Introduction to Phenomenological Research*. From Stan Lester Developments (1999), www.sld.demon.co.uk/resmethy.pdf.

Lewis, Jeffrey L., and Eunhee Kim. "A Desire to Learn: African American Children's Positive Attitudes Toward Learning Within School Cultures of Low Expectations." *Teachers College Record* 110, no. 6 (2008): 1304–29.

Lind, Vicki R. "Classroom Environment and Hispanic Enrollment in Secondary Choral Music Programs." *Contributions to Music Education* 26, no. 2 (1999): 64–77.

Lind, Vicki R., and Abby Butler. "The Relationship Between African American Enrollment and the Classroom Environment in Secondary Choral Music Programs." In *The Phenomenon of Singing*, 105–10. St. John's Newfoundland, Canada: Memorial University, 2005.

Lundquist, Barbara R. "Music, Culture, Curriculum, and Instruction." In *New Handbook of Research on Music Teaching and Learning*, edited by Richard Colwell and Carol Richardson, 626–47. New York: Oxford University Press, 2002.

Lundquist, Barbara Reeder, and Winston T. Sims. "African-American Music Education: Reflections on an Experience." *Black Music Research Journal* 16, no. 2 (1996): 311–36.

Madriz, Esther. "Focus Groups in Feminist Research." In *Collecting and Interpreting Qualitative Materials*, 2nd ed., edited by Norman K. Denzin and Yvonna S. Lincoln, 363–88. Thousand Oaks, CA: SAGE Publications, 2003.

Marlaire, Courtney L., and Douglas W. Maynard. "Standardized Testing as an Interactional Phenomenon." *Sociology of Education* 63, no. 2 (1990): 83–101.

McCoy, Travie, Philip Lawrence, Bruno Mars, and Ari Levine. "Billionaire." Edited by Mark Brymer. New York: Hal Leonard, 2010, sheet music.

McIntosh, Peggy. "White Privilege: Unpacking the Invisible Knapsack." *Independent School* (Winter 1990): 31–36.

McMahon, Brenda, and John P. Portelli. *Student Engagement in Urban Schools: Beyond Neoliberal Discourses*. Charlotte, NC: Information Age Publishing, 2012.

Mehan, Hugh. "The Structure of Classroom Discourse." In *Handbook of Discourse Analysis*, vol. 3, edited by Teun A. van Dijk, 119–31. London: Academic Press, 1985.

Milner, H. Richard, and Anita Woolfolk Hoy. "A Case Study of an African American Teacher's Self-Efficacy, Stereotype Threat, and Persistence." *Teaching and Teacher Education* 19 (2003): 263–76.

Neumann, Roland, and Fritz Strack. "'Mood Contagion': The Automatic Transfer of Mood Between Persons." *Journal of Personality and Social Psychology* 79, no. 2 (2000): 211–23.

Nieto, Sonia. "Lessons from Students on Creating a Chance to Dream." *Harvard Educational Review* 64, no. 4 (1994): 392–426.

Papoulis, Jim. *Oye!* edited by Francisco Núñez. New York: Boosey Hawkes, 2004.

Perry, Theresa. "Up from the Parched Earth: Toward a Theory of African-American Achievement." In *Young, Gifted, and Black*, edited by Theresa Perry, Claude Steele, and Asa G. Hilliard, 1–87. Boston, MA: Beacon Press Books, 2003.

PS 22 Chorus Blog, ps22chorus.blogspot.com.

"PS 22 Chorus 'Forever Young' by Alphaville." YouTube Video, 3:01. Posted by PS 22 Chorus, June 26, 2009, www.youtube.com/watch?v=KlfzbmPS3n4.

"PS 22 Chorus 'Just Dance' by Lady Gaga." YouTube Video, 3:12. Posted by PS 22 Chorus, June 15, 2009, www.youtube.com/watch?v=h0FPZolbYns.

"PS 22 Chorus 'Viva la Vida' by Coldplay at McMahon Inauguration." YouTube video, 4:04. Posted by PS 22 Chorus, January 8, 2009, www.youtube.com/watch?v=3GgMlUa5Zx0.

Reeve, Johnmarshall. "Why Teachers Adopt a Controlling Motivating Style Toward Students and How They Can Become More Autonomy Supportive." *Educational Psychologist* 44, no. 3 (2009): 159–75.

Reeve, Johnmarshall. "A Self-Determination Theory Perspective on Student Engagement." In *Handbook of Research on Student Engagement*, edited by Sandra L. Christenson, Amy L. Reschly, and Cathy Wylie, 149–72. New York: Springer, 2012.

Robinson, Kathy M. "White Teacher, Students of Color: Culturally Responsive Pedagogy for Elementary General Music in Communities of Color." In *Teaching Music in the Urban Classroom*, edited by Carol Frierson-Campbell, 35–53. Lanham, MD: Rowman & Littlefield Education, 2006.

Rodriguez, Carlos X., ed. *Bridging the Gap: Popular Music and Music Education.* Reston, VA: MENC, 2004.

Schunk, Dale H., and Carol A. Mullen. "Self-Efficacy as an Engaged Learner." In *Handbook of Research on Student Engagement*, edited by Sandra L. Christenson, Amy L. Reschly, and Cathy Wylie, 219–36. New York: Springer, 2012.

Scruggs, Bernadette, Patrick K. Freer, and David E. Myers. "Constructivist Practices to Increase Student Engagement in the Orchestra Classroom." *Music Educators Journal* 95, no. 4 (2009): 53–60.

Shade, Barbara J. "Understanding the African American Learner." In *Teaching Diverse Populations: Formulating a Knowledge Base*, edited by Etta R. Hollins, Joyce E. King, and Warren C. Hayman, 175–89. Albany: State University of New York Press, 1994.

Shade, Barbara J., Cynthia Kelly, and Mary Oberg. *Creating Culturally Responsive Classrooms.* Washington, DC: American Psychological Association, 1997.

Sheets, Rosa Hernández. "Urban Classroom Conflict: Student-Teacher Perception: Ethnic Integrity, Solidarity, and Resistance." *The Urban Review* 28, no. 2 (1996): 165–83.

Shernoff, David J., and Mihaly Csikszentmihalyi. "Flow in Schools: Cultivating Engaged Learners and Optimal Learning Environments." In *Handbook of Positive Psychology in Schools*, edited by Rich Gilman, E. Scott Huebner, and Michael J. Furlong, 131–45. New York: Routledge, 2009.

Sidran, Ben. *Black Talk.* Boston, MA: Da Capo Press, 1971.

Skinner, Ellen A., and Michael J. Belmont. "Motivation in the Classroom: Reciprocal Effects of Teacher Behavior and Student Engagement Across the School Year." *Journal of Educational Psychology* 85, no. 4 (1993): 571–81.

Skinner, Ellen A., and Jennifer R. Pitzer. "Developmental Dynamics of Student Engagement, Coping, and Everyday Resilience." In *Handbook of Research on Student Engagement*, edited by Sandra L. Christenson, Amy L. Reschly, and Cathy Wylie, 21–44. New York: Springer, 2012.

Standifer, James A. "Musical Behaviors of Black People in American Society." *Black Music Research Journal* 1 (1980): 51–62.

Steele, Claude. "Stereotype Threat and African-American Student Achievement." In *Young, Gifted, and Black*, edited by Theresa Perry, Claude Steele, and Asa G. Hilliard, 109–30. Boston, MA: Beacon Press Books, 2003.

Stewart, Carolee. "Who Takes Music? Investigating Access to High School Music as a Function of Social and School Factors." PhD diss., University of Michigan, 1991.

Strauss, Anselm, and Juliet Corbin. *Basics of Qualitative Research: Techniques and Procedures for Developing Grounded Theory*, 2nd ed. Thousand Oaks, CA: SAGE Publications, 1988.

Toshalis, Eric. "The Rhetoric of Care: Preservice Teacher Discourses That Depoliticize, Deflect, and Deceive." *The Urban Review* 44, no. 1 (2012): 1–35.

Twining, Mary Arnold. "I'm Going to Sing and 'Shout' While I Have the Chance: Music, Movement, and Dance on the Sea Islands." *Black Music Research Journal* 15, no. 1 (1995): 1–15.

"Viva la Vida" Choir, Blach Middle School, YouTube video, 3:33. Posted by Michael Shorts, October 6, 2010, www.youtube.com/watch?v=yDyyrdhAxMw.

Walker, Linda M., and Donald L. Hamann. "Minority Recruitment: The Relationship Between High School Students' Perceptions About Music Participation and Recruitment Strategies." *Bulletin of the Council for Research in Music Education* 124 (1995): 24–38.

Watts, Michelle, and Christopher Doane. "Minority Students in Music Performance Programs." *Research Perspectives in Music Education* 5 (1995): 25–36.

Wiggan, Greg. "From Opposition to Engagement: Lessons from High Achieving African American Students." *The Urban Review* 40, no. 4 (2007): 317–49.

Williams, Mary Lou. *Zodiac Suite*. [Recorded by Geri Allen, Buster Williams, Billy Hart, and Andrew Cyrille on *Zodiac Suite: Revisited*]. 2006, 1945 by Mary Records. Compact Disc.

Wills, John S., Angela Lintz, and Hugh Mehan. "Ethnographic Studies of Multicultural Education in U.S. Classrooms and Schools." In *Handbook of Research on Multicultural Education*, edited by James A. Banks and Cherry A. McGee Banks, 163–83. San Francisco, CA: Jossey-Bass, 2004.

"Woodlands Middle School chorus 'Velvet Shoes,'" YouTube video, 2:44. Posted by eabhorselvr, July 29, 2008, www.youtube.com/watch?v=VrgBAZdZF9c.

Yonezawa, Susan, Makeba Jones, and Francine Joselowsky. "Youth Engagement in High Schools: Developing a Multidimensional, Critical Approach to Improving Engagement for All Students." *Journal of Educational Change* 10, nos. 2–3 (2009): 191–209.

About the Author

Ruth Gurgel, assistant professor of music education, is a specialist in elementary music education at Kansas State University. She teaches graduate and undergraduate courses in music education and supervises student teachers. Dr. Gurgel holds a PhD in music education from the University of Wisconsin-Madison, with minors in sociology and educational policy. She also holds a Master of Arts degree in Curriculum and Instruction from Colorado Christian University in Lakewood, Colorado, and degrees in flute performance and instrumental music education from Lawrence University in Appleton, Wisconsin.

Dr. Gurgel began her career teaching elementary music in large city school districts both in Colorado and Wisconsin, instructing students in the areas of general music, band, choir, and orchestra. She brings an eclectic approach to her music instruction, integrating the techniques of Kodály, Orff, Dalcroze, and Gordon with Culturally Relevant Pedagogy. She continues to present her research and teaching practices nationally.